"Open your eyes, woman."

At Dillon's brusque command, Leonora's lids flickered, then lifted. For a moment they went wide with fear. Then she blinked, and he could see them narrow fractionally, and darken with anger.

"Release me at once. I am not some serving woman who yearns to satisfy the lord of the manor."

"Nay, my lady." A dangerous smile touched the corners of his lips, and she felt the tension humming through him. "You are not even worthy to be called a servant. You are my prisoner. Never forget that."

"You . . ." At his arrogance, she swung her hand out, intent on slapping his face.

He caught it and pinned it without effort. "That is better, my lady. I prefer your anger to your fear."

"I do not fear you, savage."

"Most unwise, my lady." She struggled as he lowered his mouth to hers and claimed her lips once more. . . .

Dear Reader,

Harlequin Historicals welcomes you to another sizzling month of romance. With summer in full swing, we've got four titles perfect for the beach, pool—or anywhere!

From popular author Miranda Jarrett comes another swashbuckling tale set on the high seas—*Mariah's Prize,* her next book in the thrilling SPARHAWK series. In this story, a desperate Mariah West convinces Gabriel Sparhawk to captain her sloop, never guessing at his ulterior motives.

Scottish chieftain Dillon Campbell abducted Lady Leonora Wilton as an act of revenge against the English. But one look into Leonora's eyes and it became an act of love, in *The Highlander* by favorite author Ruth Langan.

In Julie Tetel's stirring medieval tale, *Simon's Lady,* the marriage between Simon de Beresford and Lady Gwyneth had been arranged to quell a Saxon uprising, yet this Saxon bride wants more from her husband than peace.

And finally, if you liked Merline Lovelace's first book of the DESTINY'S WOMEN series, *Alena,* you'll love her second book, *Sweet Song of Love.* When knight Richard FitzHugh was called to battle, he left behind a meek bride given to him by the king. So who was the curvaceous beauty who now greeted him as *husband?*

Next month, our big book selection is *To Share a Dream,* a reissue by author Willo Davis Roberts. Don't miss this moving saga about three sisters who dare to build a new beginning in the American colonies.

Sincerely,

Tracy Farrell
Senior Editor

Please address questions and book requests to:
Harlequin Reader Service
U.S.: 3010 Walden Ave., P.O. Box 1325, Buffalo, NY 14269
Canadian: P.O. Box 609, Fort Erie, Ont. L2A 5X3

RUTH LANGAN

THE HIGHLANDER

Harlequin Books

TORONTO • NEW YORK • LONDON
AMSTERDAM • PARIS • SYDNEY • HAMBURG
STOCKHOLM • ATHENS • TOKYO • MILAN
MADRID • WARSAW • BUDAPEST • AUCKLAND

ISBN 0-373-28828-X

THE HIGHLANDER

RUTH LANGAN

traces her ancestry to Scotland and Ireland. It is no surprise, then, that she feels a kinship with the characters in her historical novels.

Married to her childhood sweetheart, she has raised five children and lives in Michigan, the state where she was born and raised.

To Kelsey Langan Bissonnette,
Our latest celebration of life and love.
And to her big sisters, Aubrey and Haley,
And her proud parents, Carol and Bryon.

And always, to Tom.
Always.

Prologue

The Scottish Highlands, 1281

"Soldiers! God in heaven, English soldiers!"

A cry of terror shattered the silence of the idyllic summer day in the Highland meadow. Men hastily retrieved weapons. Women who had moments earlier been enjoying a bit of gossip scurried in search of children playing in the tall grass.

With a call to arms, the leader of the clan leapt upon his horse, drawing his sword. The horse reared up, then dropped to its knees, a knife embedded in its chest. As its rider fell, two English soldiers jumped on him and crushed his skull with a mallet.

A woman screamed and tried to escape, but her voice was abruptly stilled. When a younger woman rushed to her aid, she found herself surrounded by men whose eyes glittered with bloodlust.

Throughout the afternoon, the leaden skies reverberated with the clang of sword against armor, and the sound of terrified cries. By the time the sun had made its arc to the western sky, the grass of the Highland meadow was stained red with the blood of its people. Men, women, children, even infants at the breast, had been slaughtered.

Fortified by their successful attack, the soldiers turned their mounts toward home.

An eerie calm settled over the scene of carnage as an aged monk emerged from the woods. Walking among the dead, he began to administer the Last Rites.

When a movement caught his eye, he turned and studied the body of a lad, then shook his head, convinced that it had been merely the breeze rippling the boy's clothes. Surely no one could have survived such a bloody massacre. Much to his surprise, the lad moved again. The monk hurried over, knelt, and touched a hand to his shoulder.

The boy lifted his head and peered at him through a haze of pain. His face had been split from temple to jaw by a blow from a sword.

"Praise God. You're alive, then? Here, lad." The monk pressed a square of linen to the boy's wound. "This will stem the flow of blood."

When the lad was assured that this was indeed a peaceful man of God, he rolled aside, revealing a depression in the ground in which were hidden twin boys, about six years, and a girl of three or four. All were bloody and dazed, but alive.

Recovering from his surprise, the monk helped them to sit, then removed a flask of spirits from his waist and held it to their lips. They drank greedily. All, that is, save the eldest, who refused nourishment as he stared through glazed eyes at the scene of carnage.

"Who are your people?" the monk asked.

"We are from the Clan Campbell," the twins answered in unison. "Our father, Modric, was leader."

"But how did you survive such a brutal attack?"

"Dillon," the little girl said proudly, pointing to her beloved older brother. "He shielded us with his body."

The monk studied the silent lad with interest. Heroism in one so young was a rare and precious thing.

"Did any of your clan manage to escape?"

The oldest stared around bleakly, then shook his head, overwhelmed by the fact that he and his brothers and sister were all that remained of an entire clan.

"Then you shall come with me to the monastery," the monk said. "There we will offer thanks to God for your deliverance from the English swords." As he began herding the children toward the distant spires, he said softly, "My name is Father Anselm. You will be safe with me. The monks will see to your future. And you, lass. What is your name?"

"Flame," the little girl said proudly.

He cleared his throat. A most un-Christian name. "You will be sent to the nearby abbey, Flame, where the good sisters will educate you in the ways of a lady."

He had gone some distance when he realized that the older lad was not with them. He returned to find the lad kneeling beside a man and woman. The man, like all the others, had been savaged nearly beyond recognition. The woman, her clothes torn from her, had been brutalized by the soldiers before death had mercifully claimed her.

"Come, lad. We will return on the morrow to bury the dead," the priest said softly.

Still the boy continued to kneel, his eyes narrowed, his face expressionless.

"You must forget what you see here, lad," the monk said.

"Nay." For the first time, the boy broke his silence. His fists clenched at his sides. "I shall never forget."

The monk was surprised by the hard, merciless look in the eyes of one so young. He had seen that look before. But only in the eyes of seasoned warriors.

"When I am old enough," the boy added through gritted teeth, "I swear on the souls of my father and mother that I will avenge this deed. The English who did this thing will one day answer to Dillon Campbell."

Chapter One

England, 1292

"Oh, Moira. I see the savages!" Leonora, daughter of Lord Alec Waltham, stood on the balcony of the keep, her gaze sweeping the green lands of her beloved England. For as far as the eye could see, the land belonged to her wealthy father, most of it given to him by a grateful King Edward in appreciation for a lifetime of service to the Crown. Alec Waltham was one of the king's most trusted friends, and Edward's generosity to his friends was legendary, as was his volatile temper. It was well known in wealthy circles that Edward was an autocratic, short-tempered monarch who became violent even against his most trusted friends if they dared to criticize him.

"God save us. Where?" Her aged nurse waddled across the room and lifted a gnarled hand to squint into the bright light.

"On that distant hilltop. See how the sunlight reflects off their swords?"

"Aye." The old woman crossed herself. "I would ne'er have believed that I would live to see heathens such as these sleeping under the same roof with civilized people, and even sharing food at your father's table. Ah, the things I've heard about them.''

"Heard? Have you never seen a Highlander, then?"

The woman who had been nurse to Leonora's mother, and her mother before her, shivered. "Nay. But I've heard stories about the savages. They are giants, child, who bare their limbs even in the harshest weather, and who wear little more than rags.'' Seeing Leonora's shocked reaction, she went on, "Aye, those who have seen them say they are wild, unkempt creatures, their manner of speech crude, their hairy faces horrible to behold."

Leonora's eyes widened. "Oh, Moira. Whatever shall I do? Father has ordered me to join him in welcoming these...creatures." She lifted a delicate hand to her throat.

"If he'd been wise, he'd have ordered you to remain locked in your chambers until the Highlanders departed. Who knows what villainy might befall us?" The old nurse lowered her voice. "There are those who say they eat English children, and drink their blood."

"Hush, Moira. I cannot believe such nonsense. Father would never invite such monsters into his home."

"Never forget, 'twas not your father's choice. The king ordered this meeting."

"Aye, and would the king place his most trusted friend in danger?"

The old woman gave no reply, but wisely kept her thoughts to herself. There were spies everywhere. Woe to any who fell out of favor with the Crown.

Leonora watched three horsemen urge their mounts toward the moat. At a shout, the drawbridge was lowered, and the heavy portcullis raised. The three clattered across. Immediately, the portcullis was lowered and the drawbridge was raised, leaving them no means of retreating.

"These Highlanders are either very foolish," Leonora said, turning to take leave of her chambers, "or very brave.

After all, there are only three of them, and over a hundred of the king's finest soldiers positioned within these walls.''

'''Tis said that it takes but one Highlander to crush an entire English army.''

"You go too far with such treasonous talk." Leonora opened the door and flounced from the room, eyes flashing. "These are not gods. They are mere mortals." Over her shoulder she announced haughtily, "And, since we are well fortified, I intend to see them for myself."

When she was gone, her nurse crossed herself again and dropped to her knees to pray. The lass was young, barely ten and six, and a bit headstrong. Soon enough she would see for herself that the rest of the world was not as civilized as England.

"What if they ask us to relinquish our weapons, Dillon?"

"Rob said we must do as we are bid if we are to convince them of our willingness to make peace." Dillon Campbell dismounted and handed the reins to a young lad, whose mouth dropped open like one staring at an apparition.

Dillon, choosing to ignore the effect he had on the English lad, shook the dust from his traveling cloak and tossed it rakishly over one massive shoulder. Then he shook his head like a great, shaggy beast, before straightening.

His younger brothers, Sutton and Shaw, followed suit. Though they were identical twins, with hair the color of straw and eyes more green than blue, their natures were very different. From infancy, Sutton had imitated his older brother, relishing every opportunity to wield a sword in battle. Gentle Shaw, impressed by the fine minds and generous spirits of the monks who had raised him and his brothers, had already pledged himself to the Church. It was only a matter of time before he would enter the monastery, to begin a life of prayer and contemplation.

"All of our weapons?" Sutton asked.

Dillon's lips curved slightly as he sought to hide his smile. "It matters not what Rob said, for he is safe in Edinburgh and we are the ones who must sleep with the enemy. I trust not these English dogs. We will give them only those weapons they can see. 'Twould not hurt to conceal a dirk or two," he muttered under his breath, "for it could mean the difference between life and death."

"Aye." Relieved Sutton touched a hand to the knife hidden at his waist. He'd had no intention of giving it up to these English tyrants.

"Remember what I told you," Dillon commanded softly. "Trust no one. Leave nothing to chance. Look always to your safety."

A heavy door leading to the courtyard was thrown open and several soldiers stepped out and formed a guard of honor on either side of the doorway. Like the lad who stood holding the reins of the strangers' horses, they gaped at the sight of these three Highlanders, who stood head and shoulders above even the tallest in their midst.

Behind the soldiers came a man in the robes of a bishop, followed by several formally dressed men. As each of them stepped outside, they shot speculative glances at the three strangers, then formed a half circle and turned expectantly toward the doorway, where their host paused, a young woman standing close behind.

The man in elegant fur-trimmed doublet and satin breeches could only be the lord of the keep. His silver hair, neatly trimmed moustache and pointed beard framed a handsome face whose most notable feature was a pair of lively, intelligent eyes.

"I am Lord Alec Waltham. I bid you welcome to England and to my home."

Dillon stepped forward, carefully shielding his brothers. "Thank you, Lord Waltham." Presenting his sword, he said, "I am Dillon Campbell, and these are my brothers, Sutton and Shaw."

Following the lead of their older brother, the two offered their swords to their host. Lord Waltham accepted, and handed the weapons to the captain of the guard.

Drawing his daughter beside him, Lord Waltham said, "May I present my beloved daughter, Leonora."

"My lady." Dillon, keenly aware of the contrast between his own rough clothing and that of his host, stepped forward and lifted her hand, brushing his lips lightly over her knuckles.

Up close, the female smelled of crushed roses. Her skin was as pale as alabaster, and her hair as black as a raven's wing. She glanced up, then away, but in that brief instant Dillon found himself looking into eyes the color of the heather that bloomed on the Highland meadows. They were the most unusual eyes he'd ever seen. Almost at once he released her hand and took a step back.

Leonora nodded her head stiffly, too overcome to speak. The Scotsman's voice was as cultured as any Englishman's, except for a slight burr. The hand that had touched hers was rough and callused, with a grip so strong it could have broken every bone in her tiny palm. When his lips touched her flesh, she felt a tremor along her spine unlike anything she had ever experienced before.

Moira had been right. These men were indeed giants. Rough, crude, unkempt giants who smelled of horses. Their Viking ancestry was clearly visible in their massive size and the red glints in untrimmed hair that fell in disarray to their shoulders. Their clothes were little more than rags.

The one called Dillon was probably considered handsome by the coarse women of his own land. Perhaps he would be, Leonora thought, if it weren't for the thin scar that ran from temple to jaw, clearly visible beneath a growth of red-gold beard. He wore no shirt beneath his cloak, and her gaze fastened on his naked, muscled shoulder. No English gentleman would dare to offend a lady's sensibilities in such a manner. Yet, for some unexplained reason, she could not seem to tear her gaze from the offensive sight.

Lord Waltham directed their attention to the others who stood beside him. "May I present the Bishop of York."

"Your grace," Dillon said, lifting the bishop's hand to his lips.

"You are Christian?" The bishop couldn't hide his surprise.

"Aye. After the...untimely death of our parents, my brothers and I were raised by monks in the monastery of St. Collum."

The bishop beamed with pleasure. He'd expected these barbarians to be heathens. The fact that they'd been raised by monks made the prospect of peace talks with these Scots all the sweeter.

Lord Waltham motioned another man forward. He wore a beautifully tailored velvet doublet in shades of blue and scarlet with blue silk breeches. "This is an emissary from the king himself. May I present George Godwin, the Duke of Essex."

The man kept his expression bland, but Dillon could read hostility in his eyes. This was better, he thought. He would prefer to know what was in a man's heart before he agreed to sit at table with him. In the manner of a warrior, Dillon lifted his right hand from the empty scabbard and held it aloft. Essex did the same.

"This is Lord James Blakely and his son, Alger," Lord Waltham said.

Father and son were handsome, with neatly trimmed hair and beards, and the fierce bearing of soldiers. The older man nodded stiffly. His son kept his hand on his sword and took a step closer to the lady Leonora, while he took the measure of the man he faced. It was obvious that he considered the lady his personal responsibility, and feared that these strangers might be a threat to her safety.

Something about these two troubled Dillon. Some long-buried dread began to surface, but he pushed it aside, reminding himself sternly that any English soldier would arouse such feelings.

Lord Waltham indicated a stooped, balding man who leaned on a walking stick. "This is the king's own counsel, Lord John Forest."

Dillon studied the man, who studied him just as carefully. There was neither friendship nor hostility in his eyes; merely veiled curiosity.

"Welcome," John Forest said as he offered his hand.

"I thank you."

Lord Waltham had carefully gauged the reaction of these strangers to all who had been introduced. It was essential, with men who harbored ancient enmity, that their first meeting be one of ease and trust. It was obvious that there was little of either on both sides.

"You must be weary after your long journey," he said. "You will wish to refresh yourselves before you are shown to your chambers. Come."

When Lord Waltham turned to lead the way, with his daughter on his arm, Dillon signalled to his two brothers, who followed closely. They stepped inside the great stone walls, and made their way along a hallway made bright by hundreds of lighted tapers set in sconces. While they walked, they shot furtive glances at the soldiers who followed at a discreet distance. When their party halted, a servant pulled open a door and stood aside, allowing them to enter. The soldiers remained outside.

Inside, several chairs draped with animal hides were positioned around a blazing fire. Lord Waltham and his daughter held a whispered conference before she turned to speak to a servant. That done, her father held a chair for her beside the fire. Immediately, Alger Blakely placed himself beside her in a proprietary manner.

"Sit and warm yourselves," Lord Waltham called to his guests.

As the three Highlanders took their seats, a servant offered them tankards of ale, which remained untouched until Lord Waltham took the first sip. When Dillon determined that the ale had not been poisoned, he signaled his younger brothers, who eagerly began to drink. The tankards were quickly emptied. Another servant passed around trays of bread soaked in wine, which soon restored their spirits.

Lord Waltham sipped his ale and watched them with interest. His daughter, too uncomfortable in the presence of these strangers to eat or drink, merely watched in silence.

"Was it a difficult journey?" the Duke of Essex asked.

"Nay." Dillon stretched out his long legs toward the fire, enjoying the heat that settled in his belly after the first fiery swallow of ale. If the English hoped to render them helplessly drunk, they would have to do better than this swill. In the monastery where he'd been raised, the monks made the finest ale and spirits in all of Scotland. It was a common drink with every meal. "After a life in the Highlands, a journey of several days over your gentle countryside is child's play."

"You are not weary?" Lord Waltham lifted a brow in astonishment, knowing his soldiers would find such a journey daunting.

"Nay. Perhaps, if we had to journey all the way to your king's home in London, we would feel the need to refresh ourselves. But this required no more effort than we would make on any day in the Highlands."

"I have heard of your Highlands." The minute the words were out of her mouth, Leonora felt the heat of Dillon's gaze and cursed herself for her foolishness. She had not wanted to call attention to herself. And now the man was studying her with great intensity. She was aware only of his eyes, dark and compelling, fixed on her.

"And what have you heard, my lady?"

She glanced at her father, who smiled his encouragement. After the death of his wife, his only child had been his constant companion at court. With her fine mind, she had proved to be a valuable asset when dealing with affairs of state. Even the king had commented on her ability to mingle with her father's worldly friends. He was confident she would have no problem with these simple Highlanders.

"I have heard they are—" she licked her lips "—quite untamed."

"Aye." Dillon sipped his ale and considered his words before speaking. "That they are. Untamed. A bonny land."

Hearing the passion in his tone, she felt a shiver along her spine. Bonny. It was as if he were speaking about a woman. A beautiful, desirable woman.

"Robert the Bruce must set great store by you to have appointed you his spokesman." The bishop studied Dillon who lounged carelessly in his chair. Though surrounded by English swords, the man seemed completely at ease. Could the rumors be true? Did these Highlanders truly know no fear?

"Rob knows that my word is my bond."

"The question is," the Duke of Essex said with a sneer, "will your fellow Scotsmen consider your word binding?"

Dillon's expression never changed. His words were spoken so softly everyone in the room had to strain to hear. But all were aware of the thread of steel in his tone. And a thickening of the burr with each passionate word. "I would not be here if it were not so."

"Aye." Lord Waltham stepped forward, eager to smooth things over. It would not do to end this meeting of the two warring countries before it even began. What was needed to soothe this tension was a woman's healing touch. "If you have had sufficient ale, my daughter, Leonora, will show you to your chambers.''

Leonora shot her father a pleading glance, but he turned away, deliberately ignoring her. If the look was lost on Lord Waltham, it did not go unnoticed by Dillon. He would have found it amusing, were it not so insulting. It was obvious the lady would have rather faced a den of wildcats than lead him and his brothers to their chambers.

''I will accompany the lady,'' Alger Blakely said eagerly.

''Nay, Alger.'' Lord Waltham gave him a warning look. Turning to Dillon, he said, ''If there is anything you desire, you need only ask. We will sup at dusk. A servant will be sent to fetch you.''

''My lord. Your grace.'' Dillon bowed slightly before turning to follow Leonora from the room, with his brothers trailing.

They climbed a graceful curve of stairs to an upper level. As they walked, they studied the walls lined with tapestries. Everywhere they looked, servants scurried about, polishing sconces or carrying armloads of linen. It was clear evidence of a well-ordered and opulent existence.

Dillon's attention was fixed on the lady in front of him. Even at Edinburgh, the seat of power in his country, he had not seen a female so richly gowned. The fabric shimmered in the light of the candles. With each sway of her hips, he found himself more and more fascinated by the feminine contours hidden beneath the voluminous skirts. Her hair, secured by gold netting, bobbed primly at her shoulders. His fists clenched at his sides as he found himself wondering what those raven curls would look like when set free to cascade past her waist. Almost at once he chastised himself for such foolish thoughts.

Leonora paused before huge double doors. Throwing them open she stepped inside a sitting room and motioned for the servants to leave. Seeing the strangers, they bowed from the room, leaving behind the proof of their diligence. A fire blazed on the hearth. Several chaises had been positioned around it for comfort. On a table were a flagon of ale and goblets of hammered gold.

"Is this to be our bedchamber?" Sutton asked, opening a second door.

"Aye. It is one of several," Leonora called to his retreating back. He had already disappeared inside, with his twin brother behind him.

A few moments later Sutton and Shaw returned to the sitting room holding aloft brightly colored garments. "Look, Dillon. These were draped across the beds. Feel how fine and soft is the cloth."

Dillon glanced at the garments with a frown of distaste. "You have no need of such things, my brothers. Return them to the lady Leonora."

"But—"

"At once." His tone was abrupt.

As they reluctantly handed them over, Dillon turned to the young woman. "What was the reason for this?"

"We had heard . . ." She bit her lip and wondered how to proceed tactfully. She couldn't possibly tell him that she had pitied him his coarse garments. She had requested permission of her father to furnish him and his brothers with something more befitting their sumptuous surroundings and their lofty position as representatives of their country. Nor could she tell him of the rumors she had heard, of savage Highlanders who would be nearly naked even in the company of women. "We had heard that your journey would be long and difficult. I thought you might desire a change of clothing."

He never altered his tone, but his words had the sharp sting of a whip. "We are Highland warriors, my lady. Our clothes may appear to you to be coarse and simple, but they were woven with love." He thought of the hours his sister and the nuns at the abbey had spent at the loom, weaving the cloth of green and blue and black that so pleased him because it reminded him of the green glens of his beloved Highlands, the blue of the heather that blossomed on the meadows and the black of the rich Scottish soil. "Would you deny us our heritage and turn us into peacocks like your countrymen below stairs?"

"Nay. I did not mean..." Feeling her cheeks flush, she lowered her gaze. "Forgive me. I meant no harm. I will send a servant to fetch the garments you are wearing. I assure you they will be clean and dry in time to sup."

His Scottish burr thickened, the only sign that his anger still simmered. "There is no need. We may be simple, but we are not savages. We have brought other clothes. If you will be good enough to send a servant to the stables, they are with our horses."

"As you wish." She backed away, eager to escape this harsh, angry man who made her feel so uncomfortable.

He would not allow her to flee so easily. He walked with her to the door and held it open. As she moved past him, her breast came into contact with his arm, sending a tingling sensation clear to her toes. She felt a rush of heat that had nothing to do with the warmth of the fireplace. Feeling the way his gaze burned over her, she lowered her head to hide the betraying blush that she knew was on her cheeks.

"A servant will summon you when it is time to sup."

"You are most kind, my lady."

Most kind indeed. She gritted her teeth as she hurried away. That infuriating Highlander had just made a mockery of her attempt at hospitality. And for that, she would never forgive him.

Chapter Two

The great hall was filled with the rumble of masculine voices, all raised in speculation about the Highlanders. At one end of the room stood the soldiers, who swapped stories about their battles with the fearsome Scots warriors. At the other end, in front of a roaring fire, stood Lord Waltham and the English noblemen.

Leonora stood beside her father, awaiting the arrival of their guests. Over Moira's objections, she had taken great pains with her appearance. Her gown of red velvet had a low, square neckline and fitted bodice. A girdle of lace defined her tiny waist and hips. The voluminous skirt, gathered here and there with clusters of jewels, fell to the tips of kid slippers. The sleeves, inset with ermine, were full to the elbow, then tapered to points at each wrist. At her throat was a delicate filigree of gold interspersed with diamonds and rubies. Matching earrings dangled from her lobes.

The last time Leonora had looked so splendid, she had been in the presence of the king. Though her nurse had argued that such finery was wasted on the savage Highlander, Leonora would not be dissuaded. She would make Dillon Campbell regret that he had rejected her hospitality. When he arrived in his coarse garments, he would find himself surrounded by luxury such as he'd never imagined.

Alger Blakely bowed over her hand. "You look lovely, my lady."

His father beamed his approval as his son continued to hold Leonora's hand longer than was necessary. Lord James Blakely was aware of his host's vast wealth and sprawling estates. The lady's dowry was rumored to equal that of royalty. And of even more importance was her father's close friendship with the king. The man who won Leonora Waltham's hand would inherit great power. His son had all the qualities necessary to win a lady's heart. Alger was strong of limb and fair of face. It was James's intention to see that the two become betrothed before his son was sent back into battle.

"Such beauty will surely dazzle the Highlanders in our midst," James said softly.

Lord Waltham gave his daughter an admiring glance. "Aye. It pleases me that you have taken such pains with your appearance, my dear." He drew her close and pressed a kiss to her cheek. "I know that these Highlanders frighten you, but it is the wish of our monarch that we establish bonds of friendship. It is imperative that we find a peaceful solution to our differences, or we will find our fair English knights facing them on a field of battle."

"Aye," James said. "Including my beloved son Alger."

Leonora shivered at the thought of anyone having to face such giants.

Seeing it, her father nodded. "They would be formidable foes indeed, my dear. It is far better that we offer our hands instead of our swords."

"Do you truly intend to befriend these buffoons?" The Duke of Essex lifted a goblet of ale to his lips.

"Aye." Lord Waltham felt a ripple of annoyance at the man's open display of hostility. "As one who enjoys the king's friendship, Essex, you know the importance of this meeting."

"I would as soon put a dagger to their throats as sup with them."

"Then you should have made your feelings known to the king before you agreed to come here."

"And miss the opportunity to see for myself what these savages look like?" The duke emptied his goblet and looked around at the others, who chuckled in agreement. "I wonder that Edward would even waste our time on the likes of them. We would do better to put them in a pen with the swine. Mayhap then they could draw up a treaty with those of their own kind."

Even the bishop couldn't stifle his laughter at such a remark. "They are indeed a ragged band. I wonder that our monarch would give a care to such beggars." He turned to Lord Blakely and Alger. "You two have faced their kind in battle. What say you? Are the Highlanders fearsome warriors? Or is it all a myth?"

"It is no myth," Alger said. "I have never faced more worthy opponents." Seeing that he had Leonora's attention, he couldn't help boasting, "Not that I fear them, your grace. I would welcome the chance to meet the Highlanders in battle again. Mayhap I could teach them a thing or two about handling a sword."

"But this is not a field of battle." The duke plucked another goblet from a serving wench's tray. "Prowess with a sword will not serve them in good stead here. What is needed to draw up a peace treaty is a fine mind, and—" he winked slyly at the others "—judging by the three in our midst, the Highlanders are sadly lacking in that. Could it be that the bigger a man is, the smaller is his brain?"

While the duke and bishop laughed, Lord Waltham said softly, "I would not be so eager to dismiss these strangers. Robert the Bruce could have chosen any number of men to represent him. They may appear rough and crude to us, but

I would caution you to treat them with the same respect you would give their leader."

"This is the only respect I give the Bruce." The Duke of Essex touched a hand to the sword at his side.

Leonora saw the smiles fade abruptly from the faces of several of the men. She turned to see the three Highlanders standing directly behind her. It would have been impossible for them to avoid overhearing the crude remarks made about them.

How long had they been standing there? How much had they heard?

Dillon's features showed no emotion. His younger brothers, however, who were not as schooled in diplomacy, wore identical scowls. When Sutton's hand went to the knife hidden at his waist, Dillon hastily put his hand over his brother's to still his movements.

"Nay," he said softly. "Now is not the time."

"But Dillon, they utter calumny—"

Dillon placed his arm around his brother's shoulders, effectively pinning the younger man's arms at his sides. Drawing him close, he murmured, "You must learn to be patient with fools, Sutton."

His reactions, as well as his words, were not lost on the English, who watched in stunned silence. Only Lord Waltham showed any remorse.

"Forgive us," he said. "We did not see you enter the hall."

"That was obvious." Dillon's eyes narrowed as he studied each man. Anger seethed within him, but he had learned long ago to give nothing of his thoughts away. The English, in turn, looked away rather than face his accusing stares.

Despite the turmoil he might have felt, Dillon bowed slightly and caught Leonora's hand in his. "Good even, my lady."

As his lips grazed her knuckles, she felt the rush of heat and blamed it on the blaze on the hearth. Looking at him through her thick veil of lashes, she prayed he couldn't detect the color that flooded her cheeks.

He had shaved. Without the ragged growth of beard, his face, despite the scar, was indeed handsome. His brow was firm, his face graced with a straight, even nose, wide firm lips and an angular jaw. He wore a saffron shirt of soft lawn, and on his legs, black hose. Over these he wore a loose garment woven of cloth of blue and green and black that fell to below his knees, with a matching length of fabric tossed rakishly over one shoulder like a cape, and fastened by a clasp of hammered gold. Little droplets of water still glistened like diamonds in his russet hair.

His brothers were dressed in similar fashion.

Though Leonora had never before seen such a manner of dress, she had to grudgingly admit to herself that these Highlanders looked splendid. Tall. Rugged. Earthy. By comparison, the English looked like... The phrase Dillon had tossed at her with such sarcasm rushed to mind. Peacocks.

"Ale, my lords?" A serving wench held a tray of goblets aloft.

"Aye. Thank you." As the three Highlanders accepted the goblets, Leonora saw the servant's admiring gaze move slowly over each man, and linger on Dillon's rugged face.

"That will be all, Verda." Leonora spoke a little too sharply, and found herself wondering at the sudden flash of feeling. Jealousy? She immediately dismissed such a ridiculous thought. She had never before given a care to the flirtations that passed between the servants and guests in her father's house. And surely these men meant nothing to her. "You may begin to help serve the meal."

The servant turned away with a pout.

When Dillon turned to look at her, Leonora felt the flush rise to her cheeks once more. She had the distinct impression that he could read her mind, and that he was laughing at her. This only served to stiffen her spine and deepen her frown.

"I trust your chambers are comfortable," Lord Waltham asked.

"Most comfortable." Dillon sipped the ale to give himself time to bank his still-simmering temper. He was well aware that these English had been making sport of him and his brothers. That didn't bother him nearly as much as the thought that such feelings would spill over to include all his countrymen. *That* he would never allow. If they were to agree to a peace between them, it must be worked out in an atmosphere of mutual respect.

Respect. He sensed that the Duke of Essex had been deliberately attempting to goad him and his brothers into a fight. The temptation to comply with the duke's wish had been almost overpowering. Still, Dillon knew that a battle, though the simplest solution, would shatter their fragile attempts at peace.

"Come." Their host offered his arm to his daughter, relieved that the Highlanders had managed to suppress their anger, at least for the moment. "We will sup."

With Leonora beside him, Lord Waltham led the way to the head table, which resided on a raised platform at one end of the hall. At this table would sit the bishop, as well as the honored guests from Scotland.

At the next tables sat the nobles, and the local dignitaries from the nearby villages, who had been invited to witness this historic visit between the Scots and English. At the far end of the room sat the soldiers, who had grown unusually quiet since the arrival of their old enemy, the Highlanders.

"Dillon, I would be pleased if you would take the seat of honor beside my daughter." Lord Waltham indicated a wooden bench that ran the length of the table.

As they were seated, Leonora felt the brush of Dillon's thigh against hers and reacted as if she'd been burned.

With a look of alarm Lord Waltham turned to her. "Are you in some discomfort, daughter?"

"Nay, Father." She felt Dillon's gaze upon her and cursed the heat that flooded her cheeks. "I am merely—" she struggled with her scrambled thoughts "—concerned that this first meal please our guests."

Looking past her to Dillon and his brothers, Lord Waltham explained, "Since the death of her mother, Leonora has taken charge of my many households and performed admirably. She is becoming a young woman of many accomplishments."

"Then you are indeed blessed, Lord Waltham." Dillon pinned her with a look that brought even more color to her cheeks. "A woman of beauty, charm and accomplishment brings honor to her father and joy to her husband."

Leonora was relieved when the servants began offering the first course. Huge silver trays of salmon were passed among the guests, followed by platters of beef and whole roasted pigs. There were baskets of hot, crusty bread, and silver bowls of thick gruel into which the bread was dipped. With each course, serving wenches kept tankards filled with ale and mead, a sweet, honey-laced brew.

At a signal from their host, musicians, standing on a gallery high above the tables, began to play.

Leonora was uncomfortably aware of the man beside her, who ate with obvious relish. Studying his hands as he broke off a piece of bread, she found herself remembering the feel of those same hands on hers. Such strength. And yet his manner with her had been surprisingly gentle.

"More mead, my lady?" She jumped at the sound of his deep voice beside her.

"Forgive me. I—"

Without waiting for her reply, he filled her goblet, then his own, and handed the empty decanter to a serving wench.

"You ate very little, my lady."

"I find I have no appetite."

He smiled. "Perhaps it is the company you are forced to keep."

There was no returning smile in her eyes. "Do you mock me, sir?"

"Nay, my lady." Though he wiped the smile from his lips, it was there in his eyes, in the warmth of his tone, causing her own anger to deepen. "One need only look at you to see that you are . . . delighted to serve your king in such a manner." He allowed his gaze to sweep the crowded hall. "As are all of your guests."

He studied Alger Blakely, whose gaze was narrowed on him. Even from this distance, Dillon could detect Alger's scowl. It was obvious the young soldier was smitten by the lady's charms, and unnerved by the distance that separated them.

"I would die for my king." Leonora lifted her chin in a defiant gesture.

"Aye, my lady. A noble sentiment. But entertaining the enemy is far less noble, is it not?" His eyes twinkled with amusement. "And far more vexing."

"It is you who are vex—"

"Sweets, my lord?" Verda, the serving girl, thrust a silver tray between Leonora and Dillon and gazed adoringly into his dark eyes.

"I will let the lady choose first."

Leonora looked away in disgust. "I desire no sweets."

"Perhaps you should reconsider, my lady." Dillon's voice was laced with humor. "'Tis said they sweeten the disposition."

Her eyes flashed fire, but with considerable effort she managed to keep her voice low. "It is plain to see that my father will not be dealing with honorable gentlemen."

"You would prefer the sly humor of the Duke of Essex, perhaps?"

So, he had indeed overheard all of the insults hurled by Essex, and not just the last, uttered with such contempt. She felt ashamed that anyone, even this Highland savage, should be so mistreated in her father's house.

Knowing he'd hit a nerve, Dillon continued, "Or would you prefer the silly flattery of Alger Blakely, my lady? Are these the Englishmen of honor you would have me imitate?"

"You go too far, sir."

"Nay. Not nearly far enough. Do not think I am fooled by these—"

"Ale, my lord? Or mead?" Verda, having handed the sweets tray to another, was determined to win the attention of the handsome stranger. She hovered next to him with a flagon in her hand.

"Aye, ale. I have a need to quench the fire that rages within." When his tankard was full, he lifted it to his lips and drained it, then waited while Verda filled it again.

"I will return soon, my lord, and see that your tankard is never empty." The serving wench gave him a wink as she strolled away with a sway of hips guaranteed to catch the eye of every man in the room.

Seeing it, Leonora turned away in disgust.

Getting to his feet, Lord Waltham lifted his tankard and called for attention. When the voices had stilled, and all eyes were upon him, he said loudly, "We drink to our guests

from across the border. May we find common ground,
where battles will cease, and peace prevail.''

For a moment there was an uncomfortable silence. Then,
slowly, one by one, the men in the room shuffled to their feet
and lifted their tankards aloft. When every Englishman was
standing, Dillon and his brothers followed suit. Tankards
were drained, and the men began pounding them on the ta-
bletops to get the attention of the serving wenches.

Lord Waltham signaled to the musicians, who began to
play once more. A jester stepped up on the platform and
began to juggle colored balls, to the amazement of the
crowd. When he had finished, and picked up the coins
scattered around the floor, more toasts were made, until,
replete, warmed by the ale and the blazing fires on the
hearths, the men began drifting from the great hall to the
upper floors where they would seek their sleeping pallets.

''I trust you have had sufficient food and ale,'' Lord
Waltham asked his guests as they pushed away from the table.

''Aye.'' Dillon was careful not to stand too close to Leonora, lest she bristle at his touch. ''My compliments to you,
my lady, and you, Lord Waltham. It was a meal that would
have pleased even your monarch. And now, my brothers
and I bid you a good evening.''

Leonora stood beside her father and watched as the three
giants walked away. Those few soldiers who had remained
by the fire fell silent and turned to watch them pass. The
Highlanders looked neither right nor left, but stared straight
ahead as they strode purposefully from the great hall.

''What think you of our guests, Father?''

Lord Waltham continued to watch until the three were out
of sight. Then he turned to her.

"I think," he said softly, "they are not at all what they seem. We would be wise to treat our Scottish neighbors with respect. Our future, our very lives, may be in the hands of this Highlander, Dillon Campbell."

Chapter Three

Dillon paced the floor of the sitting chamber. In the next room, his brothers could be heard arguing. The door to their sleeping chamber was suddenly yanked open, and Shaw entered carrying an armload of bed linens.

"What are you doing?" Dillon asked.

"Sutton has ordered me out of the chamber. I will sleep in here beside the fire."

"Why?"

Shaw shrugged and stared pointedly at the floor. "You will have to ask him yourself."

Storming into the room, Dillon said, "What foolishness is this? Why have you sent your own brother from this chamber?"

"The wench, Verda, has offered to warm my bed." From a basin, Sutton splashed water on his face and chest, and dried himself with a square of linen.

Dillon's eyes narrowed. "And you agreed?"

Sutton blushed. From the time he was a mere lad, women had been his greatest weakness. But, as he had often had to explain to Father Anselm whenever he'd arrived at the monastery late for vespers, it was not his fault that women young and old threw themselves at his feet. There was just something about him that caused such things to happen.

"She said she is quite taken with me. She personally saw that my tankard was never empty. And she fed me the finest cuts of meat from the platter."

"The wench would do the same for a dog if he had a fine pallet that she could share." Dillon stormed back into the sitting chamber and picked up the bed linens, flinging them through the open doorway.

"But she said she liked the way I look," Sutton shouted.

Dillon stood in the doorway, legs far apart, hands on hips. "And for the sake of a little flattery, you would let an English servant endanger all our lives?"

Sutton looked astonished. "You think one small female could bring us harm?"

"One small dagger, perfectly aimed by the female's hand, is all it would take to snuff out your life while you slept beside her, Sutton. Is the wench worth the risk?"

His brother ran a hand through his hair, then looked away. "I was not thinking. I... peered down her bodice and..."

"So did every man in that room," Dillon said with a sigh. "'Twas as she planned it. The wench is well aware of her charms, and how to use them." Dillon smiled. "But remember, brother, we are not here for pleasure. We represent our countrymen. Every Englishman we meet will judge all Scots by the way we behave."

His brother began to relax. Though Dillon's temper was legend, he had learned, after years of effort, to curb it in favor of humor.

"Forgive me." Sutton shook his head. "I give you my word, Dillon. When the wench knocks this night, my door will be barred to her." He held out his hand.

Dillon nodded his approval and crossed the room to accept his brother's handshake.

"Now, Dillon, tell us what you think of the Englishmen," Shaw said as he began to hastily remake his sleeping pallet. He was relieved that his older brother had intervened. His twin's easy way with the women was often difficult for Shaw to take. Especially since he had chosen a life of celibacy for himself.

Dillon poured a goblet of ale from a flagon and took a seat by the fire. "Lord Alec Waltham seems an honorable man. The king has chosen wisely. Our host will set the tone of the meetings that begin on the morrow. George Godwin, the Duke of Essex, on the other hand, is obviously unhappy with this meeting. I think he will do all in his power to see that the peace council fails."

"You will challenge him?"

"I will."

"How?"

Dillon's tone remained as easy as if they were discussing the weather. But his brothers heard the threat underlying the words. "It will all depend upon Essex and what he chooses to do."

"What of the aged man who walks with a cane?"

"Lord John Forest, the king's own counsel, is more difficult to discern. He seems a cautious man, and one who will decide only after all the terms have been agreed upon."

"What of the Blakelys, father and son?" Shaw asked.

Dillon's hand closed imperceptibly around the stem of the goblet. "Lord James Blakely is shrewd. And a soldier. Those two traits make him a dangerous opponent. He has learned to keep his true feelings hidden until he is upon the field of battle. But this much I know. As a soldier, he will gain nothing by a peace between our two countries."

"His son, Alger, is also a soldier," Shaw said.

"Aye. But he is too blinded by his heart, which shines from his eyes."

Shaw smiled. "I saw the way he kept you and the lady Leonora in his line of vision throughout the evening. The poor dolt is in love."

"But does he love the lady," Sutton asked with a chuckle, "or the lady's dowry? Judging by her father's estates, 'twould be considerable."

"It is of no concern to us." Dillon gave a shrug of his shoulders. "It is enough to know that Alger Blakely will do whatever pleases the lady. And the lady is a dutiful daughter. Though she mistrusts us, she will do all in her power to bring about the success of her father's mission for his king."

"What of the bishop?" Sutton asked.

Dillon glanced at their brother Shaw, who was pledged to the Church. "I mean no disrespect, but the Bishop of York, though a man of God, seems no more than a puppet. A lifetime of ease and comfort, enjoying the friendship of the king, has blinded him to truth. I think he will put aside moral judgments and follow wherever the others lead."

"Then what chance have we of succeeding?" Shaw asked as he climbed between the covers. "The only Englishman who is on our side is Lord Alec Waltham."

"We are Highland warriors, sent by Robert the Bruce, at the invitation of the King of England." Dillon stood, placed the empty goblet on a table, then strode to the door. Both his brothers were already in their pallets. Fueled by their arduous journey and the amount of food and ale consumed during the evening's feast, their eyes were heavy with the need for sleep. "All our lives, we have been outnumbered. But we have always kept our goals clearly in our line of vision." His tone lowered. "If King Edward's emissaries are like-minded, we will return to Scotland with the fragile hope for peace between our countries still alive."

"Aye." Sutton stifled a yawn, while Shaw gave in to the need for sleep. "On the morrow, then, the tale will be told."

Dillon smiled and closed the door, knowing that his brothers were already dreaming. Though the hour was late, he had no desire to sleep. Pausing before the fire, he thought again about the men with whom he would be dealing.

Throughout his life, he had nurtured a hatred for all things English. He touched a hand to the thin scar that ran from his temple to his jaw. That hatred had heated his blood through many a cold winter, and had driven him to become the fiercest warrior in all of Scotland.

Now the fates had decreed that he would be the one to talk of peace. At first, it had stuck in his throat like a stone. But now, slowly, rationally, though it was still bitter, he had begun to swallow it, and even to accept the taste. Peace. Though he still burned with the need to avenge the murders of his father and mother and his entire clan, he would try, for the sake of his younger brothers and sister, and the generations of the Clan Campbell not yet born, to put the hatred to rest.

The morrow would tell the tale. If these English were willing to deal fairly, he would do the same.

Feeling restless, he tossed his cloak over his shoulders and strode from the room. A walk in the garden was just what he needed to clear his head before attempting sleep.

Leonora sat on a stone bench, listening to the sounds of the night. Insects hummed and chirped. A night bird cried as it swooped past like a dark shadow.

Looking up at the stars, she felt a wave of loneliness. Always, in times of crises, she missed her mother. That good woman would have known just what to say to make these strangers feel welcome. She would have offered wise counsel to her husband, who could be heard pacing in his chambers before Leonora had stolen away into the garden. She chewed on her lip. Her mother would have known how to soothe the tensions between her own countrymen and these strangers in their midst. And most important of all, she would have known just how to ease her daughter's fears.

Fear. Aye. Fear and—more. What was it about this savage, Dillon Campbell, that had her so unnerved? Even at

Westminster, pitted against royals and noblemen, she had never felt so out of her element. There, at least, she could rely on propriety and good manners. But here, in the company of this man, she had no rules to guide her.

Hearing a footfall, she got to her feet, expecting to see one of her father's soldiers. Instead, she found herself face-to-face with the man who had just been occupying so many of her thoughts.

She lifted a hand to her throat. "You . . . startled me."

Dillon studied the figure in the hooded cloak, who blended in with the shadowed hedges and trees. "Forgive me, my lady. I had expected to be alone in the garden at such an hour." He glanced around. "Is it safe for you to be here?"

She felt offended by such a question. "You ask if I am safe in my father's own keep? I assure you, if someone wished me harm, they would face the wrath of a hundred soldiers who stand guard."

"The soldiers have been fortified with wine, my lady. Even now, they lie asleep. If someone wished you harm, you would be helpless to defend yourself."

Her eyes narrowed. "Why do you try to frighten me with talk of savagery? Is this the way of your people?"

He gave a sigh of impatience. This female was as unpleasant as the rest of her countrymen. "I do not wish to make you uneasy, my lady. It is just that, in my country, the women no longer feel safe even within the walls of a keep."

"And why is that, sir? Have your men become so depraved that they would attack even helpless women?"

His tone deepened with anger. "It is not my men they fear. It is yours, my lady."

He made a move to walk past her, but her hand shot out, catching the sleeve of his cloak. She would teach this savage manners while he was under the roof of civilized men.

"You would accuse noble Englishmen of attacking innocent women?"

Without a word, he stared down at the offending hand. Almost at once she removed it. The look in his eyes caused her to take a step back.

"Aye. And helpless children, as well."

Had she not been so angry, she would have recognized, by the thickened burr, the deep well of anger in his words. But her own temper was propelling her to disregard common sense.

"You go too far, sir."

Leonora's reaction was so spontaneous, even she was stunned by it. She slapped him as hard as she could, her hand swinging out in a wide arc and landing with a resounding crack against his cheek.

Reflexively, his arm snaked out. For a moment, she could only stare at him as his hand closed around her wrist. Strength. She had never felt such controlled strength in any man. She could feel anger pulsing through him as his fingers bit into her flesh. Though his anger was a terrible thing to behold, she refused to apologize or back down, now that she had made such a dangerous miscalculation.

"You are hurting me."

He tightened his grip and drew her closer until she could feel the sting of his breath against her temple. "You do not know what it is to be hurt, my lady." He nodded toward the torches that burned on either side of the castle door. "All your life, you have taken such safety and comfort for granted, while my people have had to live in fear of the next raid by your hated English soldiers."

Lifting her chin in a gesture of defiance, she said, "If you raise your hand against me, you are no better than those you accuse."

"I do not raise my hand against women. That is the way of the English." He released her as though the very touch of her offended him.

Rubbing her bruised wrist, she turned away, eager to flee to the safety of the castle. "Never before have I been so brutalized in my own father's garden."

"Brutalized?" His voice was a strangled whisper of fury.

He caught her roughly by the arm and twisted her to face him. With his hands gripping her upper arms, he held her fast when she tried to free herself. "My lady, if it were my intention to harm you, you would be already lying dead at my feet."

Fear and anger made her careless with her words. "The Duke of Essex was right. You are nothing more than a ragged, dirty savage, who does not belong among civilized men."

She saw something dark and dangerous flicker in his eyes. His fingers tightened on the soft flesh of her upper arms until she cried out, but he was beyond hearing.

"A savage, am I?" Drawing her close, he whispered, "Let this be a lesson to you, my lady."

She knew that she had pushed him beyond the limit of his control. Fear skittered along her spine as he dragged her against him.

She stiffened. Sweet heaven, he was going to violate her. Her heart slammed in her chest. Her pulse accelerated. She felt light-headed. Her breathing stilled.

He bent his head. "Never invite a snake into your garden, my lady."

His lips brushed the hair at her temple, then moved lower to graze her cheek. He experienced a sudden shock. Her skin was the softest he had ever touched.

"Aye, a snake is what you are. But I did not invite you, sir. You are here unbidden." She stiffened in his arms. His mouth hovered mere inches from hers, teasing her, taunting her. Her heart lodged in her throat, threatening to choke her. She felt afraid, yet strangely exhilarated. She felt as if she were standing on a precipice. One step, one tiny movement, and she would find herself hurtling through space.

Dillon moved his hands along her shoulders. Staring down into her eyes, he could read fear and innocence there. And something more. Defiance. Though the female was terrified of him, she stood her ground. He found himself responding to that underlying strength in her. Despite her youth and innocence, here was a woman who would be a match for any man. He could sense an almost simmering sensuality in this Englishwoman. A sensuality of which she seemed completely unaware.

Common sense told him to walk away and leave her as he had found her. But he saw the way she lifted her head defiantly, determined to fight him. His gaze fastened on her mouth. It would take only the slightest movement to taste those lips.

He hesitated, and thought briefly about fighting the desire. Then swearing under his breath he bent to her. That haughty lift of her chin, those pouty lips, were too great a temptation.

His mouth covered hers, sending shock waves crashing through her. One moment she was cold from the night air. The next moment she was on fire.

At first, the kiss was harsh, bruising. But the moment his lips found hers, he forgot that his intention had been to punish her.

God in heaven. Her lips were soft, and warm, and...trembling. He knew at once that this was the first time she had ever been kissed so brazenly.

He lifted his head and held her a little away. "My lady." His tone was gruff. He was amazed at how difficult it was to speak.

She opened her eyes and looked up in surprise.

"How is it that you have never kissed a man before?"

She blinked, humiliated that he would dare to ask such a question. "You are not a man. You are a savage—"

A smile touched his lips. "And you are even more beautiful when you are angry." He dragged her against him and covered her mouth with his. She smelled of crushed roses and some vaguely remembered scent from his childhood that evoked a rush of tenderness that left him shaken. Despite his anger, the kiss softened, until his lips moved over hers with gentle persuasion.

Leonora had been prepared for the worst. Her eyes were scrunched tightly shut. Her hands were balled into fists, which she held as a barrier between their two chests.

She could have withstood an assault; it would have fueled her hatred of this brute. But she was totally unprepared for this tender side of his nature.

Hadn't she always wondered what it would be like to be kissed by a man? Not one of the groping peacocks at court, but a strong, virile man, who would make her blood heat and her knees tremble. Would her eyes be open or closed? Would their noses bump? Would she be able to breathe, or would she be forced to hold her breath until she suffocated?

Now she no longer had to wonder. His lips were gentle, coaxing hers with feather-light kisses. Heat spread from his hands on her shoulders, from his mouth on hers, to her blood, which coursed like liquid fire through her veins.

She breathed in the musky scent of him. At that moment, he changed the angle of the kiss. Their heads turned just enough so that their noses didn't touch. She was surprised and pleased at the way the angles and planes of his body accentuated the softness of hers.

Against her will, her hands opened and her fingers curled into the front of his cloak. Though she was unaware of it, a sigh escaped her lips, and she gave herself up to the pure sensual pleasure of the moment.

His lips were warm and firm and practiced, and moved over hers with the skill of one who was accustomed to such sweet diversions.

She had no defenses against the sensations that pulsed through her. Sensations that were so new, so frightening, they left her trembling.

His grip on her shoulders tightened, drawing her firmly against him. She gave a little gasp of surprise when his tongue traced the outline of her lips, then darted inside her mouth. Her hands clutched at his back and she felt the heat of him all the way through his cloak.

Lifting his head, Dillon stared down at the young woman in his arms. She tasted sweet, alluring. Her eyes were wide, luminous, too big for her face. He could read confusion in those eyes, and something more; the first flush of desire. His arms came around her, until he felt the softness of her melting into him. His lips covered hers in a searing kiss that left her dazed and breathless.

Her breath caught in her throat. The heat became a fire, leaving her weak and clinging. Fear became excitement. Pleasure became need, a need she had never before experienced.

He was so strong, he could crush her. Yet he held her as carefully as if she were a fragile flower. She could feel the tightly controlled power, which only seemed to inflame her more.

He felt her fear fade into acquiescence. With her breasts flattened against his chest, he could feel her, warm and pliant in his arms.

Something deep inside him tightened, and he felt the rush of desire, swift, pulsing, before he banked the need. He had to end this now, quickly, before it got out of control. Had he not just lectured his brothers to be cautious of these

Englishwomen? Fool, he berated himself. He was a guest in her father's home, here in her country on a mission that would determine the fate of generations. What kind of fool would jeopardize everything for the sake of one small female?

Calling on all his willpower, he pushed her from him and took a step back.

She struggled to maintain her balance. Her eyes widened for one brief moment before she lowered her lashes and looked away in shame. She had not merely submitted; she had been a willing party to what had just transpired. Now she must find a way to ease her conscience.

Wiping the back of her hand across her mouth, she whispered, "You have just proven to me that the Duke of Essex was right. You are nothing more than a filthy savage."

"Aye." He bowed grandly and his eyes glittered as he reached out a hand and dragged her close.

Instantly they both felt the flare of heat. And both denied it.

"So, beware of savages and snakes, my lady." He caught her chin and stared down at her. Her lips were still moist and swollen from his kiss. The sight of it brought a rush of desire that left him shaken.

Leonora felt a warmth spread through her limbs at even that brief contact.

"Next time, this snake may devour you."

She twisted herself free of his grasp. "If you dare to touch me again, Highlander, you will face the wrath of my father's soldiers."

She saw the gleam of laughter in his eyes before he swung away. Over his shoulder, he taunted, "If I wanted you, my lady, there would not be enough soldiers in all of England to stop me."

With trembling legs, Leonora sank upon the stone bench and dragged cold night air into her lungs to steady her nerves.

He had been right about one thing. She had never before been kissed like that. Even at court, where passions were boldly played out in front of all, her father had gone to great pains to shelter his only child. There had been men who, emboldened by wine and caught in the grip of power, had attempted to seduce her. But their clumsy attempts had always repelled her. This man, on the other hand, had elicited a response from her that had left her shaken to the core.

Oh, Mother, she whispered, pressing a hand to her trembling lips. What have I done? How will I ever face him on the morrow?

Refusing to give in to her fear, she lifted her skirts and stalked to the door of the castle. Damn the savage! she thought as she fled to the safety of her room. And damn the fates that had brought him to her father's castle.

In the garden, the man who occupied her thoughts was pacing the darkened paths like a caged animal. And muttering a few rich ripe curses of his own.

Chapter Four

A single candle dispelled the darkness in the tower room. Two hooded figures faced each other. On the table between them was a flagon and two goblets. The night sky was visible through the balcony window.

"You saw for yourself." The voice was little more than a whisper. "The Highlander cannot be goaded into a fight."

"Aye." The second man's lips curved into a smile. "But I saw something else, as well. I think I have discerned his weakness."

The hand holding the goblet paused in midair. "A weakness? I saw none. The man is fearless."

"For himself, perhaps. But did you not see how quickly he prevented his brother from displaying his anger?"

"Because he is sworn to uphold the peace."

"Nay." White teeth gleamed in the light of the candle. "I saw the look in his eyes when he thought his brother's temper would explode. That, then, is the Highlander's weakness. Not fear for himself. Fear for his brothers."

There was a long silence.

"Perhaps."

"I know it. The Highlander has set himself up as protector of his younger brothers. We will use that to our advantage."

"How? They are always together. They have not been out of his sight since he arrived."

"No matter. Have your men in position on the morrow. When I give the signal, the brothers must be taken quickly. The Highlander will have no choice but to do our bidding."

"If Lord Waltham should learn who plotted this deed, he will go to the king."

"Aye. Unless, of course, he believes that the order comes from Edward himself. The king." The whispered voice was a sneer of disgust. "Because of Edward's unpopularity, he cannot even raise enough taxes to fund a war against the Scots. Thus we are forced to bargain with these savages instead of facing them on a field of battle. Aye, we will let Lord Waltham think that the order comes from his monarch. If this is what it takes to bring down the throne, so be it."

"Hush, man." Eyes wide with fear peered around, as if expecting to see ghosts armed with swords leap out of the shadows. "Such treasonous talk could find your tongue silenced forever."

"Is it treason to desire a strong, independent England?"

"Nay."

"'Tis for that reason I live. 'Tis for that reason I am willing to die. That is why these peace talks must be stopped now. Do you stand with me?" He paused for emphasis. "Or do you stand against me?"

The man took a sip of ale, considering. "You really believe the Highlander will concede rather than see his brothers die by the sword?"

"I do. And once he has affixed his mark to the parchment, he will be bound by it, as will all Scots. Then, at least, we will have peace on our terms, and not on his."

The man took a deep breath, then held out his hand. "I stand with you in this."

"The deed must be done on the morrow, before any talk of peace can begin. You will see to it?"

"Aye."

He lifted his goblet. "To England."

"To England."

Both men drank until their goblets were drained. Then, they quickly stole from the tower room and made their way to their sleeping chambers.

Dillon stood on the balcony watching dawn creep slowly across the land. It was not the rich, verdant hills that held his interest, nor the fattened flocks of sheep. His gaze was fixed on the horizon, on that unseen boundary between England and Scotland.

Home. He yearned for it. Ached for it.

He was uneasy. All night he had tossed and turned. He knew that much of his unease was due to the female. He cursed again the fates that had thrown them together. Though he despised all things English, he could not deny the attraction to Lord Waltham's daughter. The kiss they had shared in the garden would not soon be forgotten. Nor the passion that kiss had unleashed. Dillon Campbell was a man who prided himself on control in all facets of his life. What had happened in the garden last night must never happen again.

But some of his unease was also due to the peace council that would commence this day. The council had been planned by men of good will, but all his senses told him that there was little of that in this place. He was a man who had always trusted his instincts. And ever since his arrival in England, his senses had been shouting danger.

He rubbed his shoulder, which ached from an old wound. How much of the danger was real and how much imagined? After a lifetime of hatred, was it possible to put aside such feelings and start anew? Could he ever truly trust these English?

He swallowed the knot of uneasiness. For the sake of his brothers and sister, he would do whatever was necessary to establish an honorable peace between their two countries. But he would never forget that he was a warrior. He would never give up the freedom hard-won on the field of battle. Those were rewards the English would never take from his people. Too many had already given their lives for a few precious freedoms. He would see that their deaths had not been in vain.

"Did you sleep at all, Dillon?"

He turned to where his brother stood in the doorway of the sitting chamber.

"Some. And you, Shaw?"

"Like a bairn."

"Good." Dillon smiled fondly at this gentle, religious brother, so unlike himself. Perhaps Shaw's sleep was always so peaceful because it mirrored his soul. "I want you and Sutton to be well rested before the talks begin."

Sutton poked his head around the doorway, looking abject. "How could I sleep knowing the serving wench was forced to endure a lonely pallet in the scullery?"

"A *lonely* pallet?" Dillon winked at Shaw. "There were at least a score of titled gentlemen at table who were eager to sample the wench's charms. I'll wager a gold sovereign she did not sleep alone."

"All the more reason that I should have insisted she stay with me," Sutton retorted. "At least then, the wench would wake this morrow with a satisfied smile."

Dillon threw back his head and roared. These two beloved brothers, the sun and moon of his life, could always make him forget his worries.

"Come," he said. "Let us dress and hurry below stairs."

"Aye. I am eager to break my fast." Sutton splashed water on his face.

"You are just eager to see the serving wench," Shaw muttered.

Sutton's lips curved into a wide smile. "That, too, my brother. But not nearly as eager as the wench is to see me."

Shaw was still shaking his head when Dillon turned away to dress.

Leonora stood in the great hall, directing the servants. Since the council would begin as soon as the men had broken their fast, she was determined that this first meal of the day would be sumptuous. Her mother had always said that a man must first fill his belly before he could bare his soul.

The cooks had labored through the night to roast wild pigs and lambs, platters of doves and all the fish that could be caught by the nearby villagers. The room was redolent of the fragrance of bread baking on the hearth.

As she had the previous night, Leonora had taken great pains with her appearance this morning. It was not, she told herself, to impress Dillon Campbell. She was doing this for England.

Over Moira's objections, she had insisted upon wearing a rich violet gown that accentuated the color of her eyes and put a bloom on her cheeks. A deep purple amethyst the size of a hen's egg rested in the shadowed cleft of her breasts, secured by a rope of gold around her neck. Her waist-length hair, as always, was swept into a loose netting that bobbed at her shoulders.

Her old nurse hurried toward her, carrying a shawl of exquisite lace, which she tossed over Leonora's shoulders.

"Ye'll catch a chill without this, child."

"What would I do without you, Moira?"

"Aye, what indeed? I've been dressing you, spoiling you, pampering you, since the day you were born. Ye'd be lost without old Moira."

Leonora gave her a gentle smile. "I thought you were too afraid of the Highlanders to come below stairs."

"That I am. The heathens," she growled contemptuously. "But 'tis too early for the likes of them to be showing their faces. I'll be safely in my chambers before any of them can see me. Now let me look at you, child." She gave a sigh that could have been pleasure or exasperation. "Ye're growing up too fast. In no time ye'll be leaving your father's home and making a life with some handsome nobleman."

Leonora hugged the old woman. "If I do, Moira, you shall be coming with me."

At that, her old nurse beamed and turned away, then gave a little gasp and stopped in midstride. Leonora turned, and felt the heat rush to her cheeks at the sight of the three Highlanders standing in the doorway. She immediately cursed her reaction. Why did the sight of Dillon Campbell always cause that little flutter in the pit of her stomach? He was only a man, after all. And not even a particularly handsome one.

Dillon strode forward, trailed by his brothers.

"Good morrow, my lady." He lifted her hand to his lips, ignoring the jolt that danced along his limbs as soon as they touched.

Flustered, Leonora found herself staring at his mouth. She could still taste him. Earthy. Overpowering.

To deflect his attention, she said, "This is my nurse, Moira, who has been with our household since before I was born."

"Madame." He nodded to the old woman and watched with amusement as she immediately crossed herself and moved closer to Leonora like a mother hen protecting her chick.

His gaze settled once more on the young woman standing before him. He noticed the color of her gown brought out the deep violet of her eyes. "I trust you slept well, my lady, after your walk in the garden."

"Aye. Very well, sir." She would not give him the satisfaction of knowing that she had tossed and turned the entire night.

"I hope you encountered no more snakes, my lady."

"None," she said haughtily. She saw Moira cast a suspicious look in her direction and silently cursed Dillon Campbell. The old woman had heard her pacing through the night and had inquired about her disturbed sleep. Now that she knew that her young charge had met this Highlander in the garden, the questions would never end. Leonora could never bring herself to tell Moira about the kiss she and the Scotsman had shared. It was far too intimate a secret. And much too troubling.

They looked up as Lord Waltham and the other English nobles entered the great hall. While their host greeted his guests, several serving wenches approached with trays of goblets.

Accepting a goblet, the Duke of Essex said, "Tell us about your first night under an English roof, Highlander. Were you able to sleep? Or did the thought of our soldiers standing guard keep you awake throughout the night?"

Dillon gritted his teeth at the smug look on the Englishman's face. "I trust those soldiers are here for my protection as well as yours. Having come here in the name of peace, my sleep was undisturbed by the thought of English soldiers."

"I am pleased to hear that." Lord Waltham stepped between the two men and hoped his daughter would prove a pleasant diversion. "Does not my daughter look as fresh as a rosebud?'' Drawing her close, he pressed a kiss to her cheek. "It does my heart good just to look upon you, Leonora."

She felt Dillon's gaze burning over her and knew that her cheeks were suffused with color. "Are you ready to break your fast, Father?"

"Aye."

Out of the corner of his eye, Dillon saw the wench, Verda, whisper to Sutton. The lad smiled broadly, then followed her a short distance away before he stopped and leaned down to whisper in her ear.

Though thus distracted, Dillon heard James Blakely say, "Perhaps the younger lads, Sutton and Shaw, would prefer to join my son at our table this morrow."

Before Dillon could refuse, their host nodded his head enthusiastically. "It would do them good to befriend one another. I thank you, James." Lord Waltham turned to Dillon. "You will join my daughter and me, while Sutton and Shaw break their fast with Alger Blakely and his father."

Dillon gave a curt nod of his head, annoyed that he had been manipulated so easily. But to refuse now would be a display of bad manners. He could not insult his host. With little enthusiasm he said, "Shaw, if you would be good enough to fetch your brother."

"Aye."

Shaw crossed the room and dropped a hand on Sutton's shoulder. While Dillon followed Leonora and her father to the table of honor on the raised platform, the twins walked a short distance away to sit with the English noblemen. Though Dillon tried to keep both brothers in his line of vision, he soon found it impossible. The soldiers entered the hall and took their places at table. Dozens of servants milled about, offering food from steaming platters. It was a scene of great confusion.

Forcing himself to relax, Dillon turned to Lord Waltham, who began plying him with questions.

"Tell me about your clan, Dillon. As clan leader, are you like a king?"

"Nay, I am no king," Dillon replied honestly. He sipped his ale and wondered how he could describe a life so vastly different from what this man knew and understood. "In the Highlands," Dillon went on, "a clan leader is as dependent upon the people as they are on him. He must be a fearless warrior, but he must also be the father of his people, governing the territory for the benefit of all, dividing the land in such a way as to provide for each member, including the elderly and the sick."

"Is that not what our king does?" Lord Waltham asked gently.

"It is said that your king rewards his friends with vast estates, while stripping his enemies of everything they have ever owned." Dillon's voice lowered. "Worst of all, when he dies, his heir assumes the throne, without having to prove himself fearless in battle, or even honorable in his dealings with other men. Why should your people have to accept such a man as king?"

"It is his right because he is of royal lineage," Leonora said as patiently as if she were lecturing a child.

"Aye. But such lineage does not guarantee that a man will be worthy of the crown. Often the heir is a tyrant, and the people must suffer until he dies and another, perhaps even crueler, takes his place."

Leonora was scandalized. "What you speak is treasonous."

Dillon smiled at her. "Only the English must guard their tongues, my lady. Since Edward is not my king, I need not fear his wrath."

"If the son of a clan leader cannot inherit his father's title, how is a new clan leader chosen?" Lord Waltham asked.

"In my land, when one clan leader dies, another is chosen by the clan. They must choose wisely. In times of peace, he is the final arbiter of any dispute, and in time of war, he must lead his clan to battle. In return, the members of the clan give him utter and undying loyalty."

"You make your leaders sound like gods." Leonora couldn't hide a trace of sarcasm.

"Nay. Far from it, my lady. We are mere men, with all the faults, all the failings of men. But our loyalty is unquestioned. I am here, not out of personal choice, but because Robert the Bruce commanded it. Though he is not king, he is the acknowledged leader of all the Scots and a trusted friend. And no matter how difficult, I will work out the terms of peace, as long as those terms are honorable for my people."

"And if they are not?" Leonora asked.

"Then I shall—"

They looked up at the sound of a scuffle. The English noblemen had surrounded Sutton and Shaw and pinned their arms behind their backs. The soldiers were already preparing to join the fray.

Dillon cursed his carelessness. Ever since their arrival, he'd sensed danger. But he'd allowed himself to ignore the warnings. Pushing away from the table, he scrambled to his feet. Before anyone could stop him, he leaped upon the head table and ran, scattering food and drink as he jumped from the raised platform to the tables below. As he ran he pulled a knife from his waist.

From his position at the head table, Lord Waltham thundered, "Unhand those men! They are guests in my home."

"Nay." Seeing the Highlander bearing down on him, the Duke of Essex held a knife to Shaw's throat, while beside him, both James Blakely and his son, Alger, struggled with the kicking, biting Sutton, who was not going to be subdued without a fight. "The lads drew weapons from a place of concealment and threatened harm."

"'Tis a lie, Dillon," Shaw shouted. "We did not draw our weapons until we were forced to by the man who attacked us."

"Who attacked you?" their host asked.

"It was—" A hand covered Sutton's mouth, stifling any further attempt to speak.

Dillon's eyes flashed in fury as he swung into the crowd. By now, a hundred soldiers hurried forward, swords at the ready. Those closest to the Scot fell back at the sight of the knife glinting in his hand. They had expected him to be an easy mark, without weapons. All had heard the rumors of the skill of the Highlanders with both sword and dirk.

Leaping onto another table, Dillon turned to Lord Waltham and cried, "My brother Shaw has pledged himself to the Church. He would never utter a falsehood. If he says this thing is a lie, then it is so."

"I am also a man of the Church," the Bishop of York cried, getting to his feet so quickly the bench upon which he'd been sitting fell backward. "And I saw these lads draw their weapons."

"As did I," the Lord John Forest said calmly. "In my capacity as counsel to the king, I demand that these men be taken to the dungeons, in order to secure the safety of all."

"This is a trick. Unhand my brothers," Dillon shouted as he moved menacingly closer. All in his path fell away, eager to avoid his wrath.

"Do as the Highlander asks," called Lord Waltham.

Immediately, the Duke of Essex countered Waltham's order with one of his own. "Blakely," he shouted, "I command you to summon your soldiers at once."

Alger Blakely and his father looked from one man to the other for direction. The elder Blakely asked, "By whose command, my lord?"

''By order of the king.'' Essex's voice rang with authority.

''Forgive me, Lord Waltham,'' James Blakely shouted. ''But all loyal Englishmen must put the orders of their king above all else.''

Instantly, the two signaled to the soldiers, who drew their swords and advanced. Though he had nothing but a knife, Dillon leaped into the throng. Despite their fear of him, their sheer numbers made them bold. And though he fought like a man possessed, his knife was no match against so many English swords.

His two brothers, held fast and unable to join him in the fray, were forced to watch helplessly.

Leonora clutched her father's arm and watched in horrified fascination as the Highlander lashed out at those who would disarm him. The sight of one lone man standing against an army of swordsmen left her breathless. Despite her loyalty to the soldiers who confronted him, she could not help but admire the magnificent warrior.

At last, with his shirt hanging in tatters, and his arms and torso bloodied from a dozen wounds, Dillon's knife dropped uselessly to the floor and he was pinned against the wall by a dozen sword tips. The soldiers, angered by his display and shamed by his superior skill, now took every opportunity to inflict further pain with their blades. The floor beneath his feet ran red with his blood.

Leonora covered her mouth with her hand and turned away in shock and revulsion. He had fought nobly. He deserved better treatment at the hands of her father's soldiers.

Lord Waltham, equally sickened by the violence, held up his hands as the soldiers formed a circle around the Highlanders, while Essex and the Blakelys, father and son, held knives to their throats.

"Even though the peace has been broken," Lord Waltham cried, "we will find a way to settle this thing now and continue as we had planned."

"Nay!" Essex shouted louder, drowning out the voice of moderation. "Before we speak of peace, these three savages must be taken to the dungeons and stripped, to see that all their weapons have been removed from them."

"This is a trick, Dillon," Sutton shouted. "Once they have separated us, we will never see each other again."

"Aye." Dillon, seeing the attention of the soldiers focused on their host, grasped at the last chance to escape, no matter how slender. "But it will not work."

With what remained of his strength, he thrust his elbow into Alger Blakely's midsection, knocking the wind from him with such force that the young soldier dropped to his knees in agony. While the younger Blakely writhed and moaned, Dillon again leaped across the tables and vaulted to the platform. In the blink of an eye, he pulled a knife from his boot. When he straightened, he wrapped an arm around Leonora's neck and held the razor-sharp blade to her throat.

There was a collective gasp from everyone in the hall. That the Highlander should sully a fair English maiden was unthinkable. The sight of his bloody hands leaving their mark upon her flesh subdued the entire crowd into stunned silence.

All eyes were on them as Lord Waltham shouted, "You will unhand my daughter at once."

"Only when my brothers are released," Dillon said in a dangerously soft voice.

In desperation, Lord Waltham turned to the soldiers. "Release the Highlanders."

The soldiers fell back, but the noblemen who were holding the twins prisoner refused to follow suit.

"Essex," Lord Waltham called. "Did you not hear me? Release those men at once so that my daughter will suffer no further indignities."

"The Highlander may be a fool, but even a fool knows he cannot escape this castle, even using the Lady Leonora as a shield. He must first answer to the swords of a hundred English soldiers. And if that is not enough, he must travel a hundred miles across English land." Essex gave a laughing sneer. "Do you not see, Waltham? If we release his brothers, he will be free to take his revenge against your daughter. You saw these three. Though they made a pretense of relinquishing their weapons, they kept their knives. How many other weapons do they still have concealed upon them?"

Lord Waltham turned to the Highlander, who continued to stand as still as a statue, holding the precious Leonora at the point of his knife. "By all that is holy, I beg you to release my daughter, and this thing between us will be forgotten."

"That is what you say, Lord Waltham." Dillon's voice was deadly calm. "But I would hear it from the others."

Lord Waltham turned toward the Duke of Essex. "I beg you, Essex. Stop the madness."

"We will release his beloved brothers," Essex stated, "when the Highlander affixes his mark upon this peace treaty that has already been prepared."

He tossed down a scroll, which was picked up by the bishop and handed to their host.

Lord Waltham read the scroll, then looked up sharply. "Who is responsible for this?"

"'Twas written at the request of the king," Essex said.

"Nay. Edward would not have brought the Highlanders here under such falsehoods." Lord Waltham's face was a mask of outrage. "This is a trick."

"It is no trick. Now, Highlander, affix your mark to the scroll..." Essex tightened his grasp on Shaw, and held the blade of his knife against the lad's tender flesh until a trickle of blood stained the front of his tunic. "Or you will be forced to watch me slit your beloved brother's throat."

Dillon's fury was a terrible thing to behold. His dark eyes flashed with a deadly fire. His voice was as cold, as cutting, as the knife in his hand.

"Englishman, you have sealed the woman's fate." Before anyone could stop him, Dillon flung Leonora over his shoulder like a sack of grain and raced up the steps leading to the door of the great hall. Turning to face the stunned noblemen, he shouted, "Whatever you do to my brothers will be done to the woman. And unless they are returned to me unharmed, you will never see her again."

With Lord Alec Waltham and the others watching helplessly, he and his captive disappeared through the archway.

Chapter Five

A cold, dark terror welled up in Leonora's throat, threatening to choke her. This could not be happening. It was all some terrible, horrible nightmare.

Everything Moira had told her flashed through her mind. Heathens. Savages. Drink the blood of English children. One Highlander can defeat an entire English army.

Leonora's last glimpse of her father, before she disappeared up the stairwell, was his face contorted in shock, his eyes wide with fear.

Fear? His fear fueled her own. She had never before seen such a look in her father's eyes. He had always been the proud, strong, capable man whose life was well ordered, disciplined. Since her childhood, she had taken her safety for granted, as befitted the daughter of a trusted friend of the king. No one would dare to harm her. No one, until this . . . Highland savage.

In the courtyard, Dillon dropped her unceremoniously in the dirt and whirled as a stable boy approached. The boy, seeing the knife in the Scot's hands, released the reins of the horse he was leading and took a step back.

"I wish you no harm, lad," Dillon growled as he seized the horse's reins. "But if you do not turn and flee now, I will be forced to kill you."

"But the lady—"

"Is of no concern to you, lad." Dillon brandished the knife. "If you value your life, you will leave us."

His features were so hard, so fearsome, they could have been carved from stone. Seeing this barely controlled fury, the boy clamped his mouth shut on the protest he was about to issue. Without another look, he turned and fled.

Leonora scrambled to her feet, determined to escape, as well. But before she could take a step, Dillon pulled himself into the saddle and, leaning down, scooped her into his arms. Though she kicked and fought and bit at the hands holding her until she drew blood, she was no match for his strength. At last, fighting tears of frustration, she was forced to endure the prison of his arms.

"Please, I beg you." She struggled to keep the terror that gnawed at her from being revealed in her voice. "It is not too late to let me go. Even now my father will forgive you and find a way to begin anew."

"Forgive *me?*" His voice shook with a terrible fury. "It is he who should beg my forgiveness. It is he who lured us here with lies of peace."

"They were not lies. He believed in this peace."

"As did I. And see how I am rewarded. I would gladly give my life for my brothers. They are worth more to me than anything in this world. Instead, I am helpless to free them."

"Helpless?" she snapped sarcastically, thinking of the number of soldiers who were inside nursing wounds inflicted by this man's vicious attack.

His eyes glinted with fury. "Aye. I must take one puny hostage in return for their safekeeping, and pray it is enough."

"Puny! I would remind—"

"Hold your tongue, woman. I will hear no more." He dug his heels into the sides of the horse and urged him into a run toward the bridge that spanned the moat.

"But surely you cannot hope to escape my father's keep."

"The English castle was not built that will hold a Highlander against his will."

Above the thundering of her heart, Leonora could hear the pounding of footsteps as the soldiers burst through the doorway and raced toward them.

"You see? You are surrounded," Leonora cried. "Free me and toss down your weapon. It is your only salvation."

She saw the fire in his eyes as he urged his mount faster. Even before they reached the drawbridge, the call had gone up to stop his escape by any means.

Dozens of men began pulling the heavy ropes that secured the drawbridge and portcullis. Dozens more knelt and took aim with bow and arrow. When the bridge began to lift, and the portcullis began to lower, Leonora gave a sigh of relief. Their only escape route was being cut off. Now her nightmare would end and she would be returned to the safe embrace of her father.

Her relief turned to horror when she realized that the Highlander had no intention of bringing his steed to a halt. Instead of slowing down, he whipped the animal into a frenzy. As the drawbridge lifted even higher, and the iron bars of the portcullis dropped lower, Dillon wrapped his arms around her and bent low over the horse's neck. Their mount reached the end of the drawbridge and leaped.

For the space of long seconds, Leonora's heart forgot to beat. Closing her eyes, she clung to Dillon's strength and waited for death to claim them both. Then, as quickly as the fall had begun, their horse landed on hard ground with the force of an explosion. For a moment, the animal's legs buckled and he stumbled. Just as quickly he regained his footing and, under Dillon's expert guidance, continued as though there had been no interruption.

When at last Leonora found the courage to open her eyes, the drawbridge had been raised. She knew it would take precious time to lower it, effectively blocking any attempt by the soldiers to follow them with any speed.

Her last glimpse of her father's castle brought a lump to her throat and the sting of tears to her eyes. How could this have happened? Captured. By a vicious Highland savage.

But not for long, she thought, clenching her fists. She would cling to one hope. Her father had an army at his command. And her captor was but one man. In no time, her father's soldiers would rescue her, and then it would be Dillon Campbell's turn to endure the indignity of defeat. And the humiliation of capture.

Mile after mile, Leonora held herself stiffly, uncomfortably aware of the arms that encircled her, and the big hands holding the reins that rested just below her ribs.

She'd been forced to straddle the horse's back like a peasant, her skirts hiked up to reveal more leg than was decent. What was worse, she could feel the Highlander's thighs pressed against her naked flesh. That fact was so repugnant to her, she could not force herself to stop thinking about it. She knew that if she were to allow herself to relax her guard, even for a moment, her back would come in contact with her captor's chest, barely covered by the tattered remnants of shirt. That indignity she would never allow.

As their mount kept up a steady gait, she stared around in confusion. This was a part of England Leonora had never seen before. All day they traveled through dense forest, and never once encountered a living soul. At times, they would scare up a covey of quails or a brace of pheasants. Then the air would be alive with the whir of wings and the spectacular sight of dozens of graceful birds. At other times, they would catch glimpses of whole herds of deer disappearing silently into the underbrush.

The trees and vines were so thick that not even sunlight could penetrate. To Leonora, it was a confusing maze. Yet Dillon never slowed their torturous pace, nor showed the least hesitation as he urged his steed to ford streams and slip into mist-shrouded dells.

Throughout the long day, Dillon allowed only one stop. At the edge of a stream, he suddenly pulled on the reins and slid from the saddle. When he helped Leonora to the ground, her legs were too weak to hold her. She sank into the wet grass and watched while he knelt on the banks of the stream and drank as greedily as the horse beside him.

He turned to her. "You must drink," he said curtly. It was the first time he had spoken since their escape.

She shot him a hateful look. "I do not kneel in the mud and drink like a wild creature."

"Suit yourself, my lady." He splashed water over his hands and face, to wash away the rivers of congealed blood. Immediately, the blood began flowing afresh from the deeper wounds, though he seemed oblivious to his pain. "I will not stop again."

"Not even for something . . . necessary?"

He caught the challenge in her gaze. Studying the thrust of her chin, he felt the corners of his mouth lift, though only slightly. Her comfort was of no concern to him. "If you have the need to relieve yourself, my lady, you had best do so now. For you will not be given the opportunity for some time."

Her dignity was assaulted by his callousness. "Essex was right. You are no better than a swine."

He caught her roughly by the shoulders and lifted her to her feet. "You will see to your needs now, my lady, or not at all. When next we stop, we will be in Scotland."

She glared at him. "You will grant me some privacy."

He led the horse a short distance away, leaving several trees and low-hanging bushes as a screen between them.

Kneeling on the banks of the river, Leonora cupped her hands and scooped the cold water to her mouth, sighing as it trickled down her parched throat. Never had she tasted anything so wonderful. But never would she admit such a fact to this hateful man.

She glanced over her shoulder and could just make out Dillon's profile as he checked the horse's reins. Knowing this might be her only opportunity for freedom, she sprang to her feet and made a desperate dash toward the forest.

Twigs and branches snagged her hair and clothing, slowing her progress. Brambles tore her delicate flesh, causing tiny streams of blood to ooze. She was unaware of anything except the need to escape. Behind her could be heard the sound of a horse's hooves, and she knew that Dillon was close on her trail.

Seeing a thicket, she made a dive for it, stumbling, rolling through burrs and brambles. But instead of coming to a halt in a bog, she realized too late that the thicket had masked a sheer drop-off. Unable to stop, she continued rolling until, with a cry of terror, she found herself hurtling over a precipice and dropping through space. She landed with a thud on the forest floor. And looked up to see herself surrounded by a band of ragged soldiers.

"A female," one of them cried.

"Dropped from the skies, like a gift from the gods," another shouted, bending down to lift her skirts.

She slapped away his hand, scrambled to her feet and cried delightedly, "English soldiers?"

"Aye. What else would we be?"

"Oh, praise heaven. I am saved." She glanced around. "Who among you is leader?"

A squat, ragged man, with long, matted hair and faded tunic that could not cover his protruding stomach, shoved his way toward her, looking her up and down with admiration as he did so. "These men do as I say." He fisted a hand in her hair and yanked it so sharply tears stung her eyes. "And I say that we forgo collecting taxes from the peasants and think about more . . . pleasant diversions."

The touch of him made her skin crawl. While the others joined in the laughter, he dragged her close and ran his hand possessively up her back and across her shoulder.

She struggled free and, in a breathless voice said, "You must listen to me. I am Leonora Waltham, daughter of Lord Alec Waltham. I have been abducted by a Highland savage, who's forcing me to accompany him to Scotland. You must save me."

"Oh, we shall save you, my lady." The leader bowed grandly, before his hands snaked out and caught her roughly by the front of her gown. With one quick yank, the bodice was torn in two, revealing a sheer ivory chemise that barely covered her breasts.

Stunned, she clutched the torn fabric in both hands, striving for some semblance of propriety. "You do not understand," she pleaded desperately. "My father is a very wealthy man. He will reward all of you for returning me safely to him."

"Perhaps what we have in mind is worth more than gold," the leader said, to a chorus of laughter from the others.

"Aye," called a skinny old man whose teeth were missing. "And when we've finished with her, we can still return her to her father for the gold."

Leonora was outraged. "He would pay you nothing if you dared to harm me."

The leader roared with laughter. "Who is to stop us from taking our pleasure with you, and then killing you, my lady? We can return your lifeless body to your father for the gold, and blame your death on this Highland savage you claim has abducted you."

The others moved in closer, their eyes glittering with lust. As she turned from one to the other and saw not even one soldier who would be willing to protect her, Leonora felt a deep welling of despair. "You call yourselves English soldiers? You shame me. And disgust me. You are no better than animals."

"Aye, my lady." The leader snagged her arm and drew her against him, pressing his mouth to hers. "Animals we are. And right now, we feel like rutting goats."

The others roared with laughter as he held her in a painful grasp and moved his mouth over hers. His sour breath filled her lungs and she sank into even greater despair. She had traded one hell for another. And this one was far worse than the first.

"I will take my pleasure with the lady," the leader said as he yanked her head back savagely and reached for the ribbons of her chemise. "And then you may all claim a roll in the grass."

"Please—" Leonora struggled helplessly in his arms. "I beg you . . ."

"You see?" he called, swaggering in front of the men. "The lady begs for what I have to offer."

The others were still laughing when his eyes widened. His hand suddenly went limp and he fell forward. As Leonora took a quick step aside, he fell heavily to the grass. The hilt of a knife gleamed dully from his back.

The other soldiers, caught by surprise, began scrambling about, hoping to retrieve their weapons. With a shriek that sent terror into their hearts, Dillon leaped into their midst, wielding a tree limb like a club.

"'Tis a giant," one of the soldiers cried.

"A Highland giant," yelled another.

They raced for their horses. Those who were unfortunate enough to move too slowly dropped to the ground as Dillon swung the club with deadly accuracy.

One of the soldiers, furious that he'd been cheated out of the fun, started toward Leonora, determined to drag her away with him. Thinking quickly, she bent to the dead leader and pulled the knife from his back. When she did so, blood spurted, staining her hands. Though the knife was slippery, she held it with both hands and stood her ground. Seeing the look of determination on her face, the soldier turned and joined his comrades in retreat.

That was how Dillon found her when the last of the soldiers had fled. With blood staining her hands and the front of her torn gown, her hair in wild disarray, she bore no resemblance to the proper English lady he had first met at her father's castle.

For long minutes, she continued to face him, the knife poised for attack.

"Do not touch me," she hissed.

"They are gone, my lady. You need not fear them."

She continued to stare at Dillon with glazed eyes. "I said come no closer. If you dare to touch me again, I will sink this blade into your filthy heart."

He had seen such shock before, on the battlefield. Men, dazed by the violence, had to be jolted back from the torment in their minds.

His hand shot out and knocked the knife from her nerveless fingers. Her eyes widened. Slowly, as one awakening from sleep, she blinked.

Dillon bent, retrieved the knife and tucked it into his waistband, then caught her by the hand.

"They did not harm you?"

Though he kept his tone impersonal, she was touched by the question, though she knew not why. "Nay. They... would have. But you..." She looked up at him. Her voice trembled. "I do not understand. They are English soldiers. Why would they do harm to an English lady? Did they not understand that I was in distress?"

"Aye, my lady." He thought about all the battles he had witnessed since his youth, and the innocent victims who had endured unspeakable horror. "War makes men into something they would otherwise not be."

"But I am English. I always believed that English soldiers did not do..." Her voice trailed off. She wrapped her arms around herself to stop the trembling. She was cold. So cold.

Without thinking, Dillon gathered her close. She did not resist him. In fact, though she was loath to admit it, she welcomed his embrace. For just a moment, she needed to feel the warmth of another body.

Looking down at her, he smoothed back her hair from her face with both his hands. His gaze centered on her mouth and he was suddenly reminded of their kiss in the garden.

The need to touch his lips to hers was nearly overpowering. Even now he could taste her sweetness. And yet... Calling on all his willpower, he took a step back. He must never forget what they were to each other. Captor and captive.

Leonora had seen the look in his eye. For a moment, she had feared that he would kiss her, as he had in the garden. In such a weakened state, she would have no way of fighting him. But could it be that she had actually wanted him to kiss her? To hold and comfort her? Would that be enough to chase away the cold that entombed her?

When he stepped back, she felt bereft. Fool, she scolded herself. Then the old anger flared. And with it, the heat flowed once again through her veins.

Catching her hand, Dillon led her to where his horse was tethered. With stoic dignity, Leonora was forced to endure being lifted once more to the horse's back.

Still caught in the grip of shock, she rode in stunned silence.

* * *

Her encounter with the English soldiers had made Leonora more aware than ever of the danger of her situation. Even if she managed to escape this Highlander, she could not trust even those in her own land. A lone woman, she realized, no matter what her birthright, was easy prey.

She thought about the strange man who held her captive. His shoulders were as broad as an ax handle; his thighs as muscular as twisted ropes. He had plowed into an angry mob without a trace of fear and had watched them flee in terror. He could lift her off her feet as easily as if she were a child. He could, if he chose, imitate those depraved soldiers and force her to do whatever he desired. He was indeed a daunting presence. And yet, though it galled her to admit it, she felt somehow... safe with him. Though she knew not why.

Then another thought intruded. She must not become complacent. Though she was safe for the moment, she would never be safe as long as she was held captive. She was no match for Dillon Campbell's strength, but she must somehow find a way to escape him before he spirited her away from England. If she were not quickly returned to her father's side, his heart would surely be broken.

When at last they emerged from the cover of the forest, darkness blanketed the land. Dillon urged his steed along a well-worn path, made clear by a ribbon of moonlight. As soon as they drew near a village, they left the path and headed across a meadow. When the village was far behind them, they began once more to follow the path worn smooth by hundreds of horses' hooves and carriage wheels.

Leonora's body protested the long hours spent in the saddle. But despite the pain and discomfort, she would not give her captor the satisfaction of hearing her complain.

Gritting her teeth, she stared straight ahead, determined to endure.

Gradually, as the horse's hooves ate up the miles, her lids flickered, then closed. Despite her best intentions, sleep overtook her.

Dillon struggled against an almost overpowering need to stop and rest. There was no longer any feeling in his hands or fingers. His body ached from dozens of wounds.

He knew he'd been weakened by the loss of blood, but he couldn't chance stopping while they were still in England. Though there had been no sign of Lord Waltham's soldiers, he knew they were behind him. Lord Alex Waltham was a man of wealth and power. The king, the most powerful man in all of England, was his friend. He would be able to command many armies to hunt for this female.

He stared down at the woman in his arms. He'd felt the gradual change in her. She slumped against him and would have fallen if he had not been holding her. He lifted her across his lap, but even that didn't rouse her.

She shivered and he wrapped his cloak around them both. Her arms encircled his waist and she sighed and buried her face in the hollow of his neck. He felt the press of her lips against his throat and had to fight the sudden, shocking arousal.

His lips curved into a grim smile. If the lady knew what she was doing to him, she would be scandalized. And as furious as a little wildcat.

He could not deny that she'd held up better than he'd expected. She was, after all, a delicate, sheltered English lady, unaccustomed to such rough treatment. Instead of a weeping, wailing, hysterical female, he had glimpsed an iron will and a defiant nature. And when she'd found herself in the clutches of that ragged band of soldiers, she'd fought back. He would long carry an image of the lady facing her tormentor with a knife in her bloody hands. He glanced down at the torn, muddy gown, the dark hair spilling wild and tangled around a face serene in repose. Her lips parted slightly, and he felt the warmth of her breath across his cheek. God in heaven, she was magnificent. At once he berated himself for such thoughts. He cared not for anything English, even a beauty such as this. He cared only that she was precious enough to her father to guarantee the safe return of his brothers. The thought that his brothers were being held in an English dungeon brought the flame of anger back to his eyes. Damn the English. And damn this female for making him forget, even for a moment, how much he hated them all.

He took his bearings from the stars and turned the horse away from the well-worn trail. Soon he would be on Scottish soil.

Chapter Six

At the sound of a twig snapping nearby, Dillon reined in his mount and took shelter in a stand of trees.

The jarring motion awakened Leonora, who stared around in confusion. Why were her arms around the Highlander's waist? How long had her lips been pressed to his throat?

She pushed herself away. This man filled her with disgust. How could she have behaved so wickedly in sleep?

Before she could make a sound, he clamped a hand over her mouth. She saw his eyes narrow at the same moment she heard the sound of many hoofbeats. Praise heaven. Her father's soldiers, come to fetch her safely home. She began to struggle. She had to shout, to let them know that she was here. But the more she fought, the stronger was his grasp upon her.

The hand clamped over her mouth was too strong to pry away. But the more she struggled, the harder it became to breathe. In desperation, she stopped struggling as stars danced before her eyes. Finally, just as she thought she would surely suffocate, the hoofbeats faded and he removed his hand from her mouth.

Gasping, she filled her lungs with precious air and turned on him with blazing fury. "You could have caused my death by keeping your hand upon me."

"And it would have been my death if you had called out to the soldiers."

She tossed her head in a gesture of defiance. "Think you that I care whether you live or die, Highlander?"

Catching her chin in his hands, he forced her to meet his angry gaze. "You had better care. For if I die at the hands of your father's soldiers, I vow that you will die with me. With my last breath I will see to it."

She tried to pull away but he tightened his grasp. "Beware, my lady. There is one thing more to consider. You have no way of knowing if the horses we heard belong to your father's soldiers, or the soldiers you found in the forest."

He saw her blanch and realized that he'd hit a nerve. Though she was desperate to escape, she would not risk falling into the hands of such depraved creatures a second time.

He turned his mount away from the path. Across a raging stream, they plunged deep into the woods, where nothing could be heard above the sound of swiftly flowing water.

In that still hour between darkness and dawn, an eerie mist had settled over the land. The horse's breath plumed as they crested a hill. In the pearl light, the thatched roof of the crofter's cottage in the distance seemed dusted with diamonds.

This time, instead of taking refuge in the woods, Dillon urged his horse straight toward the cottage. Leonora was stunned when he called out a greeting.

The door to the cottage opened. A bearded face peered out. The door was thrown open, and a man, wearing the crude dress of a peasant, stepped outside.

Dillon lifted his hand in greeting. "I am Dillon Campbell of Argyll."

"A long way from home." The man's glance swept Leonora, then returned to Dillon. "I am Brodie of Morayshire. Are ye in need of shelter?"

"Aye. And a bit of food for strength."

"Ye have it. Come." The man turned away and Dillon slid from the saddle before helping Leonora to the ground.

After so long in the saddle, she felt a wave of dizziness and was forced to cling to him for a moment before regaining her composure. With a firm grasp on her arm, he led her inside the cottage.

"Sit." The man indicated a rough-hewn table and chairs.

As Leonora took her seat, a young woman close to her own age turned from the fireplace and studied them in silence. Despite the blood and dirt that marred Leonora's appearance, it was obvious that she was a woman of noble birth. The cut of her gown, the jewelry at her throat, made a marked distinction between Leonora and the young woman who faced her.

Peeking from behind the young wife's skirts were two little boys of about three and four. From a crudely constructed cradle came the sudden cry of an infant. Ignoring the cries, the woman filled two bowls with a thick gruel and handed them to her guests, then filled a platter with slices of freshly baked bread and slabs of cold mutton.

Only after the food was served did the young woman cross the room and pick up the squalling infant. She settled into a chair in front of the fire and lifted the babe to her breast. At once the crying ceased.

Leonora was struck by the look of serenity on the young wife's face.

The two little boys leaned across their mother's lap and continued to study the strangers in their midst.

"Have you been visited by English soldiers?" Dillon asked between mouthfuls.

"Aye." The crofter's gaze continued to dart between Leonora and Dillon.

"How long ago?"

The man shrugged. "They would be all the way to Glen Nemis by now."

Dillon visibly relaxed. Being careful to eat only one small bowl of gruel and one piece of bread, he pushed away from the table. "I must rest a while before I go on."

The man stared pointedly at Dillon's blood-soaked clothing. "My woman, Anthea, knows a bit about healing."

"I would be grateful."

Leonora glanced down and realized that she'd eaten everything put in front of her, yet she couldn't remember what anything tasted like. She knew only that she had never known food to be so satisfying, or a fire to feel so wonderfully warm. Her clothes had been thoroughly soaked by the mist, and she had felt chilled to the bone.

These peasants had asked no questions. Dillon had offered no explanations. And yet, they had been taken in and treated like honored guests. What strange people, Leonora thought.

When the crofter stood and led the way, Dillon caught her by the arm and forced her to accompany him to a second room. On the floor were several straw pallets. The young woman entered and handed Leonora a sheepskin pouch. Then the man and woman walked away, leaving them alone.

Opening the pouch, Leonora caught a whiff of foul-smelling ointment and made a face. "What is this?"

"The woman uses it to heal. You will apply it to my wounds."

She tossed him the pouch and turned away. "See to it yourself. I will not touch you or your filthy wounds."

She was shocked by the bruising hands that caught her and spun her around. His voice had grown dangerously soft.

Taking the knife from his waistband, he turned it so that a
stray beam of morning light glinted off the fine, thin blade.
"You shall make this easy, my lady, or you shall make it
difficult for yourself. I care not. But this I know. You will
apply the ointment. And then I will have the rest my body
craves."

She swallowed and said crossly, "You will have to remove those rags you call clothes."

He dropped his cloak on the straw, then removed the tattered shirt, all the while staring down into her eyes. He saw
the flicker of discomfort there, before she blinked it away
and lifted her chin in that haughty way he'd come to expect.

"You are too tall. You will have to kneel," she commanded.

He did as he was bid, and watched as she dipped a hand
into the pouch. Tentatively she touched his flesh.

She had never before ministered to a man. Nor had she
touched a man so intimately. How broad his shoulders are,
she mused as she ran her hand across the wide expanse.
Hard muscles rippled beneath her fingertips. For a moment, she lifted her hand, unsure if she could go on. It was
the most purely sensual feeling she'd ever known. Chiding
herself for permitting such feelings toward a man like Dillon Campbell, she swallowed and forced herself to continue.

The ointment was indeed foul and burned like the fire of
hell when she began to rub it across his bloodied flesh. Dillon gave a hiss of pain and clenched his teeth to keep from
muttering every rich, ripe oath he'd ever learned.

She smiled at his reaction. This was the perfect way to
keep her strange, unexpected feelings at bay. "Does it burn,
sir?"

"Nay." He clenched his teeth harder. "'Tis but a prick of
my skin."

She dipped her hand into the pouch and came up with a handful, which she proceeded to smear across his shoulders and down his chest.

Despite the burning, Dillon was achingly aware of the press of her fingers on his flesh. To keep from dwelling on the intimacy of her actions, he concentrated on the pain.

Hearing his sharp intake of breath, she rubbed harder, clearly enjoying her small measure of vengeance. "And that? Is that also a mere prick?"

His fingers closed around her wrist and she let out a yelp. "Forgive me, my lady. Since you were rubbing so vigorously, I forgot my own strength."

"Have you had enough?" she asked, meeting his narrowed eyes.

"Aye. And you, my lady? Have you had enough?" He tightened his grip until she had to bite her tongue to keep from crying out.

"Quite enough."

He snatched the pouch from her hand and tossed it aside. Tearing his bloody shirt into strips, he said abruptly, "Lie down."

Her eyes widened in sudden terror. Just how far would this brute go in his quest for revenge? "What are you planning to do?"

"I am planning to get some rest. And the only way I can be assured of that is to see that you are subdued."

"Subdued?" She backed away but his hands snaked out. After tossing her to the straw pallet, he quickly bound her hands and feet.

When she began to struggle against her bonds, he said, "You waste your strength, woman. 'Twould be better if you would rest. For if you think the journey thus far was difficult, the journey that lies ahead will be far more taxing."

Without another word, he lay down beside her and pulled the edges of his cloak around them both. Almost at once his

breathing became slow and steady as he fell into an exhausted sleep.

Beside him Leonora lay, deeply troubled. At first she had
hoped that these peasants would realize her plight and help
her escape this tyrant. But seeing how quickly they had accepted him, she was convinced that she must already be on
Scottish soil. With each passing mile, her hopes for freedom were fading. Soon she would be in the Campbell
stronghold, a prisoner among savages.

The man beside her shifted. In sleep, his arm slipped
around her, his hand resting at the small of her back. With
her hands and feet bound, she was unable to escape his
touch, or even to roll away. Closing her eyes, she swallowed back the hysteria that bubbled in her throat, threatening to unravel her strength of will. She must not think of
him as a man. He was a Highland savage. Her captor. She
must endure. Survive. And above all else, escape. And one
day she would triumph over Dillon Campbell.

Dillon awoke to the softness of feminine curves snuggled
dangerously close to him. In sleep, he had tossed one leg
over hers, and had drawn her into the circle of his arms. He
lay very still, breathing in the womanly scent of her. Despite all that she had been through, Leonora was still every
bit the proper English lady.

Had he not wondered how her hair would look un-
bound? Now free of the netting, it fell in silken tangles
across one breast. He took a moment to enjoy the vision.
Spiky lashes cast shadows on her cheeks. Her skin was pale
and unblemished. Her lips, pursed in sleep, begged to be
kissed. All the graceful curves and contours of her young
body were clearly visible beneath a gown which, though torn
and mud-spattered, was still elegant. His gaze trailed to the
dark cleft between her breasts and he felt a rush of heat.

Tearing his gaze away, he glimpsed the sun through the narrow window in the cottage, and determined that it was nearly midday. Though he was eager to reach the safety of his Highland fortress, he could not begrudge the hours they'd spent sleeping. He was not certain that either of them could have traveled much farther before they would have collapsed.

He saw Leonora's lids flicker, a sure sign that she would soon awaken. He rolled aside and dressed quickly. By the time she was fully awake, he was standing by the window, surveying the green hills for any sign of soldiers.

She lay still a moment, studying his proud profile. She was grateful that he was no longer lying here beside her. She had awakened with the prickly sense of being watched, a most unsettling feeling.

"Will you unbind me now? Or will I be forced to endure this for the rest of the journey?"

Without a word, he turned from the window and touched his knife to her bonds. As soon as she was free, she rubbed her wrists. Instantly, he caught one of them in his hand and lifted it for his inspection. At the sight of the bruises that ringed her flesh, Dillon experienced a moment of regret.

"Forgive me, my lady. I had not meant to inflict pain."

"Oh, aye. That is why you bound me so tightly."

His guilt faded, to be replaced with a sudden surge of anger. "Do not forget that you brought it on yourself." He released her hand and strode to the door. "You are not my guest. You are my captive. I will take whatever measures necessary to see that you do not escape."

"Perhaps you will have to kill me," she taunted, scrambling to her feet.

He paused at the door and turned to face her. "If that is what is necessary, rest assured, my lady, I will do so without hesitation."

He strode through the doorway, leaving her to follow.

The crofter, having just returned from the fields for his midday meal, looked up from the table. His wife, standing beside him, was portioning out what remained from their morning meal. The two little boys watched hungrily.

Leonora felt a wave of shame. She had eaten everything offered to her, without thought to the cost to these poor people. They would probably have to go hungry on the morrow because of their kindness to her.

"I thank you for the meal and the pallet," Dillon said to the crofter and his wife. "And I thank you for the ointment. Its healing powers are already evident."

The woman gave him a shy smile, then looked away.

From his pocket, Dillon removed several gold coins and handed them to the man.

"I do not want y'er gold," the man protested.

"Then take it for the lads."

The little boys looked at the stranger with wide eyes, and their mother cast a pleading glance at her husband, but apparently his pride would not allow him to accept.

"Nay. 'Twas what I would do for any of my countrymen."

"Then," Dillon said, "if you will not accept my gold, accept my hand."

The two men grasped hands as a seal of friendship. Out of the corner of his eye, Dillon saw Leonora remove from her neck the rope of gold from which dangled the egg-sized amethyst. For a brief moment, the priceless jewel caught and reflected the light of the fire. When she thought no one was looking, she dropped a hand to the infant asleep in the cradle.

Seeing the young mother's inquiring glance, she murmured, "It is a beautiful babe, Anthea. A girl?"

The woman nodded, pleased that this Englishwoman would notice.

When Leonora's hand lifted away from the cradle, it was empty. The gold and jewel nestled in the babe's bunting.

"Come," Dillon called.

Leonora followed him from the cottage.

The crofter darted to the edge of a woods and returned leading their horse.

"He has been fed and rested," the crofter said. "In a place where no English soldier could find him."

"Again, I give you my thanks, Brodie of Morayshire."

"Safe journey," the crofter returned.

Dillon pulled himself into the saddle and settled Leonora in front of him.

As they rode away, Dillon said, "I saw what you did, my lady. 'Twas a kind and generous thing."

"I was merely paying my debt. I knew they would never willingly accept such a thing. Especially from an English-woman." She struggled to keep her tone impersonal, but Dillon could see beneath the facade. She could not keep the passion from her tone as she added, "It is but one of many beautiful things my father has given me. But to these people, a jewel such as that is a treasure that can assure their family food and shelter for many years to come."

Dillon fell silent as he turned his mount toward the hills of home. Who would have expected a woman of noble birth to care about the fate of a Scots peasant? There was much more to the woman than he had first thought.

He admonished himself that he must not allow her single act of kindness to soften his heart or dissuade him from his mission. This woman must remain his prisoner if he would ever see his brothers alive again.

The land soon became more challenging. The gently roll-ing hills and meadows were left behind, replaced by deeply wooded mountains and plunging ravines. Their steed slowed as it adapted to the steep climb. Snowcapped mountain peaks soared in grandeur, competing with the clouds. Tumbling rivers cascaded down wooded glens.

"Look," Leonora called suddenly.

Following her direction, Dillon watched the flight of a golden eagle soaring high above.

"Oh! What is that?" Again she pointed, this time to a sleek creature leaping from rock to rock high above them.

"Have you never seen a wildcat before?"

"Wildcat? Nay. But it is beautiful."

"Aye, and dangerous." He rubbed his shoulder, remembering. "I was attacked by one when I was a lad."

She looked astonished. "And lived to speak of it?"

He nodded. "I had no choice. I knew that if it succeeded in killing me, it would also kill my brothers. That is probably what gave me the strength to win."

She grew silent a moment. "It would seem that you have spent a lifetime protecting your brothers."

"There was no one else."

"No parents?"

"Not since I was a lad of eight years."

Eight. She thought of her own carefree childhood, adored by her parents, pampered and spoiled by the nobles at court.

She shivered and he drew his cloak around her. The air was colder here, the wind sharper.

Dillon urged his mount up a steep incline and Leonora caught her breath at the spectacular beauty of the scene before her. Between two mountain peaks lay a green, fertile valley. Sprinkled here and there were sturdy houses. Flocks of sheep and goats fanned out over the hillsides, along with herds of red deer.

She thought again of the word he'd used to describe his Highlands. Bonny. Never had she heard such passion in a single word.

As they rode along the valley, men and women stepped from their cottages to wave and shout greetings, which Dillon cheerfully returned. Many of them held children aloft, and Dillon lifted his hand to each of them, calling them by name.

A lad leaped upon the back of a pony and raced alongside Dillon's horse.

"Welcome home, my laird."

Laird? Leonora thought. This ragged brute?

"Shall I carry word to Kinloch House?" the boy asked.

"Aye, Duncan. But first, tell me. Have there been any more mysterious deaths?"

"Aye, my laird. A crofter's wife. And a lass no more than ten and three."

Leonora gave an involuntary shiver. Did these savages never get enough killing? Must they resort to murdering helpless women and children?

The boy dug his heels into the pony's sides and raced ahead. Dillon fell silent.

Soon they left the valley behind and began to climb once more. Here the land was even more primitive, and more spectacular. Rushing waters tumbled over rocks, then roared over steep ravines. Gnarled trees clung to the edges of rocky crags. Vast stretches of forest blotted out any view of sun or sky. As they climbed yet another slope, they suddenly broke free of the tangle of growth. There in front of them was a fortress built between two towering peaks. A gray and umber stone structure, its turrets and towers soared heavenward, gleaming in the soft rose hues of a spectacular sunset.

"At last. Home," Dillon breathed.

His words, spoken with such passion, made Leonora feel like weeping. Would she ever see her home again? Or would she be forced to remain here, among these savages, until death mercifully claimed her?

She studied the place that would become her prison. Because of the location of this fortress, it had no need of a moat, as did the English castles. The only way to enter or leave was through the valley, affording the inhabitants plenty of time to prepare a defense against approaching armies.

As they drew near, huge double doors were thrown wide, and an array of people and dogs spilled into the courtyard.

The hounds raced forward, barking and baying. As Dillon slipped from the saddle, he called them by name and they leaped up at him, nearly knocking him off his feet in their impatience to feel the touch of his hand.

"Welcome home, my laird," called a stooped old man who caught the reins of the horse.

"Thank you, Stanton."

"Such a bonny wee lass," the old man said, stealing a glance at Leonora.

A plump peasant woman stepped forward and squeezed his hands. "Welcome, my laird. Ye were sorely missed."

"Thank you, Mistress MacCallum. You cannot know how good it is to be home."

"Dillon! Dillon!" With high-pitched squeals of delight, a ragged youth whipped a horse into a run down a precipitous ravine.

Leonora turned to watch. "Sweet Virgin," she muttered, lifting her hand to her mouth. Convinced the animal would stumble and both horse and rider would surely break their necks, Leonora was unable to tear her gaze from the sight of them careening headlong down the incline.

They did not come to a halt until they were inches from where Dillon stood. As the horse reared up, the youth catapulted from its back into the waiting arms of Dillon.

A second horse followed at a slower pace. The young giant astride this horse dismounted and stood silently by.

"Duncan said you were coming, but I did not believe him."

Close up, Leonora was surprised to discover that the youth in Dillon's arms was a female. She wore the coarse breeches and tunic of a peasant lad, and her feet were bare. A cap slipped from her head. Long red hair fell in a wild tangle of corkscrew curls to below her waist.

The smile on Dillon's face was positively radiant. Leonora was amazed at the transformation in him. Without his usual scowl, he could almost be called handsome. The love he felt for this female softened all his features and put a light in his eyes that had, until now, been extinguished.

"And why did you not believe Duncan?"

The girl wound her arms around his neck and kissed him full on the mouth before releasing him. Pushing free of his arms, she looked around and allowed her gaze to settle on the woman astride the horse. "Because he said Sutton and Shaw were not with you."

His smile disappeared. "Aye."

The word, spoken so softly, was a deep welling of pain.

The girl turned back to him and waited, but instead of explaining, he set her down and hauled Leonora roughly from the saddle.

"Flame, this is the Lady Leonora Waltham."

The two women eyed each other warily.

"Why have you brought the Englishwoman here?" Hands on hips, the girl's eyes mirrored her confusion. "And where are Sutton and Shaw?"

Ignoring her questions, Dillon called, "Rupert."

At once, the rawboned giant stepped forward. Though he looked to be as young as the girl called Flame, he stood head to head with Dillon. His arms were already as muscular as any man's. His eyes held a vacant, faraway look, and Leonora feared that the lad was simpleminded.

"Take the lady to my chambers and see that she does not leave."

"Your chambers?" Flame's puzzlement grew. "Have you brought home an English bride?"

"Nay, lass." Dillon dropped an arm around the girl's shoulders and steered her toward the doorway, where a crowd of servants waited to greet their laird.

Behind them, Rupert closed his big hands around Leonora's arm and forced her to walk beside him. She felt a moment of terror. His were the biggest hands she had ever seen. She had no doubt that this lad could snap her bones with little effort. Still, his grasp was surprisingly gentle, and she realized that the lad would not harm her as long as she did not resist.

"Then, if she is not your wife, why is she here?" Flame demanded.

"The lady is my prisoner."

Dillon's announcement caught the attention of all who had gathered around him. The elderly stableman, the plump housekeeper, even the rawboned youth who held her, seemed to stop in midstride. A tense, expectant silence settled over the crowd.

Dillon's tone left no doubt that, here in the Highland, he was indeed laird and master, and would brook no dissent. "And she will remain so until Sutton and Shaw have returned safely from England."

Chapter Seven

"English," someone whispered.

"Aye. The laird's captive."

"Such a wee lass, for an Englishwoman," stooped old Stanton repeated.

Leonora could feel the stares, most hostile, some merely curious, as the servants drew back to allow her to pass. She had never before been treated like the enemy. It pained her to see the way some of them watched her, as though expecting her to sprout a devil's horns and tail.

Some of them spat as she passed. Others crossed themselves, and she was reminded of old Moira, who had been terrified of the strange Highlanders.

Keeping her spine straight and her head lifted at a proud, haughty angle, she glanced neither right nor left as she walked among them. And though she could not see Dillon, she could feel his dark gaze burning into her back.

Flame's voice, demanding answers, followed her up the staircase.

"But why have you brought her here, Dillon? Why would you allow the daughter of an English dog under our roof?"

With that, Leonora paused and looked over her shoulder. *Our* roof, was it? There was no doubting the possessiveness of that phrase. In one all-encompassing glance, Leonora could see why the lass owned Dillon's heart. She was beautiful, in a wild, primitive way. It was obvious that the two shared many similar qualities, including a fearlessness on horseback. And a hatred for all things English.

Leonora felt a tug on her wrist and was forced to turn and keep pace with the youth who never released his firm grasp on her until they entered what she assumed to be Dillon's chambers.

When Rupert released her, Leonora rubbed her wrist gingerly. Though he had amazing strength, she had to admit that he had not treated her harshly.

"Leave us." The lad's voice, which should have been as deep as a man's, was a curious blend of croak and hoarse whisper.

Several servants, who had been preparing for the master's arrival, looked up and scurried away without a word. When the door closed behind them, Rupert took up a position in front of it, arms crossed, feet firmly planted.

In the sitting chamber, a fire had been laid in a massive stone fireplace. Leonora moved closer, grateful for its warmth. While she warmed herself, she stared at the sword above the mantel. This was not the weapon of a poor man. The hilt of pure gold was inlaid with priceless jewels. Yet, she recalled, the sword Dillon Campbell had presented to her father had been a simple weapon, of the sort used by peasants throughout the countryside.

Had Dillon suspected, even then, that his trust in the English would be betrayed? She nibbled her lip. It would mean he had been willing to lay down his life for peace, even though he feared such a sacrifice would bring about nothing but failure. If that were true he would be doubly noble. Her mind rejected such a notion.

She studied the sword. It was so massive, it could have only been made for a man of Dillon's extraordinary size. Though the blade had no doubt been soaked with the blood of her countrymen, Leonora was forced to admire it for its sheer beauty. Her father's mantel boasted such weapons, and she knew they had seen many a battle in his youth.

If the room reflected the man who lived here, Dillon Campbell was indeed a contradiction. Primitive and cultured. Lord and peasant.

Rough timbers formed the huge beams. Several large settles, made from the same rough timbers and draped with animal hides, had been drawn up before the fire. An ancient tapestry, depicting a lion and an eagle, hung on one wall. She paused to study the intricate design that traced the clan from ancient times and ancient kings.

On a large side table rested a decanter of spirits and several exquisite gold chalices. Though she would have welcomed some ale, Leonora resisted the urge to do anything that might incite the young giant to restrain her again. It was not so much his size that she found daunting, but the strange look in his eyes.

Her wandering gaze was arrested by a balcony. What lay beneath it? She had to find out. It might offer her an opportunity to escape.

Not wanting to call attention to herself, Leonora began to circle slowly, touching a fingertip to a table, running her hand along a sleek animal pelt on the back of a settle. When she reached the balcony, she chanced a quick look over the stone rim and was dismayed to see a man standing in the courtyard below, a sword at the ready. Her hopes deflated, she turned away, and caught the fleeting grin on Rupert's lips. Her intentions had been so obvious, even this simple lad had discerned them. She would have to learn to become more secretive. Annoyed at herself, she turned away and began to explore once more.

Through an open doorway, she could glimpse the shadows cast upon the wall from another fire. The firelight illuminated a sleeping pallet, the linens carefully turned back in preparation for the night.

She wandered to the open door and surveyed the sleeping room more carefully. Candles flickered in sconces along the walls. A table held a pitcher of water and a basin for washing, along with several squares of linen. A settle, draped with animal hides, was positioned in front of the fire. The sleeping pallet was softened by the addition of several thicknesses of animal pelts.

Hearing a knock on the door, she hurried back to the sitting chamber. Rupert opened the door to admit a serving girl bearing a silver tray.

Placing the tray on a side table, the servant said, "My laird bids you to eat, my lady."

Leonora's temper, which had been simmering since her arrival at Dillon's fortress, flared. "Tell your laird it is not food I desire. It is freedom."

"Aye, my lady."

With a shy sideways glance, the girl beat a hasty retreat. Almost at once, the lass called Flame entered. With hands on hips, she studied the Englishwoman.

"Dillon said your father is holding Sutton and Shaw in his dungeon."

"Aye." Leonora faced her, lifting her chin as she did so. "And there they shall stay until I am returned unharmed."

Flame circled Leonora, as a wild creature might circle its prey. Everything about the girl seemed primitive, untamed, from the tip of her red curls, which spilled in disarray around a disarmingly beautiful face, to her bare feet, which she seemed not the least embarrassed to display.

"Your king lied. He summoned us to speak of peace, while he plotted to betray us."

"I am not privy to the king's council," Leonora retorted defensively. "But he would not have taken such steps lightly. Perhaps he knew of a similar plot by your people."

Green eyes danced with unconcealed fury. "Plot? Dillon, Sutton and Shaw came to you without an army. Does that speak of plot?'' Flame paused in her pacing to face her opponent. "They willingly handed over their swords. Does that speak of plot, Englishwoman?''

Leonora nodded toward the ornate sword hanging over the mantel. "I see that Dillon Campbell did not entrust that to my father's keeping.''

"Aye. And for that, he should be thankful. For it is all that he has left of his father, and his father's father.'' Her voice lowered ominously. "Dillon, Sutton and Shaw trusted the word of the English, and this is their reward.''

She began circling again, too agitated to stand still. "Because of their goodness, my brothers languish in your father's dungeon.''

"Brothers?'' For long silent moments, Leonora studied the girl. Of course. She should have seen the resemblance, especially in the eyes, and around the mouth. Though she knew not why, it pleased her to know that this wild, beautiful creature was Dillon's sister, and not his lover. Instantly she was annoyed at the strange path her thoughts were following. This girl and her brother were the enemy.

"I will not rest until my brothers are safely home,'' Flame said, turning toward the door.

For a moment, she paused and glared at the young woman who continued to stand, head high, back straight. Despite Leonora's torn and ragged gown, she was, in Flame's mind, the image of every Englishwoman she had ever imagined. Haughty. Regal. Arrogant. Anger, always quick to surface in the young Highland lass, spilled over. Unrepentant, was she?

With a last parting shot, Flame added, "Nor should you rest easy, Englishwoman. For Dillon has pledged that their fate shall be yours. You had best pray my brothers are treated kindly by their English jailers, or you will taste the same treatment at the hands of my brother.''

Tossing her head, she strode through the doorway.

At once, the young giant took up his position in front of the closed door.

Leonora began to pace. If she were a man, she would snatch that sword from the wall and fight her way to freedom this very moment. Aye, if she were a man, she thought, fist clenching and unclenching. But her father had raised her to be a cultured lady. She had neither the strength nor the skill to wield a sword. And she knew naught about fighting.

What weapons did she possess? She pressed her hands to her temples, as if to force her numb mind to work.

She stopped her pacing and studied the sky slowly darkening outside the balcony window. She could direct a household staff, bake and cook and sew a fine seam. She had been told that she had a facile mind. She could converse with kings and soldiers alike. But what other skills did she possess? She'd always had the ability to watch and learn, and if necessary, endure. If these were her only weapons, she would have to find a way to use them.

First, she reasoned, she must conserve her strength, so that when the opportunity to escape presented itself, she would be strong enough. Though it galled her to accept the hospitality of her captor, she would do whatever necessary to survive and escape.

She lifted the lid of the serving tray and noted the rock-hard biscuits, the cold slab of mutton. Food unfit for the hounds she had seen below stairs, if truth be told. After swallowing a few bites, she lifted a goblet of hot mulled wine and forced herself to drink.

Seeing the smug look on the face of the young giant, she turned toward the fire, deep in thought. At this moment, it mattered not that the food was tasteless and cold. It was nourishment. She would need all her strength to flee the hated Dillon Campbell.

* * *

"Whatever were you thinking, man, to bring the English female into your home?" Camus Ferguson, short, squat and stout, with legs as thick as tree stumps, paced in front of the fire, sweating profusely. Damp red hair was plastered to his forehead.

He and Dillon had met in the monastery, when both were mere orphaned lads. The bonds of friendship were deep enough and strong enough that Camus could say what he thought without fear of Dillon's displeasure. "You have sealed your own fate. The English will demand your death."

"I had no choice." Dillon sprawled in a chair, a tankard of ale in his hand, and dismissed the servant who had been busy cleaning and binding his wounds.

The hounds lay by his feet, raising their heads from their paws whenever his voice lifted in that familiar growl of anger.

"With no army and no weapons, I needed to buy time."

"Time." Graeme Lamont emptied his tankard and held it out for a servant to replenish his ale. When she shot him an inviting smile, he playfully swatted her rump. With one foot on a bench, he leaned on his knee and studied first Dillon, then Camus. Lacking a clan, since he had been born to an unmarried peasant girl, Graeme had been taken in by the monks and raised with these two childhood friends. The three had studied together, wenched together and had grown to manhood together. Of the three, Dillon was acknowledged as the finest warrior, Camus had the calmest demeanor and Graeme was unquestionably the one who won the females' hearts.

"We have all had occasion to taste English justice." Graeme's tone lowered. "How can you really believe that Sutton and Shaw are still alive?"

Dillon came out of the chair so quickly, no one had time to react. He grasped Graeme by the front of his tunic, his face twisted in fury. "They are alive. Of that I have no doubt. I would know, here in my heart, if it were not so."

Refusing to back down, Graeme persisted, "But for how long, man?"

Dillon whispered through clenched teeth, "You will not speak of such things again while in my sister's presence."

Flame swallowed back the fear that suddenly clogged her throat. It was not so much Graeme's words, as Dillon's reaction to them, that had her so afraid. Such violence was a certain sign of inner turmoil.

To cover her feelings she said, "Dillon has the English-woman. They would not dare to harm Sutton and Shaw, knowing she will share their fate."

"Perhaps." Graeme's eyes narrowed as he watched Dillon turn away. With a trembling hand, he straightened his tunic and lifted his tankard to his lips, emptying it in one long swallow. More than once he had felt the sting of Dillon Campbell's legendary temper. But never like this. This situation with the English had Dillon coiled like a viper ready to strike.

Flame's thoughts were equally dark and unsettling. Seeking comfort, she glanced toward the old monk, who had listened without a word. "What think you, Father Anselm?"

"I think Dillon is correct in his belief that your brothers are still alive. This English nobleman will do all in his power to spare their lives, in order to see his daughter safely returned."

"But what about—"

"And now I think that you and I will go to the chapel and pray, child." With effort the old monk pulled himself from the chair and got heavily to his feet. "And leave the talk of armies and retribution to the warriors."

"But I would stay and hear—"

Dillon shook his head and waved her aside. "Go with the priest, Flame. We have serious matters to discuss."

"I am not a child," she said petulantly.

Dillon caught her hand and surprised her by pressing it to his lips. "I grow more aware of that fact every day. But I would have a word with my friends." As she opened her mouth to argue, he added softly, "And I am in dire need of your prayers. As are Sutton and Shaw."

Flame clamped her mouth shut and obediently followed Father Anselm from the room.

When they were alone, Dillon glanced from Camus to Graeme. "I require an army."

"How soon?" Camus asked quietly.

"The morrow would not be soon enough," Dillon replied with a grim smile. "But it will surely be a fortnight or more before we can assemble enough men and horses and weapons."

Camus nodded. "I will ride to Perthshire and Dumfries." He turned to Graeme. "And what of you?"

After a moment's silence, Graeme said, "And I to Galloway and Cowal."

Dillon offered his hand to each man, grateful for their friendship and loyalty.

"And what of the English soldiers?" Camus asked. "Think you that they will attempt to get the Englishwoman back?"

"Let them try." Dillon walked to the fireplace and, with one hand on the mantel, stared down into the flames. "After such a shameful betrayal, it would be gratifying to spill some English blood."

"If it is English blood you desire, there is always the English female," Graeme said with a smirk.

"You would kill her?" Camus asked with a look of surprise.

"I do not speak of killing. There are other ways to seek vengeance. Especially when your captive is a female. 'Twould serve them right if she were returned to them despoiled."

Dillon's frown grew. "That would make us no better than the English."

"Perhaps. But why should we be better?"

Dillon's fist clenched by his side. "Because our cause is just."

"Just." Graeme slammed his tankard onto the tabletop. "I say it is time the English have a taste of the bitter gall we have been forced to swallow for a lifetime."

Dillon's voice lowered dangerously. "I remember what was done to my mother. I do not hold with those who despoil innocent women." He fixed Graeme with a piercing look. "The Englishwoman is merely a pawn, as are Sutton and Shaw. I have given my word that she will be safely returned, as long as my brothers are not required to forfeit their lives."

"And if they are?"

Graeme watched the flicker of emotion in his friend's eyes before Dillon composed himself. "Then she will forfeit her life, as well."

A sly smile touched Graeme's lips. "Then I ask a favor, friend, in return for the army I will assemble."

Dillon arched a brow. "Ask it."

"If she must forfeit her life, let me have a few minutes alone with her first." Seeing Dillon's angry scowl, he burst out laughing. "See what the monks have done to our friend, Camus? He cannot even jest about such things." Graeme walked closer, and slapped a hand on Dillon's shoulder. "I had only a glimpse of the Englishwoman, but you had much more time with her. Is she truly as fair of face as I thought? Or have I been too long without a woman?"

"You?" Camus asked with a laugh. "If you are forced to abstain for even a night, Graeme, I see you watching the wenches with a hungry look."

"Aye. And tonight I am feeling especially hungry. What say you, Dillon? Is the lady fair?"

Dillon shrugged his shoulders, rubbing a hand over the linens that covered his wounds. "I did not notice."

Graeme chuckled, low and deep in his throat. "You were never good at telling falsehoods, my friend. Beware. Father Anselm will ask to hear your confession."

Camus joined in the laughter. "'Tis true, Dillon. Even the servants are whispering that she is indeed a great beauty."

"Aye. All but a blind man would have been aware of such." Graeme winked at Camus. "I think our friend noticed a little too much, and wishes to keep her all to himself." Turning to Dillon, he taunted, "What think you, Dillon? Could I spend a few minutes alone with your captive? Or are you saving her for your own pleasure?"

"Enough jest." Despite the laughter of his friends, Dillon felt the ragged edges of his temper beginning to fray. "You are both welcome to spend the night at Kinloch House, before you leave on your quests for an army. But I must insist that the English prisoner be treated with the same respect you would show our Highland women."

"I would respect her." Graeme emptied yet another tankard, then stumbled as he attempted to walk to the table. "After I sampled her charms."

Camus saw the dark look that came into Dillon's eyes. "Graeme's words mean nothing. It is the ale that makes his tongue careless," he said quickly, to avoid an ugly scene between his two friends. "On the morrow, he will regret having drunk so much. Come, my friend."

Draping his arm around Graeme's shoulders, Camus steered him toward the door. He called to Dillon, "I give thanks for your safe return home. And on the morrow, we will begin the task of rescuing your brothers.''

"I thank you.'' Dillon waited until they had gone, then turned back to stare somberly into the fire.

Now that he was home and had ample food in his belly, the enormity of his situation dawned. He had abducted an English nobleman's daughter. He, and he alone, was responsible for her safe return.

Graeme's remarks, though made in jest, rankled. There would be many in this land who would share Graeme's views. They would not be above seeing the woman harmed, in retribution for the injustices done to them by the English. No matter that the female was innocent. No matter that her safe return was necessary if Sutton and Shaw were to survive. There would be many who would use the woman to satisfy their own blood lust.

He drained the tankard, tasting the bitter dregs. He would be well advised to watch her carefully. Not only because he needed her as a bargaining pawn, but because there would be many who would use her for their own selfish ends.

Leaving the hounds to drowse by the fire, he made his way up the stairs. A sense of deep sadness welled up inside him. This homecoming should have been a happy event, marking the beginnings of peace between England and Scotland. It would have been a time of merriment, celebrated in every town and village across the land. Instead, they would once again be forced to resort to violence and bloodshed.

When would it end? When would his green, beautiful land be allowed to flourish and prosper? When would his people be able to walk with freedom and dignity?

Freedom. Even without the English, there was the matter of the killer who stalked these Highland forests. Over the years, a score of women, young and old, had been brutalized. As laird, it was Dillon's responsibility to see to the safety of his people. Yet the mysterious savage remained undiscovered.

His hands clenched into fists at his sides. He was weary beyond belief, yet he could not rest. There was still the woman to deal with. And for now, for her safety, as well as that of Sutton and Shaw, she would have to be his responsibility, and his alone.

Chapter Eight

Leonora and her young guard both heard the sound of footsteps moments before the door to the chambers was thrown open. Leonora, standing stiffly by the fire, tensed in preparation for the coming confrontation. She caught a quick glimpse of armed guards taking up positions on either side of the arched doorway. Then the door was closed, and Dillon Campbell filled her line of vision. He looked even more cold and forbidding than when she had last seen him.

"Has the lady given you any trouble, Rupert?"

"Nay." The youth's lips curved into a smile. In that odd, hoarse whisper, he replied, "She saw the guard in the courtyard below, else I think she might have tried to leap to her freedom."

Dillon's head came up sharply. He would have to take better precautions. He could ill afford to have the woman leap to her death.

His tone was rougher than he intended. "That would have been most foolish, my lady. All you would gain for your efforts would be broken bones and great pain. And you would still be my prisoner."

"Unless I died. In which case, I would be free of you," she snarled.

"Nay, my lady." His tone deepened. "Even in death, you would not be free of me. If your father desired a Christian burial for his beloved daughter, he would first have to deal with me. I would hold your body ransom until my brothers were set free." He shot her a chilling smile. "So I would not advise you to harbor thoughts of martyrdom. 'Twould be a painful death, which would serve no useful purpose."

She turned away in tight-lipped silence, refusing to acknowledge him. To do so would be to admit defeat. And that she would never do.

Dillon turned to the youth. "Did she eat, Rupert?"

"A little."

Dillon lifted the lid of the tray. "Very little, it would seem." He glanced at Leonora's rigid back. Despite the torn and dirty gown, her hair spilling wild and free to her waist, she exuded a regal bearing. "I expected to find you asleep by now, after such an exhausting journey."

She turned, eyes blazing. "Did you? And where am I to sleep?"

"In my sleeping chambers."

"Your...!"

Seeing that she was about to explode with fury, Dillon pretended to ignore her, which only caused her anger to increase.

To the young guard, Dillon said, "That will be all tonight, Rupert. You did well."

The boy beamed at Dillon's praise. "I would not mind standing guard throughout the night."

"I know that, and I am grateful for your loyalty. For now, you must sleep."

"The lady is determined to escape," the lad whispered, glancing nervously at Leonora, who stood glowering at her captor.

"Fear not through the night, Rupert. I have posted guards."

The boy seemed relieved. "Will you need me on the morrow?"

"Aye." The lady would have to be guarded day and night, not only to save her from those who would harm her, but to save her from her own foolish attempts that might result in her harm or even death. "I have decided that you will become the lady's personal guard."

The boy drew himself up to his full height, which was considerable, and puffed up his chest. "I would be honored."

Leonora gave an exasperated sigh at the boy's fawning devotion to the Highlander. What inspired such loyalty?

Dillon waited until the youth had gone, then closed the door and leaned against it. His arms were folded across his chest, his legs planted far apart, in anticipation of the clash that was to come. Though he was bone-weary, he could not give in to his exhaustion until the woman was sufficiently subdued.

Leonora's eyes flashed with a light that he had come to recognize. "You cannot seriously believe that I will share your sleeping chambers."

"For now, it is the only place where I can be certain you will not attempt to escape."

"And how can you be certain of that?"

"A warrior learns to sleep lightly, my lady. If you should attempt escape, I will most certainly hear you."

She felt the wild beating of her heart and struggled to hide her fear. "You cannot expect me to...sleep in the same pallet with you."

"That is exactly what I expect. Until other arrangements can be made."

"I demand a chamber of my own."

"You demand?" His lips tightened. "You demand?" Giving in to the need to release all the pent-up fury that had been building since his brothers' capture, he stormed closer, until they were mere inches apart. "Let me remind you, my lady, that you are my prisoner. If I choose, I can have you chained in the dungeons, where you can have all the privacy you desire. Unlike your English castles, where the dungeons teem with enemies of your king, our dungeons are empty. There are no other prisoners being held in Kinloch House. Is that enough privacy to suit you?"

Leonora struggled to hide the fear that churned inside. Though she had been forbidden to go down to the dungeons, she had heard the stories from Moira and the other servants. Rats, as well as all manner of vermin, scurried across damp earthen floors. The cells were littered with human waste. The air was thick with the cries of human misery.

With a show of bravado she said, "I would prefer the dungeons to sharing your pallet."

"Aye." He stared down at her, brow furrowed in thought. "I believe you would." He turned away in abrupt dismissal. "But this is war, my lady. And those engaged in battle must learn to suffer all manner of discomfort. For your own safety, you must remain by my side."

Scalding tears burned Leonora's eyes but she blinked them away. She was well aware of the terrible things that were done to women during war. Had she not had a taste of it during her brief encounter with the soldiers in the forest? Yet she had convinced herself that this man was above inflicting such torment. Now she realized that she had only been lulling herself into a false sense of security. Here in his own land, surrounded by people who would stand by him, he fully intended to revert to his primitive ways and use her shamelessly. Was this not what she had expected from a Highlander?

She would not go meekly to the slaughter. Even if she could not win, she would put up the fight of her life.

She looked around for something, anything, to use in her defense. Spying the crystal decanter of ale, she snatched it.

With his back to her, Dillon started toward the sleeping chamber. "Come, my lady. My body cries out for sleep."

Out of the corner of his eye, he caught sight of her shadow moving along the wall. When the hand in the shadow lifted, he spun around, barely avoiding being struck on the back of the head with the blunt object in her hand. Instead, the blow glanced off his temple, stunning him momentarily.

He heard the crash of glass as the decanter splintered, then shattered on the floor at his feet; felt the cold sting of ale as it splashed across his neck and over his shoulders.

It was the final act that caused his rigidly held temper to snap. His hand lashed out. His fingers closed around her wrist so tightly that she cried out in pain.

She cringed at the full force of his fury.

"So this is how you repay me." His face was a mask of unconcealed fury. "I offer you food, while my brothers must starve."

She tossed her head, refusing to back down. "In my home, such food would not even be fit for the swine."

His eyes narrowed fractionally. "Yours is a prosperous land, while here the people have been forced to defend themselves for so long, they have little time or energy to prepare fine meals. But we offer to share with you what little we have. I offer you the comforts of my home, while my brothers suffer chains and torture."

"Your home." Though she knew she was going too far, she could not stop herself. Frightened and confused, she lashed out with the only weapon available, her tongue. "It, too, is barely fit for the swine. This hovel is cold and dirty and smells of animals."

She felt the sting of his hot breath against her temple as he dragged her closer. His thumbs pressed into the soft flesh of her upper arms until she cried out, but anger and frustration had driven him beyond caring.

"I offer you a pallet, while your father condemns my brothers to a cold dungeon floor. And this is how you return the kindness."

"Kindness?" She drew back to stare up into his eyes. "I know what you plan to do to me. You are no better than the depraved men I confronted in the forest. But you hide your lust behind noble words, Dillon Campbell. You boast of your own goodness, but I am not fooled by the mask you wear. When we are alone, you will be no better than those others who would force me into unspeakable acts for their own gratification."

"Silence, woman." His big hands closed around her shoulders. Through gritted teeth, he snarled, "May you and all your people burn in the fires of hell for the pain and suffering caused my poor people."

"And may you—"

He had not meant to kiss her. In fact, it was the furthest thing from his mind. But the fury that boiled inside him drove him to do the very thing she had accused him of plotting.

His mouth covered hers in a hard, punishing kiss. He felt her stiffen and begin to fight the hands that imprisoned her. That only inflamed him all the more.

Defy him, would she? He would show her what such defiance wrought.

His arms came around her, pressing her against the solid wall of his chest. His lips plundered hers, bruising in their intensity.

A wave of heat pulsed between them, flowing from her into him and back again. Heat so intense, both seemed consumed by it.

So, he had not imagined the heat of their first encounter in her garden. At their simplest touch, it was there again, blazing like flame to tinder between them. Nor had he merely imagined her innocence. He had thought, from the way she had responded to their first kiss, that she had never before been kissed by a man. Now he was convinced of it.

She kept her hands between them, using them as a wedge to hold him at bay. Her lips were tightly closed, as were her eyes.

Fear. He could taste her fear. Like a predator, it excited him. He wanted to feel her tremble, to cower before him. Though it would not make up for what had been done to him and his brothers, it would satisfy some primal urge in him to seek satisfaction from his enemy.

"Open your eyes, woman."

At his brusque command, her lids flickered, then lifted. For a moment, they went wide with fear. Then she blinked, and he could see them narrow fractionally, and darken with anger.

"Release me at once. I am not some serving wench who yearns to satisfy the lord of the manor."

"Nay, my lady." A dangerous smile touched the corners of his lips, and she felt the tension humming through him. "You are not even worthy to be called a servant. You are my prisoner. Never forget that."

"You . . ." At his arrogance, she swung her hand out, intent on slapping his face.

He caught it without effort. "That is better, my lady. I prefer your anger to your fear."

"I do not fear you, savage."

"Most unwise, my lady." She struggled as he lowered his mouth to hers and claimed her lips once more.

This time the kiss, though still punishing, became more possessive, fueling her resistance. The more she fought him, the stronger became his need to dominate.

Trapped in his arms, she felt her body begin to betray her. Her struggles ceased. Her skin warmed and heated beneath his touch. Her lips trembled beneath his.

The change in her triggered an equal response from him. Even while he held her captive in his arms and plundered her mouth, his touch gentled, his lips softened.

At the change in him, strange feelings curled along her spine. Feelings that she knew were neither fear nor anger. A warning sounded in her mind. Such feelings were dangerous. This man was her enemy. She must guard against any display of weakness. Yet she was incapable of holding back the sensations that rippled through her as, with lips and teeth and tongue, he awakened her to desire.

He'd meant only to teach her a lesson. But the moment his touch gentled, he was lost.

He was mesmerized by her lips. Soft as the underside of a rose petal. Cool as a Highland stream. She tasted sweet, clean, untouched. Without realizing it, his hands lifted, framing her face while he lingered over her lips.

Leonora would have never believed that a simple kiss could be so arousing. As the kiss softened, she closed her eyes, absorbing all the strange new feelings that washed over her. She was helpless against such skill. His lips were warm and firm and experienced in the art of seduction. He rubbed them slowly, gently over hers until her body began to hum with need. Each time he changed the angle of the kiss, the feelings grew until she was breathless.

He smelled of wood smoke and horses and evergreen. He tasted of ale, and some darker male taste that lingered on her tongue, taunting her, tempting her.

Her fears were forgotten. Of their own volition, her hands curled into the front of his tunic, drawing him closer.

His hands left her face to follow the slope of her shoulders and trail along her back. With each touch, she felt shivers of pleasure along her spine. As his hand pressed to her back, she was aware of the imprint of each of his fingers, burning a trail of fire along her spine.

When he took the kiss deeper, she sighed and moved into him, molding herself to the length of him.

His arms came around her, drawing her even more firmly against him, until he could feel her heartbeat inside his own chest. With his tongue he traced the fullness of her lips, then probed the intimate recesses of her mouth. She gasped and tried to pull back, but his arms imprisoned her and he kissed her with a thoroughness that left them both gasping.

Dillon felt the need building, threatening to explode with a violence that would shock the sensibilities of this gently bred young woman. He realized his mistake. The moment he'd permitted any feelings of tenderness, he was hopelessly lost. Now he was standing at the very edge of an abyss. One step, one wrong move, and he would find himself falling through endless space.

He had to end this. And yet . . .

He lingered over her lips, unwilling to step back from the heat that tempted even while it burned.

One last kiss. One last taste.

At last, calling on all of his willpower, he lifted his head and took a step back.

"Now that we have established who is laird and who is servant, we will give in to the need for sleep."

"I pray I live to see you burn in the fires of everlasting hell," she said through clenched teeth.

"If you do, my lady, it will be because you are there with me."

His hands, he noted, were shaking. The realization filled him with renewed anger that this female could have such an effect on him.

Keeping his tone deliberately bland, he muttered, "A pity to have wasted such fine ale." He stepped over the shards of glass and puddles of ale and strode toward his sleeping chamber.

She matched his dispassionate tone. "I thought it the perfect use for such swill. What better purpose than to dump on a swine?"

Rewarded with a deepening of his scowl, she knew that her barb had found its mark.

She stood perfectly still, struggling to calm her racing heart. How could it be that just moments ago she'd experienced such strong desire? How could she not only have allowed this man to take such liberties, but to have willingly cooperated?

With a deep welling of shame, she lifted her skirts and stepped across the debris. She would have to be on her guard every moment of the long night. Her captor was dangerous. In more ways than she had first anticipated.

Chapter Nine

Leonora stood just inside the doorway of the sleeping chamber, her arms crossed angrily over her chest.

Ignoring her presence, Dillon sat on a chaise and pried off his boots. He stood and yanked his tunic over his head and unselfconsciously stripped off everything but his breeches, which fit like a second skin.

After what they had just shared, she was far too aware of him as a man. She struggled to keep from staring at the wide expanse of shoulders, the muscles that rippled across his back as he bent to a pile of logs.

He crossed the room and tossed a heavy log on the fire, then sat back on his heels until the bark caught fire and began to sizzle and snap.

Across the room, Leonora watched, aware of each sleek, lithe movement. She was in awe of his strength. He'd lifted the log with such ease. A log that would have strained the efforts of most men.

He stood and dusted his hands on his breeches, then made a turn around the room, snuffing the candles, until the only illumination came from the fireplace.

He turned to her. In the dim light of the room, she could see his eyes, reminding her of the predator they'd glimpsed in the forest.

"You will lie down," he commanded, indicating the pallet.

She didn't move.

With a sigh of resignation, he crossed the room and clamped a hand around her wrist. Leading her to the pallet, he snapped, "Woman, try my patience no more this night for I am far too weary. Lie down."

Drawing the remnants of her tattered gown around her like a mantle of dignity, she settled herself on the pallet.

He felt her flinch when he lay down beside her. Reaching across her, he lifted the edge of the fur and drew it over them both. As he did, his arm brushed her breast and he felt her recoil as though she'd been struck a blow.

Tension. It was so thick it threatened to suffocate them. They were both hanging on to the ragged edge of nerves stretched far too thin. But there was nothing to be done for it. He swore and rolled to one side, making a determined effort to keep from touching her with any part of his body.

Leonora closed her eyes and concentrated on listening to the sound of Dillon's slow, even breathing. At any minute, she expected him to tear off her clothes and ravish her. The fear and expectation were almost worse than the deed itself. At least, if he would show his true, villainous self, she could have the release of fighting back. But this waiting was the worst torture she had ever been forced to endure. Saliva pooled in her mouth and she finally swallowed it, though it sounded overloud in her ears. Her fists were clenched so tightly the nails bit into her flesh, drawing blood.

Sweet heaven, how would she manage to make it through the night with this Highlander beside her, knowing that at any minute he would attack? She dared not let down her guard and fall asleep, or he would take advantage of her vulnerability.

The image of her father's dear face swam before her and she felt a lump form in her throat. How he must be suffering, knowing what his beloved daughter would be forced to endure. And Moira. That sweet old servant would be grief-stricken, wondering if and when her young charge would be returned to her. And in what condition.

Tears sprang to Leonora's eyes. Without warning, she found herself sobbing uncontrollably. To muffle the sound, she pressed her hands over her face.

Beside her, Dillon heard the sound of crying and felt her body shaking. He could sense the tremendous effort she was making to control herself.

His first inclination was to wrap his arms around her and assure her that she would not be harmed. But, he cautioned himself, this was war. She was his captive. And he had given his word that she would only be as safe as were his brothers. To say otherwise now would be to court disaster. The Englishwoman must be made to understand that her safety depended upon the safe return of Sutton and Shaw.

Though the woman's tears grated on his already frayed nerves, he refused to offer her the comfort of his arms. Hardening his heart, he lay beside her in stoic silence. Gradually, the tears ceased. Her breathing slowed. Against her will, sleep overtook her.

Morning sunshine slanted through the balcony window and warmed the figures bundled beneath fur pelts. Dillon awoke, marveling at how soundly he'd slept. Like a man drugged. Sitting up, he threw back the covers, then froze at the sight of the woman beside him.

She lay curled on her side, one hand tucked beneath her head. Her breathing was slow and easy. The torn bodice of her gown had fallen open, revealing the shadowed cleft between creamy breasts.

He took a moment to study her in the soft morning light. Dark, sooty lashes were a sharp contrast to pale, translucent skin. Her nose was small and upturned, her lips full and lush. A mouth made for kissing. The very thought conjured images of the kiss they had shared, and he experienced a rush of heat that left him shaken.

Slipping silently from the pallet, he crossed the room and stoked the fire, then walked to the sitting chamber and summoned a servant.

The sound of muted voices woke Leonora. She lay a moment, completely disoriented. These were not the smells of her father's castle. This was not the softness of her bed. Then the realization came rushing back. She was in Dillon Campbell's impenetrable fortress in the rugged Highlands. A prisoner.

She sat up, shoving tangled hair from her eyes. Just then, the door was opened and she caught sight of the hated Highlander, followed by several serving wenches.

Clutching together the remnants of her torn bodice, Leonora caught the look in the servants' eyes as their gazes slid over the rumpled bed linens. She knew what they were thinking, and felt a flush begin at the base of her throat and continue upward along her cheeks.

"Place the lady's things over here," Dillon commanded. "And leave us."

The servants added wood to the fire, and filled two basins with water from several pitchers. As the others left, one young serving girl, who walked with a pronounced limp, remained behind, laying out an array of feminine garments.

"Shall I help the lady?" she asked shyly.

"Nay, Gwynnith." Dillon's tone was sharp. "You have enough chores to see to. The lady is capable of dressing herself."

"But I have been a lady's maid. A woman of noble birth can hardly be expected to dress herself."

"You are far too tenderhearted, Gwynnith. The lady will see to her own needs."

"Aye, my laird." She began to bow from the room, her gait ragged and uneven.

"Remember that while the lady is in Kinloch House," Dillon added, "she is to be treated like a prisoner."

The girl's glance slid to Leonora, then back to Dillon. She nodded before pulling the door closed.

"Wash yourself," he said curtly to Leonora. "And we will go below stairs to break our fast."

Without waiting to see if she complied with his orders, he bent to a basin of water and began his morning ablutions.

Leonora stood across the room, glowering at his back. How she hated him. It would give her the greatest satisfaction to hold Dillon Campbell's head under water in that basin until he sputtered and begged for mercy.

The thought brought a smile to her lips. Vengeance, when it finally came, would be so sweet. Aye. And she would have her moment of vengeance.

She continued staring at him as he washed himself. Her gaze was riveted to the muscles of his back and shoulders, bunching and tightening with each movement. How different was a man's body. How strangely beautiful. The thought shocked her. And puzzled her. How could she think such thoughts about a callous brute who would spirit her away from all that she held dear? A savage who would hold her captive against her will.

Firming her resolve, she strode to the basin and began to wash. While she did, her mind worked feverishly over plans to escape. Sometime during this long day, her captor would be distracted. When that happened, she was determined to slip away.

Dillon pulled a simple wool tunic over his head, then stepped into his boots. When he glanced across the room, he felt a smile tug at the corners of his lips. Leonora had draped a length of linen around herself for modesty while she washed. Leaning a hip against a side table, Dillon crossed his arm over his chest and enjoyed the view.

With a tug of ribbons, her chemise drifted to the floor at her feet. He watched as she lathered her body, then rinsed, all the while keeping hold of the linen covering. When her petticoats dropped to the floor, he caught sight of shapely ankles and calves.

"I would wager," he said, his voice warm with laughter, "not too many of your Englishmen have been privy to such a sight as this."

She half turned, clutching the linen about herself. He saw the flash of fire in her eyes when she realized that he'd been watching. "An English gentleman would turn away and allow a lady her privacy."

"Aye." His smile grew. "The English never did have any sense."

"You go too far, Dillon Campbell. I expect you to leave me and allow me to dress without your intrusion."

"Then you expect too much, my lady." He uncrossed his arms and took a menacing step closer. "I suggest you quicken your pace. When I am ready to descend the stairs, you will accompany me, whether you are properly dressed or not."

She was clearly shocked. "You would force me to appear in front of your countrymen without modest attire?"

"The choice is yours, my lady. You have already wasted precious time."

With a sigh of disgust, she crossed the room and began to dress. Though the coarse articles of peasant clothing were rough against her skin, it was a relief to be rid of the torn, muddy clothes she'd been forced to wear for the past two days. She tied the ribbons of a pale chemise, then fastened the laces of the petticoat, before dropping the linen covering.

Dillon caught a quick glimpse of pale shoulders and tiny waist, as she slipped the simple pale woolen gown over her head. Smoothing the skirts down over the petticoats, she sat down and pulled on her soft kid boots. She shook her head, spilling her hair forward over one breast. After working a comb through the tangles, she tied her hair back with a simple white ribbon.

Peering into the framed oval mirror, she sighed. Oh, how she missed her old nurse, Moira. This was, in fact, the first time she had ever been forced to dress herself without Moira's assistance. The old woman's fingers, though gnarled and swollen, could still work miracles with needle and thread and jeweled combs.

"While you stand there admiring yourself, the morning swiftly passes. Come, woman," Dillon said gruffly, offering his arm. "There is no time to squander on such frivolous vanities."

Deliberately ignoring him, she swept past and waited at the door until he opened it. Standing just outside the door was the youth, Rupert.

"Good morrow, Rupert," Dillon called cheerfully. "I see you are armed and ready for your duty as guard of the prisoner."

"Aye." The lad beamed his pride at such an important position.

Leonora noted that the remnants of their late-night battle had been swept away. All traces of the shards of glass and puddles of ale had been removed.

As Leonora started past Dillon, he caught her by the wrist, stopping her in midstride.

"You will walk beside me." He released her, as though the mere touch of her burned him. "Or you can walk behind me in chains, with Rupert to guard you."

"I would prefer the lad's company to yours."

"And you shall have your wish as soon as we have completed our meal."

The two were still glowering at each other when they entered the great hall. Immediately, the hounds swarmed around them, leaping at Dillon, eager to be petted. In their excitement, tails switching, tongues lolling, they shoved Leonora aside.

"Nay. Sit."

At Dillon's simple command, they crouched at his feet.

He took Leonora by the elbow and led her toward a cluster of people. At a snap of his fingers, the hounds followed meekly, as did Rupert.

Leonora looked around with interest, curious to learn all she could about these Scots savages and how they lived.

The hall was similar in size to the one in her father's castle, with blackened fireplaces at each end, and rows of scarred wooden tables to accommodate the great numbers of people who took their meals here. But that was where the similarities ended. There was no raised platform for the lord's table. Apparently, Dillon Campbell did not set himself apart as leader, but ate with his soldiers. There was no musician's gallery to offer entertainment. There were no elegant tapestries hanging from the walls, nor aromatic reeds on the floor to give off their fresh fragrance.

As she approached, Leonora felt the curious stares from the people who were studying her with avid interest.

Dillon paused. "This is the Lady Leonora Waltham." To Leonora he said, "You have already met my sister, Flame."

Leonora noted the young woman's angry glare and nodded stiffly.

"This is my friend, Camus Ferguson."

The stout young man stared at her with open curiosity before bowing slightly and saying, "My lady."

Dillon dropped an arm around a gray-bearded priest. "This is Father Anselm." Though the introduction was brief, Leonora could hear the note of affection in those few words.

"Father Anselm."

"I suppose welcome is not the proper greeting, my dear, since you are here against your will. But I wish you a pleasant stay in our land, and a safe return to your home."

"Thank you, Father." Perhaps, because his was the only smile she had seen since her arrival in this country, she returned it.

"This is Graeme Lamont," Dillon said, indicating a handsome young man who stood beside the priest.

The young man insolently looked her up and down, then said to Dillon, "You chose your captive wisely, my friend. If I were going to flee England, I would choose such a traveling companion." Seeing the closed looks on the faces of the others, he threw back his head and laughed before adding, "At least the nights would pass in reasonable comfort."

Dillon's words were spoken softly. "I will remind you that the woman is to be treated with respect, Graeme. While she is in Kinloch House, let no one speak a word against her."

At once, Graeme's smile faded. A sly look flitted across his features.

Dillon led Leonora to a table and invited the others to join them. "Come. Let us break our fast."

As soon as Dillon was seated, wenches began serving the meal. There were bowls of gruel, as well as trays of freshly baked biscuits and slabs of cold meat, all washed down with goblets of ale and mead.

As on the night before, Leonora had to force herself to swallow a hard biscuit and several bites of tough meat, which she washed down with a swallow of ale. The rest of the meat she tossed to the dogs, who lay in wait for scraps beneath the table. They were soon crowded around her lap, hungry for more.

Flame, seated on her brother's right, looked up from her meal. "Will we be preparing for attack, Dillon?"

"Aye. I will send riders to the nearby towns and villages, and ask them to keep watch for English soldiers. If any are spotted, the women and children will be brought to my keep for safety. I will expect you to work with Mistress Mac-Callum in preparing food and shelter."

The girl's face fell. "Food and shelter," she scoffed. "That is the work of scullery wenches. I would work with the villagers, honing blades and preparing weapons. Or lead an army of hunters to provide game."

"All work is noble," Dillon said with a smile. "And Mistress MacCallum may have the spirit, but lacks the strength to prepare for such an invasion of villagers by herself. She needs your assistance, Flame."

The girl sulked. "Why was I born female? The men have all the adventures, and women are forced to cower behind locked doors, tending sniveling bairns."

"Aye," Dillon said softly. "Why indeed? Had you been born a lad, you could have been languishing in an English dungeon now, instead of having the luxury of complaining about your duties."

The girl stared down at the table, properly chastised. Her lower lip quivered. "Forgive me, Dillon. I did not mean to sound ungrateful."

"I know, lass." He placed a big hand over hers and squeezed. "But for now, everything we do, we do for Sutton and Shaw. Their lives depend upon us. And even the lowliest scullery maid performs heroic deeds."

Leonora watched as brother and sister clasped hands.

"Camus and Graeme have agreed to scour the countryside for men willing to fight," Dillon announced to the others.

"By the time we return," Camus said, "we will have an army big enough to take on all of England."

Leonora noted that the serving wenches smiled and hugged the two men, filling their plates and seeing to it that their goblets were never empty. Camus and Graeme were treated like heroes, though, as yet, they had done nothing. She clenched her teeth and pressed her hands together in her lap. The room had suddenly taken on a festive air, as though the thought of going to war with the English was no more than a romp through a meadow.

Dillon glanced at her. "You are not hungry?"

"Nay."

"I see. It is all this talk of war with your people."

She lifted her chin. "I do not fear war. If that is what it takes to rescue me, I welcome it. Besides, it is well known that our English soldiers far outnumber your Highlanders."

He saw through her attempt to boost her own sagging spirits, and refused to allow her to bait him. "I will not have you returned to your father weak and ill." Signaling to a servant with a tray of food, he removed several more slabs of meat and placed them in front of her with a terse command. "Eat."

Gritting her teeth she whispered, "This food is not fit to eat."

Seeing the animals pressing in around her, he muttered, "The hounds, it would seem, do not agree with you."

"Aye. It is fit for dogs. Though only those with sharp teeth can manage to chew it." She dropped the meat and the dogs fell over each other in their haste to snap it up.

His eyes narrowed. "Do as you please, woman. But there will be no more food until our midday meal. Perhaps if you are forced to go hungry, you will appreciate our hospitality."

She gave a short laugh. "Even hunger will not make this food more palatable. As for your hospitality, I have had a taste of it. I suspect your brothers fare better in my father's dungeons."

She saw him wince with pain before he composed himself. "Rupert," he called.

At once the lad bounded to his feet, as eager as any puppy to please his laird.

"Take the lady back to my chambers. See that she does not leave until I return."

"Aye," the boy whispered hoarsely. He took hold of Leonora's arm and turned away from the table.

"And Rupert . . ."

The lad halted and turned.

"Do not let the lady out of your sight for any reason. Be warned. She is most clever."

The lad's head bobbed up and down, as if to emphasize the seriousness of his responsibility. "The lady will not escape me."

With his hand clasped firmly around her wrist, he turned and led her away.

Chapter Ten

Standing on the balcony of Dillon's chambers, Leonora watched the courtyard below as Camus Ferguson and Graeme Lamont approached their waiting horses. While Camus joked with the stablemen, Graeme hauled a young serving wench into his arms and kissed her soundly. She tried to break free but her struggles only seemed to inflame his ardor. With a cruel laugh, Graeme squeezed her breasts, then tossed her aside. The wench's cries brought a frown from Camus, who spoke sharply to his friend before pulling himself into the saddle. As Graeme mounted his steed, he happened to glance upward and caught sight of Leonora on the balcony. A sneer twisted his lips. With an exaggerated bow in her direction, he urged his horse into a run until he overtook Camus at the crest of a hill. The two friends shouted something unintelligible, then went their separate ways in search of soldiers for the anticipated battle with the English.

A short time later, Leonora observed Dillon as he prepared to ride toward the village. He mounted his horse in the courtyard, calling instructions to Mistress MacCallum and Stanton, the stable master, as he did. Before setting off, he glanced up at the balcony. Though he did not acknowledge her presence, she knew that he had seen her. His smile fled.

His spine stiffened. He rode away without another glance in her direction.

Flame, dressed in the garb of a stableboy, raced across the courtyard and pulled herself into the saddle. Horse and rider left in a cloud of dust and followed a trail across a high meadow. Dillon's sister, Leonora mused, seemed always in a hurry. Leonora wondered how the lass had managed to persuade her brother to allow her to ride, thus avoiding the household chores, which she seemed to detest. Perhaps the lass was doing this without her brother's permission. Leonora smiled. That would seem more in keeping with Flame's character. Strong-willed and impetuous.

After the clatter of so many horses, a silence seemed to settle over the castle, leaving Leonora feeling alone and bereft.

By midmorning, the sound of footfalls echoed along the hallways outside the door, as maidservants bustled about, seeing to their chores. In the courtyard below, workmen could be seen going about their work. In the distant fields, peasants tended their crops.

Everyone had something to do. Even the lad who stood silently by the door, watching her, had a duty to perform.

What twisted irony, Leonora thought. How many times had she wished she could step back from the hundreds of chores necessary to keep her father's households running smoothly? Since her mother's death, she had been overwhelmed with so many responsibilities. And now, she was distraught because this enforced idleness required of her naught but to sit and wait. Wait for what? War? Rescue? Death at the hands of her captor? Nay, she thought fiercely. She must not sit and wait. She must act if she hoped to escape this prison. But how?

She paced the length of the sitting chamber, back and forth. Each time, she would pause by the balcony, and stare off into the distance. Somewhere across those green hills was England. Father. Home. Freedom.

In her mind she worked out elaborate ways to escape. The most obvious way would be to distract her young guard and slip away. A bold plan took shape. Turning to young Rupert, she announced imperiously, "I have need of something to occupy my idle fingers. I could do some embroidery, if you would supply me with cloth and needle and thread."

The poor lad had been given no such orders, and hesitated a moment before answering. "You will remain here," he said in his strange whisper.

As soon as he strode from the room, she hid herself beneath the sleeping pallet. When she heard his footsteps return, she lay as still as death, praying he would not hear her unsteady breathing.

"My lady," came his cry of alarm.

She heard his booted feet stride from sitting chamber to sleeping chamber and back. With a muttered oath, he dashed from the room, calling to the guard. Leonora waited until the sound of their footsteps receded, then she slid from her hiding place and dashed from the room.

Because she had no knowledge of Kinloch House, she knew not where she was headed. She knew only that any room was preferable to the chambers in which she had been held prisoner.

Hearing footsteps, she stepped inside a small closet and cowered beneath a pile of furs. In the hallway she could hear raised voices and hurried footfalls as the servants fanned out and began searching.

"She has not yet left Kinloch House," announced Rupert's voice very near her, "or the guards would have seen her. Send for the laird. No one is to rest until the prisoner is found."

Leonora sank deeper into the furs and remained as still as a doe in the forest when confronted by danger. By the time the morning had fled, she was sound asleep.

Leonora awoke to the sound of muffled voices. The door to the closet was yanked open. Keeping her eyes tightly closed, she prayed that she would not be found out. With heart pounding, she waited. Suddenly, the furs were torn away. Her eyes blinked open. And she found herself staring into Dillon's angry, narrowed eyes. Without a word, he hauled her from the closet and dragged her toward his chambers. Once inside, he bellowed for Rupert. The lad stood, cowering and quivering, in abject misery.

"Forgive me, my laird," he whispered. "The lady asked for needle and thread."

"And if she had requested a sword, lad?" Dillon's tone was flat as he struggled with his temper. "What would you have done?"

Rupert studied the floor.

Turning to Leonora, Dillon said, "You have what you requested." He pointed to the brightly colored threads and needles atop a pile of cloth. "You have also sealed your fate, woman. You will not leave my chambers again."

He turned and stalked out, leaving her alone with her guard.

For days afterward, everyone in Kinloch House walked softly around the laird, whose mood was black indeed.

For Leonora, the days passed in an agony of waiting. These chambers, and this silent youth who guarded her, became her whole world. Had it not been for the little she could observe from Dillon's balcony, she would have felt completely isolated. Except for her embroidery, she had nothing to do but brood and scheme.

The evenings were no better. A tray of food, consisting mainly of bread, meat and gruel, was brought to Dillon's chambers. While her youthful guard was permitted to go below to sup, another guard would take his place. When the door opened, she spied two more armed guards in the hallway. Another guard stood watch in the courtyard below the balcony. Dillon Campbell, it seemed, was leaving nothing to chance. He was not about to lose his prized pawn in this deadly game.

The nights were the worst. She slept in all her clothes, with the fur throws bundled around her for an extra measure of modesty. Oddly, Dillon rarely returned to his chambers until late into the night. And though she always pretended to be asleep, she was forced to listen to the whispering night sounds as he moved about the room, removing his clothes, snuffing out the candles, stoking the fire. When he crawled into the pallet beside her, she was forced to hold her breath, lest he discover that she was awake. The thought of his hard, muscled body lying next to her was enough to make her heart race and her blood chill. Sleep often eluded her until the first streaks of dawn light painted the horizon.

The hours of sleeplessness began to take their toll, and she found her energy fading and her nerves strung tautly.

In the mornings, Dillon always managed to be dressed and gone before she awoke, as though avoiding any contact with her. For that she was most grateful.

"I would have a word with you." Father Anselm caught up with Dillon as he paced along the darkened path of the garden. It occurred to the old priest that the laird spent a great deal of time these nights pacing the garden path. Could it be that Dillon was avoiding his own chambers? And the female who resided within them?

He studied the firm profile. Aye. The highly principled lad who had reached manhood under the tutelage of the monks would not lightly give in to the temptation of an English lass. It would be, to a man like Dillon Campbell, an admission of weakness. As laird he had to hold himself to a higher standard than others.

The priest looked at him with new respect. Dillon had never taken the easy road.

"Aye, Father. What is it?" Dillon paused and waited while the robed monk caught his breath.

"'Tis the lady."

Dillon's brows knit together in a frown. "What about the lady?"

"All of Kinloch House whispers about her confinement in your chambers. Do you think the lass should endure bread and gruel as part of her punishment?"

"Would you have me treat her like royalty?"

"Nay." The priest placed his hand on Dillon's sleeve. He could feel the knot of tension beneath his touch. "But I would ask a favor."

Dillon waited.

"I would visit the lady."

"Beware your change of allegiance, Father. Do you visit the lady as friend and comforter?" Dillon's tone was low with anger. "Or do you intend to smuggle in meat and ale, and offer her a weapon with which to defend herself against her cruel captor?"

"Nay, Dillon. You know better than that. I do not involve myself in civil strife. I go as priest and confessor." He found himself wondering about the tension in his young friend. Was it the strain of having his brothers imprisoned in England? Or perhaps the sparring with his gentle captive here in his home? Whatever the reason, the laird's tension was a living, palpable thing. "I will carry nothing on my person that the lady could use as a weapon."

Dillon rubbed an old ache at his shoulder. "Visit her, then." He turned away, then paused and turned back. His

voice in the darkness was tinged with sarcasm, as he recalled her attack with the decanter. "But keep a close watch
over your sandals and prayer book, or the woman will find
a way to relieve you of them, as well. They may be neither
food nor weapon, but she will find a way to use them to her
advantage."

The priest smiled. If he did not know better, he would
suspect that Dillon Campbell was beginning to regret his
hasty actions in taking the woman captive.

At the knock on the door, Leonora looked up in surprise. It was too early for her tray.

Rupert opened the door, then stepped aside to allow the
old priest to enter.

"Father Anselm." The pleasure in Leonora's voice was
genuine. She put aside her embroidery and crossed the room
to take his hands. "How is it that you are allowed to visit?"

"I sought permission from Dillon. I come as a servant of
God."

"Ah." She nodded and led him toward a settle pulled in
front of a cozy fire. "I am most grateful to see you. I wish
I could offer you some refreshment, but, alas, I have nothing."

The priest studied her with gentle eyes. "I need no refreshment, my lady. It is I who should be offering you sus-
tenance. But all I can offer is spiritual refreshment."

She folded her hands primly in her lap. "It is enough that
you came. I was feeling so isolated."

"Are you troubled in your mind, lass?"

She shrugged. "I try not to be. But sometimes, in the
darkest hours of the night, I find myself wondering if I will
ever see my father again."

He placed a hand over hers. "You must not lose hope, my
dear. Your father and Dillon Campbell desire the same

thing, the release of those most dear to them. With such a common bond, it shall come to pass.''

"My father is a man of honor," she said with feeling.

"As is Dillon Campbell."

"How can you say that?" Suddenly agitated, she got to her feet and began to pace in front of the fireplace.

"Because I have known Dillon since he was a lad. I will never forget the day we met. Would you care to hear the story?"

She paused and lifted her head. She had no interest in the savage, she told herself. But it would help to pass the time. "Aye. If you wish."

He told her of the sounds of battle that had drawn him to the Highland meadow, and of the bodies of the men, women and children that littered the field until the ground ran red with their blood. And of the lad, who had bravely shielded his brothers and sister with his own body, with no thought to his own safety.

She became so caught up in the tale that, by the time he had finished, she was forced to turn away to hide her tears. She thought of her own childhood of wealth and privilege. She had taken for granted her safety and comfort.

"Who took them in?" she asked, keeping her gaze on the fire.

"Dillon, Sutton and Shaw came to live at the monastery. Flame was sent to a nearby abbey, where she lived until her brothers sent for her."

Knowing how the girl adored her brothers, Leonora said softly, "It must have been terrible for the child to have been separated from them for so many years."

"Aye," he said thoughtfully. "That long separation has made Flame guard her brothers jealously. She sees every woman as a rival, my lady. Especially the woman who might turn the head of her eldest brother. To her, Dillon is her strong, noble protector."

Leonora turned slowly and saw that the priest was watching her closely. She felt the sting of heat on her cheeks, but blamed it on the fire and returned to her place beside him on the chaise.

"What sort of child was Dillon, Father?"

"A serious lad. He seemed to stand apart from the others. Though he indulged in many of the pranks and mischief that most children indulge in, he seemed impatient to reach manhood and avenge the death of his parents. The anger that burned inside him was frightening to see."

"Anger at the English?" she asked.

"At first. But that faded with time. It became a deeper anger. Aimed at all injustices. That is why he was the perfect choice to meet with your father to discuss peace between our countries. He is known throughout Scotland as not only a just man, but a fair one."

"Would a fair man confine me to this prison?" she challenged.

In answer, he glanced around the comfortably appointed chambers, at the cozy fire, the fur-draped chairs. Getting slowly to his feet, Father Anselm said gently, "I would ask if you believe Dillon's brothers are confined to such as this, my lady. Or are they, perhaps, languishing in a cold, cruel dungeon?"

Leonora hung her head in shame.

Father Anselm touched a hand to her shoulder. "Would you like my blessing before I go, my lady?"

"Aye." She knelt and he lifted his hands in a benediction.

With a brief word to Rupert, he was gone.

Leonora began to look forward to the priest's visits. The hours passed quickly in his company. Moreover, because of his fondness for a sip of spirits in the late afternoon, he began to smuggle in small amounts of wine, hidden in the folds of his robes. The two of them would sit together, enjoying a bit of wine and the warmth of the fire.

Father Anselm was a fine storyteller. Through his words she began to see a portrait of Dillon's early years. The picture that emerged was of a strong, deeply moral lad who bore the full weight of responsibility for his brothers and sister. A natural leader who, by his very nature, drew others to trust and follow him.

"How did he become laird?" she asked one afternoon.

The monk lifted a goblet of wine to his lips and drank deeply before answering her. "'Tis not enough for a Highlander to be a natural leader among men. The real test of his manhood lies on the field of battle. And there, my lady, Dillon Campbell has no equal. He is both fearsome and fearless. A most compelling force indeed." Father Anselm's voice lowered. "I have seen him after a battle. There is a look in his eye..." He shook his head. "He is a man driven. Woe to anyone who faces Dillon's wrath. 'Tis both terrible and wonderful to behold."

Leonora thought about the way Dillon had leaped to the defense of his brothers. Even the swords of a hundred soldiers had not stopped him. There had been a look about him. She sipped her wine. Magnificent. That was the word that always came to mind when she recalled the scene in her father's castle. Dillon Campbell had been the most magnificent warrior she had ever seen.

In frustration, Leonora asked her solemn guard, "What do you do when you are not watching me?"

Rupert blinked. For a moment, he seemed uncertain what to do. After a long, uncomfortable pause, he seemed to have decided that the beautiful Englishwoman deserved a reply.

"Ofttimes I ride with Flame. The lass is my responsibility."

"Your responsibility?"

"Aye. Decreed so by her brothers. The lass is headstrong, and takes many foolish chances. It is my duty to see that she does not come to harm."

"Does Flame know you are watching out for her?"

The boy blushed. "Nay. Dillon swore me to secrecy. The lass would be furious if she knew that her brother had ordered me to be her protector." He seemed suddenly aware of what he had revealed. "You will not tell her?"

Leonora shook her head and smiled gently. "It will be our secret."

Rupert looked greatly relieved.

"Besides," Leonora added, "I doubt the lass will ever have occasion to speak with me. It is obvious that she shares her brother's hatred for the English."

The lad flushed and she realized she'd hit a nerve. Everyone in Dillon Campbell's fortress, in all his land, it seemed, shared such a hatred.

"What do you do when you are not looking out for Flame?"

For the first time, a slow smile touched Rupert's lips. "I tend to my doves."

"Doves?"

He nodded. "I constructed a pen up on the rooftop of the inner wall of the fortress. The doves are my friends. They know the sound of my voice, and whenever I climb up to feed them, they perch on my hands and head and shoulders."

"How wonderful." Leonora smiled at him. "I wish I could see them."

His face became animated; his eyes danced with an inner light. "Would you like to?"

"Aye."

"I shall ask Dillon if you can be allowed to leave his chambers and accompany me to the tower."

She folded her hands behind her back and stared at the floor. "Dillon would never permit it."

"Aye. I fear that is true."

She glanced up, favoring him with her most persuasive smile. "We could see the doves now, and be back in his chambers before he returns."

Oh, how Rupert wished he could visit his precious doves. He sorely missed them. But not even the woman's smile could induce him to disobey his laird's orders again. He shook his head. "That would not be right. My laird said you must not leave these rooms."

"But it would be our secret. Dillon need not know."

"But I would know. I have been given a task. I will perform it, or die trying."

The lad was so solemn, she could think of no argument that would persuade him to change his mind. Besides, if the truth be told, she felt a twinge of guilt for having tried to trick the slow-witted Rupert into defying Dillon's orders again. Perhaps Dillon Campbell was a harsh taskmaster. Perhaps, if this lad disobeyed him, and she managed to escape while under his watchful eye, Dillon would have him put to death. It was what she would expect from these Highland savages.

"I understand, Rupert," she said, lost in thought. "I would not have you punished by your laird."

"The laird would never punish me, my lady. 'Twould be punishment enough to know that I displeased him."

The lad turned away in sadness. He wished there was some way to put the smile back in the beautiful English-woman's eyes.

"The lady has asked to see my doves, my laird."

Dillon glared at him.

First, she had charmed the priest. Dillon had sniffed the scent of wine in his chambers. The next day, keeping watch on Father Anselm, he had seen the priest accepting a decanter from Mistress MacCallum and hiding it in the folds of his robes before going up for his daily visit with the Englishwoman. It was obvious that even that sweet old man of God was falling under her spell.

And now, though he had ordered Rupert not to speak to the prisoner, it was obvious that the lad had told her about his doves.

"You spoke to the woman?"

Rupert ducked his head, his face flaming. "I...may have said a word or two. The lady has a natural curiosity about all things, my laird. But I warned her that she would not be permitted to see them."

After a pause Dillon surprised him by saying, "I see no harm in it." The truth was, he was feeling guilty at the harsh punishment meted out to the lass. But she had to learn the rules of war. It was the way of all prisoners. Why should she be any different?

Leonora's only food had been tasteless biscuits and thick gruel, which had gone untouched. And, of course, the wine Father Anselm had managed to sneak in.

Each night, as he lay beside her, he had to fight an almost overpowering desire to kiss her again. But he knew that, under cover of darkness, one kiss would lead to another. And that would only take him over the edge. Hating him the way she did, she would never consent, and the thought of taking a woman, even an enemy, by force, went against everything he had ever believed in.

He found himself often prowling the gardens until late into the night. When he returned to his chamber, he managed, through sheer willpower, to endure the endless nights. By day, he avoided her as much as possible.

Though the woman had grown considerably thinner, her spirit had not been broken. If anything, she had become even more defiant, not only by refusing food, but by refusing to speak to him unless commanded to do so. To fill the lonely hours, Rupert reported that she had begun imitating the voices of the women around her. Her favorite was Mistress MacCallum. She could mimic every inflection of the housekeeper's speech. Perhaps, Dillon mused, if he let her see the doves, this show of good faith on his part would soften her demeanor.

The rawboned youth's eyes darted with genuine pleasure at the prospect of sharing his precious doves with the prisoner. "Will you tell her, my laird, or shall I?"

"I will tell her, Rupert. You may go to the tower."

Dillon made his way to his chambers and dismissed the guards. When the door opened, he saw her standing on the balcony, her gaze fixed on the horizon, a look of hunger in her eyes.

"If only you could fly like a little bird." His words bespoke her innermost thoughts, twisting the knife in her heart.

She turned. "Aye. I would be free. Free of you. Free of this hovel."

He ignored her taunt. "You wish to see Rupert's doves?"

She tried to hide her surprise. She had expected that this request would be coldly refused. "Aye. With your permission."

"I grant it." At her arched look he added, "I will accompany you."

"To make certain I do not fly away?"

He merely smiled and turned away. With a frown of impatience, she followed him down the hallway and up several flights of stairs until they reached a tower. Rupert stood eagerly awaiting their arrival.

She and the lad had spent so much time together, that, even though they rarely spoke, they had developed an easy camaraderie.

"From this position atop the highest tower, you can see clear to England, my lady." He pointed and she followed his direction.

"Is it truly England?"

"Aye."

Behind them Dillon watched the way she clasped her hands together until the knuckles were white. He allowed her a long time to drink in the view of green, fertile lowlands and beyond them, a sweep of English countryside, before saying gruffly, "We will see the pigeons now, Rupert."

"Aye, my laird."

The lad opened a heavy door that led to a walkway ringing the tower. Outside was a wooden pen with tiny compartments. Each compartment held a cooing bird.

As they approached, the cooing grew louder. Rupert threw open the tiny doors, freeing the birds. There was a great whir of wings as gray and white and black doves lifted into the air and circled gracefully. From his pocket Rupert removed a handful of seeds. As quickly as the doves had ascended, they descended, landing on the lad's head and shoulders and hands. For a moment, their wings continued moving, like giant butterflies. Then their movements stilled, and they cooed as they gently pecked at the seeds he offered them.

Leonora was enthralled. "Look how they trust you," she said softly.

"Aye, my lady." The lad's words were spoken almost reverently.

Beside her, Dillon flinched. Trust. If only he could trust the woman. But that was something to be earned through mutual respect. Something a Highland laird and an English noble could never hope to achieve.

"Did it take a long time to earn such trust, Rupert?"

"Aye. But it was worth it." He lifted a dove to his lips and the bird touched its beak to his lips. "I am mother and father to them. And friend. No matter how far away they might fly, they will always return to me. And no matter how long they are gone, I know they will ne'er forget me."

"Then it is more than trust. It is truly love."

Dillon felt a shiver pass through him at her words.

The lad turned to her. "Would you like to hold one, my lady?"

"Oh, aye." She clapped her hands in excitement. "Would they permit me to touch them?"

"If you do as I say. You must make no sudden moves, my lady. Stand very still and let them get to know you."

He took her hand and transferred one of the doves to her finger. The pale gray bird watched her as she lifted it close to her face. In a gentle voice, she began to murmur words of endearment. As if mesmerized, the dove began to coo.

Dillon stood back, watching her with wary eyes. How gentle she was. How in tune with this big, gentle lad. When had these two dissimilar people formed such a strange bond?

His gaze slid to the dove. With gentle coaxing, it had grown calm and trusting.

Rupert handed her several grains, which she offered to the bird. Though hesitant at first, it finally pecked at the grains. At the first touch of its beak, she drew her hand away with a jerk.

"Nay, my lady. Do not be afraid. It will not hurt," Rupert assured her.

She flattened her hand and tried again. This time, the bird pecked at the grain and she didn't flinch. When the grains were gone, she laughed delightedly.

"Oh, Rupert. They are all so lovely. I can see why they bring you such pleasure."

The lad beamed with joy at her words. "Most here at Kinloch House think me a fool for spending so much time with the doves. After all, they are not useful like the horses, or protective like the hounds."

"All of God's creatures serve a purpose, Rupert. Even if it is only to make our world a more beautiful, gentle place in which to dwell. In fact, they may be the most noble purpose of all. To add light and beauty to our dark lives."

At her words, Dillon turned his head to study her more carefully.

"Aye, my lady. That is what my doves have brought to my life. Light and beauty. But the others do not understand."

"That is because they have not seen you with them. If they saw what I just saw, they would not only understand, but share your love for these beautiful creatures."

He lifted his arms and the flock took to the air with a great flapping of wings. For long minutes, they circled. Then, at his simple command, they returned to perch all over him.

Realizing that the lad needed to be alone with his doves after having been denied them for so long, Leonora said, "Thank you for allowing me to see your doves, Rupert. I will leave you now."

She turned and followed Dillon back inside the tower. When she glanced out the window, Rupert was still surrounded by his beloved birds. On his face was a look of radiance.

Dillon led the way down the darkened stairway toward his chambers. His thoughts were not on the darkness, but on the light and beauty cast by this complex woman.

Chapter Eleven

Leonora paced the length of Dillon's chambers, then back. As she did, she wrinkled her nose at the odors that drifted up from the floor. Looking up at Rupert, who stood guard at the door, she asked, "How long ago were these rushes strewn?"

The lad shrugged. "I helped cut them a year ago or more."

"A year..." She stooped and lifted a handful to her face. "They are sour. They need to be burned and replaced with fresh reeds."

"There is no one to perform such chores, my lady. Everyone is needed to prepare for the siege."

"And what have the servants been doing for the past year? Preparing only for sieges? Is that all your people do? Fight? Is there no time for civilized behavior? Does no one see to the running of this keep?"

He flushed clear to his throat. "Dillon has entrusted Flame to oversee Mistress MacCallum and his household. But the lass prefers riding the hills with the lads to working inside these walls, so the work goes undone. Flame calls such household chores drudgery."

"Drudgery, is it? Then I have been performing drudgery since I was weaned from my mother's milk. It would seem, since you and I have nothing to do for these long, endless days, Rupert, that we can give Mistress MacCallum a hand with the drudgery of household chores. At least in these chambers." Leonora rolled up her sleeves and began to gather up the rushes into bundles. At last she had found a way to vent her anger and frustration. Hard work had always been her release. "I have never been one to sit idly by. Especially when there is a need as pressing as this."

The lad watched in amazement as the proper English lady carried an armload of rushes to the balcony and tossed them over the edge. She was further rewarded by the sound of the guard's curses, which could be heard from the courtyard below as the bundle dropped on his head.

"But my lady, who will cut fresh rushes?"

"You and I are young and strong."

"You cannot leave these chambers. And I must remain here to guard you."

Would nothing move this lad? Ah well, at least she had tried. She gave him her most innocent smile. "Then it would appear that Flame and Mistress MacCallum will have to order one of the servants to see to it. As for me…" She bent and scooped up another armload of rushes and dumped them over the balcony railing. "I shall not spend another night in a room more befitting animals than humans."

While her young guard stood by helplessly, Leonora stripped the floors. When they were bare of rushes, she said, "You had best send for a servant, Rupert." When the lad hesitated, she added, "Dillon Campbell did not say I could not clean his chambers. He merely commanded that I could not leave them."

"Aye, my lady." Reluctantly the youth hailed a passing serving wench and instructed her to send for Mistress MacCallum.

A short time later, the plump housekeeper waddled into the room, sweating profusely. It was obvious that the climb up the stairs had caused her some discomfort, and added to her dour disposition. When she caught sight of the bare floors, she turned on Rupert accusingly.

"Now what have ye done wi' the laird's chambers, ye young dolt?"

"'Twas not me, Mistress MacCallum." In his agitation, Rupert's whisper was even more pronounced. "'Twas the Englishwoman."

With her hands on her ample hips, the housekeeper turned a suspicious eye on Leonora, who was busy shaking out the fur throws and draping them over the balcony to air out.

"What do ye think this'll gain ye, lass?"

"A breath of fresh air." Leonora walked to the sleeping chamber and began to strip the linens from the pallet. Bundling them into the arms of the housekeeper, she said, "I will need clean linens and freshly cut rushes for the floor."

"I do not take orders from the likes of ye. I suggest ye take this up wi' the laird."

Leonora, who had been anticipating just such a response from the housekeeper, merely shrugged. "As you wish, Mistress MacCallum. Of course, I do not think Dillon Campbell will be too happy to find his floors bare of rushes and his sleeping pallet unmade when he returns tonight to his chambers." With that, she turned away and busied herself polishing a side table, using a square of linen moistened with water from the basin.

For long moments, the housekeeper watched her, then seemed to come to a decision.

"Ye shall have ye'r rushes, my lady. But I cannot spare a servant to help ye set the laird's chambers right. Ye and the lad here will have to see to that ye'rselves."

"Thank you, Mistress MacCallum. We will manage very well."

Leonora continued polishing the table, and kept her face averted until the housekeeper was gone, so that her smile of satisfaction would be hidden from view. If she could not escape the confines of this room, at least she would make it as tolerable as possible, under the circumstances.

Having found a purpose, Leonora felt a renewal of strength and spirit.

A knot of servants gathered in the hallway outside their lord's chambers, chattering like magpies. When Gwynnith limped toward them, their voices stilled.

"Why are you here?" she asked. "If Mistress Mac-Callum should discover that you are not doing your chores, you will taste her anger."

"The arrogant English lady has demanded that fresh rushes be cut for the floor of the laird's chambers," one of the servants said, standing beside a cart laden with freshly chopped reeds. "I had to go into the forest and cut rushes and evergreen boughs."

"And I had to wash and hang bedding for the laird's pallet," another added, displaying an armload of crisp linens.

"Aye," piped in another, "and I had to gather beeswax."

"I had to pick sage and thyme from the garden," said one servant with a nervous laugh.

"And what has Mistress MacCallum said about these requests?" Gwynnith asked.

"She ordered us to comply with all the lady's wishes."

"Then see to it," Gwynnith said briskly. "Why are you standing about? Take them into the laird's chambers."

"But we cannot," one of the servants said with alarm.

"And why is that?" Gwynnith folded her arms across her chest.

"Because," the servant whispered, "she is English. Evil. If we are in her presence, she can cast a spell upon us, and we will be helpless to protect ourselves."

The young serving wench put her hands on her hips in imitation of Mistress MacCallum. "Where did you learn such nonsense?"

"For what other purpose would she want sage and thyme except to cast a spell?" asked one servant.

The others nodded and murmured.

"Foolishness," Gwynnith responded.

"'Tis true," one of the others said, her eyes wide with fear. "It is said the English parents cut out the hearts of their enemies and give them to their children to eat. What if the English lady has eaten the hearts of our fathers?"

Without a word, Gwynnith knocked on the door of Dillon's chambers. Rupert opened the door wider and stood aside to allow the servants to enter. Leonora, her sleeves rolled to her elbows, her face flushed from her activities, hurried toward them. At once the servants fell back in fear. Seeing this, Leonora looked from Rupert to Gwynnith.

It was Gwynnith who found herself explaining, "They are afraid, my lady."

"Afraid of what?" Leonora asked in puzzlement.

"Of you," Gwynnith said softly. "They have heard that—" she licked her lips before continuing "—the English eat the hearts of their enemies."

Leonora thought of her old nurse, Moira, and the stories she had repeated about the Highlanders. "I have heard similar stories about your people," she said gently.

They all looked shocked at her admission.

To the servants, who cowered just beyond the doorway, Leonora said, "I see you have brought the things I asked for. I am grateful." She walked to the far side of the room to allay their fears, calling over her shoulder, "You may set them anywhere and leave. Rupert and I shall see to them ourselves."

Keeping a close watch on her, the servants hurriedly deposited the things they had brought and fled.

When Leonora turned, only Gwynnith remained.

"Are you not afraid of me also?" Leonora asked.

"Nay." The young servant stood just inside the doorway, looking unsure whether to stay or flee.

"And why is that?"

"Rupert is here to protect me."

Leonora suddenly laughed at the absurdity of it all. She was a prisoner in a Highlander fortress. Held against her will by a wild, dangerous warrior. Guarded by a giant of a youth. And the servants saw *her* as the object to be feared.

The sound of her laughter brought a smile to the lips of the lad and lass who faced her. This Englishwoman, described by the servants as dangerous and arrogant, was wearing a peasant gown, her hair a bit mussed, a smudge of dirt on her nose. In such circumstances, she seemed far less formidable. In fact, she seemed almost like one of them.

"Would you like some help, my lady?" Gwynnith asked shyly.

Taken by surprise, Leonora arched a brow. "I would not take you away from your chores, Gwynnith. You might incur Mistress MacCallum's wrath."

"Aye, lass," Rupert said. "You'd best leave us now so you can help prepare for the midday meal."

Gwynnith nodded and said, "If you need anything else, my lady, you need only ask and I will see to it."

"Thank you, Gwynnith. I am grateful for your help."

When they were alone, Leonora began removing rushes from the cart and spreading them over the floor. Along with the rushes she added the aromatic herbs to give the room a pleasant fragrance.

From his position at the door, Rupert watched as the lady moved across the floor on her knees, laying the rushes in a crisscross pattern as intricate as any woven tapestry. Though her muscles must have been protesting, she never stopped or rested. When she turned to retrieve another armload of rushes, she was surprised to see Rupert standing behind her, removing the branches from the cart.

As he handed them to her, she gave him a smile. "Thank you, Rupert."

"You are most welcome, my lady."

Each time she used up the pile of rushes, she would find a fresh pile beside her. She continued working without rest until the floors in both the sitting chamber and the sleeping chamber were completed. Then, while Rupert again took up his position in front of the door, she polished the tables to a high shine, and made up the sleeping pallet with fresh clean linens.

Rupert had never seen a room shine so. He breathed deeply, inhaling the fragrance of herbs and freshly cut rushes. In the space of a few hours, this Englishwoman had transformed the laird's chambers. The laird. Rupert frowned, wondering what Dillon Campbell would say about all this.

As if in answer to his thoughts, the door suddenly burst open and Dillon filled the doorway.

Leonora, on her knees in front of the fireplace where she was polishing the sooty stones, looked up in surprise.

"What have you done to set off Mistress MacCallum?" he thundered. "The poor woman was ranting about evil spells and the servants fearing you would eat their hearts."

"They need not fear," Leonora said, getting swiftly to her feet. "It is not their hearts I intend to eat, Dillon Campbell. It is yours."

Behind him, Rupert swallowed back the smile that threatened. It seemed impossible that this gentle woman, who had just spent hours on her knees, could be transformed into a wildcat in the blink of an eye. Yet here she was, facing down the Campbell himself as though she were a warrior going into battle.

"What have you done in here?" Dillon's eyes narrowed suspiciously.

Turning on Rupert, he demanded, "Did you disobey me, lad? Has the woman left these rooms?"

"Nay, my laird." Rupert pulled himself to his full height, standing as stiff and tall as a giant oak. "You know I would die before I would disobey you."

"Then what is all the fuss? What has my captive done to Mistress MacCallum and the servants to cause such a stir?" Dillon breathed in deeply, aware of an odd, sweet fragrance in the air. He glanced around the room, seeing the sunlight reflecting off highly polished wood. The rushes beneath his feet were soft and springy, and gave off a most delicious evergreen aroma.

"The lady has done nothing, except clean your chambers."

"Clean?" Dillon crossed to where Leonora had been kneeling before the fire, pushed her aside and examined the stones. They were so clean, the firelight's gleam could be seen reflected in them.

"What trickery is this?" he demanded.

Leonora's temper, which she had kept bottled up for so long, exploded.

"Trickery? Trickery?" With her hands on her hips and a look of fury in her eyes, she advanced on him, uncaring that a matching blaze of fury burned in his eyes. "It is bad enough that I am here against my will, and that I have been forbidden to leave these filthy chambers."

"Filthy—"

"Aye, filthy. If this is to be my prison, I will at least make it tolerable. Perhaps a Highland warrior cares not whether his chambers are fit for nothing more than wild creatures, but an English lady expects better."

Without turning away from her, Dillon said, "Rupert, leave us."

"Aye." The lad, who had been watching wide-eyed, felt a twinge of disappointment. Never had he heard anyone speak to the laird in such a manner and live. Though he had no doubt that Dillon could best any man in the land, he would not like to make a wager on the outcome of this battle with this small female. He turned away reluctantly. He would give the Englishwoman this—she had spirit.

As the door closed behind him, Dillon turned on her with all the fury of a wounded boar. "Woman, you are not in England now, living the life of a spoiled, pampered nobleman's daughter. In my home, I am lord and master. What I command is done instantly. And if I so order it, your very life will be forfeited."

She faced him, lifting her chin in a haughty manner that further added to his fury. "I do not fear you, Dillon Campbell. You cannot order my death until you learn the fate of your brothers."

"Aye." His hand shot out and closed around her throat.

He saw her eyes widen in surprise and felt a small victory. At least, for the moment, he had her attention.

In the garb of a peasant, with her hair loose and streaming down her back in a riot of damp curls, she appeared younger, more vulnerable. Up close he caught sight of the dirty smudges on one cheek and the tip of her nose.

More than anything, he wanted to kiss them away.

The thought was like a blow to the midsection. From what source had such a thought come? She was nothing more to him than a pawn in a deadly game. He must never forget that fact. Still, this was precisely why he had been avoiding her. Being forced to lie beside her each night without touching her was the worst sort of torture. Yet he knew that if he despoiled this woman, his cause was lost.

Angry at the sudden lapse in his composure, he tightened his fingers around her throat and met her defiant gaze with a look of contempt.

"Be warned. There are far worse things than dying, my lady." He saw the flicker of fear and knew that he had made his point. To underscore it, he whispered, "So, while you are under my roof, you would be advised to hold that wicked tongue of yours. Woe to you if you should push me beyond my limit."

She pulled herself free of his grasp and took a quick step back. She had seen the way his gaze had burned over her mouth and had felt the tensing of his fingers. He had come very close to kissing her again. That she must never allow.

The man was dangerous. When he touched her, strange things happened to her heart. Even though she knew he was the enemy, he had a way of making her forget everything except the pleasure of the moment.

Even now her heart was racing. Her throat had gone dry. all the work in the world would not be enough to help her forget how tenuous was her position here. She must find a way to hold this savage at arm's length, if she were to survive this captivity... intact.

Chapter Twelve

"Mistress MacCallum has prepared a midday meal. Wash yourself," Dillon commanded curtly.

As he turned away, he noted that his hand trembled slightly. It was not the thought of kissing the woman, he told himself. It was the fury she always managed to arouse in him. He thought of several rich ripe curses that would bring a flood of color to her cheeks if he were to utter them in her presence.

Delighted at this unexpected release from her prison, Leonora filled a basin with water and began to wash.

Dillon stared around the room, marveling at the transformation. How could one small female have made such a difference? Sunlight danced on freshly polished wood. Even the fireplace, which had been layered with the soot of a hundred fires, now sparkled. The room smelled as clean as the forest.

His gaze settled on the woman, who, having washed all trace of grime from her hands and face, was busy trying to comb the tangles from her hair. When she had succeeded, she smoothed down her skirts before turning to face him.

He experienced the sudden jolt he always felt whenever he caught sight of her. Though she was dressed in a coarse peasant gown of unbleached wool, and wore no adornment, she still bore the unmistakable manner of a gently bred English noble. She was so beautiful she took his breath away.

"Come. We have wasted enough time." To cover his feelings, he crossed the room and tore open the door.

She brushed past him without a word. At that simple contact, he felt his body strain toward hers.

They descended the stairs side by side, making certain they did not touch. When they reached the bottom of the stairs, Rupert stood waiting, as patient and long-suffering as the hounds that lay at his feet. The moment Dillon appeared, the dogs leaped up, eager for an affectionate pat of his hand.

With the dogs dancing at their feet, and Rupert trailing behind, they made their way to the great hall. Inside, the room resounded with the voices of the men from the village, who had gathered to make plans for battle.

Leonora glanced around at the men wearing all manner of strange dress, excitedly talking and laughing, and felt a shock of recognition. All her life she had been witness to such gatherings in her father's keep. Before every battle there was the same air of anticipation. The same heightened sense of adventure. The same feeling of camaraderie.

"Dillon." Flame, still wearing the tattered breeches and tunic better suited to a stableboy than the sister of the laird, strode across the room and caught her brother's hand. "I rode to Kilmartin and have been pledged arms by ten and two men of the village."

Dillon glanced around. "Are they here, then?"

"Nay, not yet. But they have given their word that they will join you within a fortnight."

He smiled and tousled his sister's hair. "I should have known you would best both Camus and Graeme, and be first to bring me pledges of arms."

She beamed at him, clearly overjoyed to win his approval. Her smile faded when she caught sight of Leonora. "Why is the Englishwoman here?"

"Would you deny her food?" Dillon asked.

"If I had my way, I would deny her life," Flame snapped, turning her back on Leonora. "I do not think we should be forced to look upon the woman whose father holds Sutton and Shaw captive."

The men standing around them nodded in agreement and began grumbling among themselves about the wicked English.

In a low voice, Dillon admonished, "You will keep a civil tongue, lass. I cannot permit an uprising here in my own home. The blood of this horde is already hot for battle. The simplest word could fan the flame of hatred and unleash an outpouring of violence against the woman."

"As if I would weep for her loss."

Dillon caught his sister roughly by the arm. His voice was low, with a barely controlled hint of anger. "Then weep for this. Any harm done to her will assure the same harm to Sutton and Shaw. Do you wish to see them suffer?"

Flame shivered and cast a hateful look at the woman who had caused her brother to speak so to her. "Nay, you know I do not."

"Then think, lass, before you speak."

She turned away, sulking.

They both fell silent as Father Anselm crossed the room and made his way to Leonora's side. "Ah, my dear. I bid you good morrow."

"Thank you, Father." Leonora felt herself visibly relax in the old priest's presence. His smiling face gave her heavy heart a lift.

"I have heard talk among the servants, lass." The priest accepted a goblet from a serving wench. "They say you made several strange requests."

"Aye. I...managed to find work for my idle hands," she remarked.

"Ah. What is it you did?"

"The lady cleaned my chambers." Dillon clearly intended that such a statement would humiliate her.

Father Anselm arched a shaggy white brow. "You...cleaned, my lady?"

"Aye." She held herself as proudly as she could manage, knowing that the conversation around them had faded in order to hear what she was saying.

Flame gave a cynical laugh. "Fitting work for an English dog."

At the girl's outburst, Father Anselm chided gently, "Hush, lass. You might take heed of this. To serve others, in any manner, is noble work."

Intrigued, several of the serving wenches paused in their work to listen and observe. They looked at the Englishwoman with new respect. A woman of noble birth had lowered herself to clean the laird's chambers?

"Did Rupert lend a hand?" the priest asked.

Leonora glanced at the lad, who looked away nervously. Her heart went out to him. One word from her, and he would be shamed in front of his countrymen. She could almost taste his fear, it was so palpable.

"His task was to guard the door so that I could not escape. To that end, he performed admirably."

Rupert shot her a grateful smile before dropping on one knee to pet the hounds. Relief had him trembling.

Dillon, who had been watching and listening, caught the look of relief on the lad's face. With a frown, he handed a goblet of ale to Leonora, then plucked another from the tray for himself. His unconscious gesture of kindness was not lost on the priest. Nor on his sister, who stood beside him glowering at the Englishwoman.

While the servants bearing trays began to circulate among the tables, the men took their places. Leonora found herself seated between Dillon and Father Anselm, and though she kept up a running conversation with the priest, she was uncomfortably aware of the silent man on her other side whose shoulder and thigh brushed hers as she ate.

"Did you do such work in your father's home?" Father Anselm asked.

"Nay. We had many servants. But I soon learned that the chores were better accomplished if I took an interest in what the servants were doing. Ofttimes I worked alongside them until they knew how I wanted something done. It takes many willing hands to maintain such large quarters, but many of the younger lasses from nearby villages had never performed such duties before. My father used to boast that, though I could be demanding, I was a patient taskmaster."

Dillon listened to this exchange in silence. He did not know what surprised him more, that the lass knew how to work, or that she was patient. He would have expected neither virtue from the spoiled daughter of an English nobleman.

"Do you live here, Father Anselm?" Leonora deftly changed the subject, hoping to deflect interest from herself. Besides, she had often wondered why the monk spent so much time in this fortress.

"My home is at the monastery of St. Collum," the old priest said. "But Dillon has built a chapel here at Kinloch House so that the villagers, when they must stay for prolonged periods during a siege, have a place to worship."

"I should like to see it." She cast a sideways glance at Dillon, aware that he was listening. "And to worship there, as well, Father."

Beside her, Dillon scowled. The female was a most clever adversary. The little witch was actually challenging him. Now that he had permitted her to leave his chambers, she would push for more freedom. She knew that he could hardly deny her request to worship.

Father Anselm's face was wreathed with smiles. "I look forward to seeing you at morning Mass, my child. Perhaps you can persuade Dillon to accompany you."

Dillon's frown deepened.

"Dillon's brother Shaw has long attended daily Mass," the priest added, "and for years has lived a life of poverty and chastity."

He could see that he now had the Englishwoman's complete attention.

"But why?" she asked.

"To prepare himself for a life in service to God. It is his intention to pledge himself to the Church."

Leonora glanced at Dillon and could see the pain etched on his features, along with the pride. The mere mention of his young brother brought a fresh wave of grief. For the first time, she realized that his pain and suffering were as deep as that of her father. Could it be that these savages actually mourned their losses in the same way as civilized people?

As if reading her mind, Father Anselm murmured, "'Twould be a great loss, not only for Dillon and Flame, but for the Church, if Sutton and Shaw should not be returned to us."

"My father is an honorable man," she said fiercely. "They will be returned to you. Unharmed."

"You had better pray it is so," Dillon muttered. He tore apart a loaf of bread with a vengeance that sent a tremor of alarm through her.

She watched as he ate mechanically. Though she had worked up a hunger, she found she could barely swallow the flavorless food set before her. She managed to choke down several bites before pushing it aside.

"Again you do not eat," Dillon commented.

"I am not hungry."

He spoke quietly so the others wouldn't hear. "Already you grow thinner. You will eat, else your father will accuse me of having starved his child."

"I am not a child." She felt her temper rising. This man had a way of making every statement sound like a command from on high. Did he do it deliberately to goad her into a fight? If so, he was succeeding. "And I will not be ordered to eat this swill."

"You will be still," he ordered. "To insult our food is to incur the wrath of every man in this hall."

"They already hate me because I am English. Will they hate me all the more because I will not eat this unpalatable swill?"

His hand, hidden beneath the table, clamped around her wrist in a painful vise. He brought his mouth close to her ear. Through clenched teeth, he hissed, "Woman, say not another word to incite my anger. If you will not eat, at least you will keep a civil tongue."

"Like your sister?" Her face was pressed close to his, her eyes blazing.

He winced. How was it that he could control hundreds of men, but could not control two clawing, spitting females? His sister and this Englishwoman were so dissimilar, and yet, in temperament, so alike. Both were headstrong. And both knew how to try the patience of saints and men.

"Not another word." He released her wrist and lifted a goblet to his lips, drinking deeply.

Beside him, Leonora rubbed her tender wrist and soothed herself by imagining that it was poison in Dillon Campbell's goblet. Glancing around, she saw the dark, baleful stares from his countrymen, and realized that this man might be the only one standing between her and death. What strange irony. This man constantly threatened to harm her. Yet, without Dillon's protection, she would find herself in a den of vipers.

She was reminded of the incident in the forest. Was she willing to trade a known danger for an unknown one?

If it killed her, she would placate him. She bent her head and managed to consume several more bites of bread dipped in gruel before pushing it aside. Through it all she maintained a discreet silence.

Beside her, Dillon drained another goblet of ale, his thoughts in turmoil. Every day that Sutton and Shaw remained in an English dungeon, the danger to them grew. Though he trusted Lord Waltham to do the honorable thing and release them in exchange for his daughter's safe return, there were others who would benefit from their deaths, thereby destroying any hope of peace between England and Scotland. If such men proved stronger than Waltham, all would be lost.

Time. His hand clenched around the stem of the goblet. So little time. To raise an army. To fight off the anticipated English attack. To ride back to England and free his brothers in exchange for the woman.

The woman. He preferred to think of her as the woman instead of Leonora. A beautiful name. A beautiful woman. Damn her for being beautiful. He hated the way the mere thought of her distracted him from important duties. With a snort of disgust, he pushed back from the table.

"It is time to return you to my chambers. There is work to be done, and I have no more time to waste."

"Goodbye, Father Anselm," Leonora said as she got to her feet.

"Goodbye, my dear." The aged monk gave her the benediction of his smile. "I look forward to seeing you at chapel."

Her gaze slid over Flame, and the girl returned her look without a word. Leonora turned away to walk beside Dillon, taking care not to touch him. The hounds milled around them, and Rupert scrambled to his feet to follow along behind.

After climbing the stairs, they stepped into Dillon's chambers and paused in midstride. Inside, Mistress MacCallum and more than a dozen serving wenches looked up in surprise. Several of them were on their knees, inspecting the rushes and evergreen boughs that covered the floors.

Dillon's tone was stern. "What is the meaning of this, Mistress MacCallum?"

The housekeeper blushed in embarrassment. "We wanted to see the sort of work the English lady had done, m'lord." She turned to Leonora. "How is it that these chambers smell so fresh, m'lady?"

"The rushes must be freshly cut," Leonora said, "and mingled with evergreen and sprinkled with sage and thyme. Not only will the herbs smell sweet, they will also repel vermin."

The old woman seemed greatly relieved. "Ye sprinkled the herbs on the floor?"

"Aye. Why else would I have asked for them?"

"Why indeed?" Mistress MacCallum looked aside, and muttered to the servants, "Evil spells indeed."

"What is this about evil spells?" Dillon asked.

"Nothing, m'lord." The old woman's jowls wiggled from side to side as she shook her head. "Just a foolish notion one of the wenches had. Now about the wooden tables, m'lady. I have ne'er seen them shine so."

"Beeswax," Leonora explained. "And endless polishing." A bold plan leaped into her mind. Dare she try it? Without taking time to think it through, she asked, "Would you like me to show the servants?"

"Ye would do that?" Mistress MacCallum's brows shot up in astonishment.

"I would be happy to. It would help me to pass the lonely hours." Leonora turned to Dillon. "That is, if your laird does not object."

"M'lord?" Mistress MacCallum asked hopefully.

Dillon's eyes narrowed. He had to admit that his rooms had never been quite so pleasant. They put the rest of Kinloch House to shame. A pity to keep such talent locked away. Besides, it would keep the woman busy and out of his way, since he had to be away from Kinloch House for several days recruiting soldiers. And the servants might gain some knowledge. Why not learn some of the ways of the English while the woman was his prisoner?

"So long as Rupert remains by your side every minute of the day, I suppose you can be allowed to move freely about Kinloch House. But be warned, my lady, if you should attempt to escape you will be confined to my chambers, and bound hand and foot, as well. Is that understood?"

Leonora felt the bile rise to her throat, not only because of his threatening words, but because he chose to say them in front of so many curious servants. By evening, everyone in the keep would be aware of the insults she had been forced to endure. Still, she cautioned herself to swallow her pride. More freedom meant more chances to escape.

Dillon saw the flash of fire in her eyes before she lowered her gaze and said softly, "Aye, I understand."

"The woman will be below stairs shortly, Mistress MacCallum. Now leave us. And fetch my sister. I would have her learn the English ways along with the others."

The housekeeper waddled to the door, followed meekly by her serving wenches. When Rupert held the door for them, Dillon said to him, "You may wait in the hallway, as well. I would have a word with the woman alone."

When the door closed behind him, Dillon turned to the woman who had strolled to the fireplace, where she stood warming herself.

His voice, as cutting as the blade of a knife, sliced through the silence. "I am not fooled by your innocent face, woman. I know the game you play."

She turned to him, her chin lifted, and braced herself for what was to come. She knew that Dillon held on to his temper by a tenuous thread.

"Game? I merely wish to fill the long, lonely hours. Would you prefer that I remain in your chambers, lying abed, weeping over my lost freedom?"

He walked closer, fists clenched by his sides. "Somehow, that is not how I envision you, woman. Weeping and wailing does not become you."

"Nor idle threats you, my lord."

"Idle?" He grabbed her and hauled her up against him. Caught by surprise, she was unable to wedge her fists between them. Instead, her hands hung limply at her sides.

"I am laird," he said through clenched teeth. "If I ordered you flogged, it would be done without question."

She struggled against the fear that welled up and threatened to paralyze her. She must never permit this brute to see what effect his words had on her. "If you dared to have me flogged, you would answer to my father."

"I answer to no man. Least of all, the English tyrant who holds my brothers prisoner."

"Tyrant?" She tossed her head. "Look to yourself. You are no better."

"Aye. Remember that, woman." His thumbs dug into the soft flesh of her upper arms as he drew her fractionally closer, until she was forced to stand on tiptoe, staring into eyes as dark as the night. His scar stood out in pale relief against sun-bronzed skin. His lips twisted into a dangerous smile. "There are other ways to punish a woman. Ways that would break your spirit, and wrench your father's heart from his chest."

When the horror of his words dawned, fear lodged in her throat, threatening to choke the breath from her. "You are a savage."

"Aye." His gaze fastened on her mouth. His burr thickened with anger. "As wild, as untamed as the land that spawned me."

His mouth claimed hers in a harsh, brutal kiss.

The moment their lips met, heat poured through him, turning his blood to liquid fire. And even though he loosened his grip on her arms, he remained lost in the kiss, unable to pull back from the heat that drew him closer, closer, until he knew he would be burned.

He had not intended any of this. He had planned only to warn the woman, to frighten her into submission. But now, holding her, breathing in the heady woman scent of her, tasting the clean, freshness of her, he forgot everything except the need for more.

He took the kiss deeper and felt the slight trembling of her lips. Could it be that the little wildcat was trembling over a simple kiss? Simple? Nay. What he felt, and struggled to resist, was far from simple. And though he had fully intended to punish her, he found himself moved by her fear. Though he had not planned a seduction, he found his hands moving gently along her back, soothing, arousing, as his mouth nibbled and tasted and rubbed over hers with sweet invitation.

Strange new sensations leaped and pulsed as Leonora was held captive in his arms. Never had she known such feelings. This savage was the enemy. She hated him. And yet, she had never been so aware of a man.

Her hands, which had been clenched at her sides, now lifted until they were clutching his waist. She forgot to breathe. Her heart forgot to beat. She seemed, for the moment, suspended in time. She steeled herself against feeling anything at all for this man. But though she tried to resist, she found herself responding against her will to the gentleness of his touch.

Feeling the tremors she couldn't hide, Dillon lifted his head and stared down into her face. Her eyes were squeezed tightly shut.

"Woman, open your eyes."

Her lids fluttered open. In those violet eyes he could see a reflection of himself. He felt, for one breathless moment, as if he were drowning in her eyes. The thought left him shaken.

He had intended to torment her further with his kisses, to set a trap for her until she begged him to stop. Now, he realized, he was the one who had fallen into a trap. A trap of his own making.

He wanted her. Wanted her as he had never wanted any other woman. Not as punishment for her father's crime of imprisoning his brothers. But because she was a beautiful, desirable temptress and his blood was hot to have her.

He caught her by the upper arms and drew her a little away. Through narrowed eyes he studied her. What had this woman done to him? Somehow she had bewitched him. If he was not very careful, he would be the one imprisoned.

Perhaps it was fortunate that he would be gone for a while. He needed to put some space between himself and the woman.

"Now that you understand just how easy it would be for me to take you, my lady, I will warn you again. Do not try my patience." His eyes were hard, his voice a low growl. "If you do anything to anger me, my vengeance will be swift and terrible. As laird, I will be the one to mete out your punishment."

He dropped his hands to his sides as though the touch of her offended him. In truth, he was afraid to touch her again, lest he take her here and now. The need for her still pulsed through him, heating his blood, causing his tone to be harsher than he intended. "Do you understand?"

"Aye." She was amazed at how difficult it was to speak. Filling her lungs with a deep breath, she shot him a hateful look. "I would leap to my death before I would allow you to carry out your threat."

To regain control, he deliberately turned his back on her and strode across the room. At the door he turned. "If you incur my wrath, my lady, we shall have a chance to see if you are as good as your word."

She turned away as Rupert entered and took up his position in front of the closed door. With her back to him, she pressed her hands to her fevered cheeks.

She hated Dillon Campbell. Hated him as she had never hated any man before. And yet... Her cheeks flamed anew at the thought of how she had reacted to his kiss. The feelings he aroused in her were contrary to everything she had ever believed. This man was a Highlander, a savage. She was English nobility. If she allowed this man to sully her, she would be forever soiled. No decent man would ever have her.

And yet... A tremor pulsed along her spine at the thought of his arms holding her, his lips plundering hers. No other man, with their fumbling hands and clumsy kisses, had ever made her feel the way she felt in his arms.

What would she do if he made good his threat? The answer came to mind clearly, instantly. She would have to leap to her death rather than submit. To do otherwise would bring dishonor to her father's name.

Chapter Thirteen

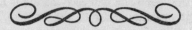

"My lady." Rupert waited until she had stopped her agitated pacing.

She turned to where he stood in front of the door, as solid, as sturdy as a giant oak. "Aye, Rupert?"

"I wish to thank you."

"Thank me?" With thoughts of Dillon still crowding her mind, she seemed unable to focus on the lad.

"For keeping secret the fact that I helped you."

"Ah." She gave him a gentle smile. "It was little enough to thank you for your kindness. It shall remain our secret. Now—" she crossed the room "—it is time to join Mistress MacCallum and the servants below stairs."

Now, more than ever, she was eager to use her newfound freedom to seek a means of escape. And her best means of escape was to learn as much as she could about the structure of this fortress.

Rupert opened the door and held it for her, then moved along by her side.

They found the housekeeper and her legions of serving wenches in the scullery, where duties were being meted out. Heads turned and voices stilled as the Englishwoman stepped into their midst.

Flame, her arms crossed over her chest, watched in silence.

Mistress MacCallum seemed truly flustered. It was obvious that she had never before given orders to a woman of noble birth.

Realizing how important it was to gain her confidence, Leonora decided to make it easy on the housekeeper. "Perhaps you would like me to start in the great hall," she offered.

From the first time she had seen the hall, Leonora had known that it was the center of the fortress. There were many doors leading from there to outer passageways. It had to offer her a route for escape.

Whatever guilt she felt at betraying Rupert, she cast aside. This was war. She had to try to make it safely back to her father.

The housekeeper blinked and looked incredulously at Flame. The cavernous great hall was the largest room in the keep. The task of keeping it clean was a daunting one, and only the lowliest of scullery maids was ever assigned to it. Flame, sharing the older woman's thoughts, allowed a smug smile to touch her lips. It was the sort of work she would have gladly meted out to the English dog.

"Aye, m'lady," the housekeeper said. "A fine place to begin. Tell me what ye will need."

"Little more than strong backs and brooms and buckets of water. Since the day is already half over, we will gather the old rushes into bundles for the fire, and sweep and scour. The morrow will be soon enough to lay clean rushes." She looked up. "Do you agree, Mistress MacCallum?"

"Oh, aye." The woman nodded so vigorously, her jowls jiggled. Then, remembering her manners, she turned in deference to the sister of the laird. "And ye, lass. Are ye in agreement, as well?"

Flame shrugged. "My brother has said I must remain and observe. But he did not say I had to share the work or speak to the prisoner. Continue, Mistress MacCallum."

To make certain that everyone understood that she was in command, the housekeeper said to Rupert in a stern voice, "Ye will remain beside the prisoner at all times. And of course, I shall look in on ye from time t' time to be certain the work is being done properly."

With a knowing smile, Leonora made her way to the great hall, with the servants and Flame trailing behind her in silence. When they reached their destination, Rupert took his usual position in front of the closed door. Silently Leonora began gathering the rushes into bundles, which she tossed next to the fireplace, to be used for kindling. With each turn around the room, she noted the location of the doors, determined to see where each one of them led.

After watched her for several minutes, the servants began to follow suit, bundling the rushes. Though they worked alongside her, they followed Flame's lead and spoke not a word. Leonora sensed that, along with the animosity, there was a great deal of curiosity about her, but she could not find a way to break through their wall of reserve.

After more than an hour, Leonora was relieved when Gwynnith joined them. Her open smile and friendly demeanor were welcome amid these closed, unsmiling faces.

"Here, my lady." Seeing Leonora on her knees gathering rushes, Gwynnith caught her by the arm and helped her to her feet. "The servants and I will gather the rushes and bring them to you. You will stand here by the fireplace and see that they are bundled."

"You need not pamper her, Gwynnith," Flame said curtly. "The woman has boasted that she is capable of hard work."

"Aye. If I were not aware of that," the girl said, "the sight of the laird's chambers would have convinced me. But she has done enough for one day. The lady will pay dearly for the work done this day, I will wager."

Leonora's muscles were already protesting the hard work, but she was determined to ignore the discomfort. "Do not fret, Gwynnith. I have a need to be busy."

Though Gwynnith insisted, Leonora continued to kneel and gather rushes alongside the others. As she worked, she asked, "Were you born here in the village, Gwynnith?"

"Nay, my lady. I was born some distance from here, in the village of Cawdor."

"And how is it that you make your home in Kinloch House?"

"My village is gone. As is my family. They were all killed in a terrible battle with the..." The girl paused, clearly uncomfortable. Licking her lips she continued in a rush, "With the English. When Dillon Campbell found me, he brought me here to live."

"And made you a servant," Leonora said with a trace of contempt to cover her own discomfort at the thought of the pain inflicted by English soldiers.

"Nay, my lady. He gave me a home. It is my choice to repay his kindness by serving him." She glanced down wryly at the deformed foot that caused her pronounced limp. "Without the kindness of Dillon Campbell, what would my life be?"

Leonora asked, "How did it happen?"

The girl looked away. "One of the soldiers trampled me with his horse. I was not supposed to live."

Leonora shuddered at the image of a young girl having to endure such mistreatment at the hands of soldiers. She saw the pain in the girl's face as Gwynnith muttered, "No man will have a wife who bears such imperfection. But if I cannot be wife and mother, at least here at Kinloch House I have purpose. These people have become my family."

The other servants had gathered around to listen.

"The laird rescued me, as well," said another servant shyly. "The English killed my mother and father and my four sisters. I was still a bairn, and I was left to die in the cold. But Dillon's brothers found me and brought me here, where I was taken in and given shelter. I have been here ever since."

"And I," volunteered another. "Both my brother and I were forced to watch the murder of our family. Dillon found us wandering in the forest and brought us home with him. My brother is learning to care for the horses in the stables, and I am learning to care for a household. Without the laird's kindness, we would have perished. As would that one," she added, motioning toward young Rupert, who stood guard across the room.

"Tell me about Rupert," Leonora asked gently. "Was he also rescued by Dillon Campbell?"

"Aye, my lady." Gwynnith paused, and Leonora noted that her look softened. It was clear that the little servant had feeling in her heart for the lad.

"How long has he lived here at Kinloch House?"

"Since he was no more than eight or nine years."

"Has he no family?"

"None. They were all killed in battle."

Though the lass was careful not to mention English soldiers, Leonora knew by now that many of the wounds inflicted in battle had come from her countrymen.

"Why did he not perish with his family?"

"Dillon proclaims it nothing less than a miracle. When he found Rupert, the lad was more dead than alive."

"From a sword wound?" Leonora asked.

"Nay, my lady. The soldiers had hanged him. That is why, even today, the words come so slowly. He cannot speak above a whisper."

Leonora felt a welling of tears in her eyes and turned away to hide them from view. It pained her to think about sweet, gentle Rupert having endured such brutality. Her mind was in turmoil. The lad had every right to hate her for what her countrymen had done to him and his family. As did Gwynnith. Yet these two good people did not hate.

How could she do less?

She pondered all she had heard. She had hoped to hear of the savage's faults. Instead, these people made him sound like a benevolent father. She thought back to the words Dillon had spoken so passionately in her father's house, about a Highland laird's duties to his people. She frowned as another thought intruded. English soldiers. With every horror story, it seemed, came the mention of the cruelty inflicted by English soldiers. Until her capture she would not have believed such things about her beloved countrymen. But since her own experience in the forest at the hands of such animals, she now knew it to be true. All her life she had heard only about the savage Highlanders. Now she was hearing a very different story. What had Dillon said in the forest? All men are changed by war.

"Are all Scots as noble as your laird?" she asked.

The servants exchanged looks. It was Gwynnith who said, "Nay, my lady. There is one in our forests who stalks like a wild creature. A score of females have been killed at his hands, and still no one has found him out. No lone woman would dare to venture into the forest."

Leonora shivered. She was grateful for the hard, physical work. Somehow, the thoughts that troubled her were more easily dealt with while her hands were busy and her back was aching.

That evening, Leonora ate sparingly, and wrapped the rest in a square of linen, which she tucked into a pocket of her gown, to be concealed later beneath the pallet in Dillon's chambers.

A plan was taking shape in her mind. A plan that would require careful thought. She must attempt another escape. She would need food, weapons and warm clothing to survive the wilds of the Highlands. Even the fear of the one who stalked the forests could not discourage her from her need to escape.

When darkness settled over the land, she was grateful to sink between the fur throws, where she fell into an exhausted sleep.

Leonora awoke, eager for the day. This would be her first full day of freedom from these chambers. She was determined to make every moment count.

Once the morning tray had been delivered and she had broken her fast, Rupert accompanied her below stairs, where she joined the servants and Flame in the great hall. Since the floor was bare of rushes, some of the servants began to sweep, while Leonora showed the others how to scrub the soot and grime from around the fireplaces by using a finely ground powder of stone. When she saw their reluctance to try new ways, she coaxed them by working alongside them.

Now that the servants had begun to relax in her presence, the talk flowed more freely. The only one who did not join in was Flame. The lass continued to stand apart, watching and listening, and sulking at having lost her freedom to roam the countryside at will.

"Tell us about your home in England," Gwynnith coaxed.

"Is it as fine as Kinloch House?" asked another.

"It is much like this." Leonora sat back on her heels, idly rubbing at the stone she'd been polishing. "We do not have the protection that nature provided you here in the Highlands, but we have a moat and drawbridge to keep out invaders." Her tone softened, and the love and longing was evident in her voice. "When I was a child, the stables were my favorite place to be."

At that, Flame's interest was piqued. She had thought this Englishwoman too frail to sit a horse.

"But after my mother died," Leonora continued, "I was kept too busy to ride. Now, I think, the gardens are my favorite place in my father's keep. They are where I escape when I am troubled."

"How did the laird manage to steal you away?" one of the servants asked boldly.

The others held their breaths, eager to hear the tale, though none of them had had the courage to ask. At once, Flame sat forward, as eager as the others.

"When his brothers were threatened, he fought off a hundred of my father's soldiers and carried me away as his hostage."

The servants gasped. Flame nodded. It was what she would have expected from her brother. When Leonora told of the dramatic leap from the drawbridge, and their escape into the forest, all of them were completely caught up in the story.

"Oh, my lady," Gwynnith said, her hand at her throat, "you must have been frightened."

"Aye. And sad." Wistfully she said, "I miss my home and my father."

"The tale near takes my breath away," breathed a serving wench.

"Aye," whispered another. She peered at the Englishwoman. "The laird is strong and handsome, is he not?"

Leonora blinked. "I had not noticed." She went back to her polishing with a vengeance, while several of the servants exchanged knowing looks, which were not lost on Flame.

Soon Leonora began spreading the rushes and evergreen boughs in an intricate pattern. When she had finished several rows, the servants followed suit.

As they worked, their chatter continued. "The laird is handsome," said a dimpled lass. "But I much prefer his younger brother Sutton."

"Oh, aye," came a chorus of eager voices that had even Leonora laughing aloud.

"And what of Shaw?" Leonora asked.

"He is as handsome as his brothers, but he does not take notice of the women," a shy lass said quietly. "He has pledged himself to the Church."

"But that does not prevent you from trying to catch his eye," Flame taunted, causing the lass to blush furiously.

When Mistress MacCallum entered the great hall, she found the women, including Flame and the prisoner, talking and laughing among themselves with ease.

"So." The housekeeper stared around, pleased by what she saw. "Once again you have made a room shine. What is your secret, m'lady?"

"It is not to my credit. This is the result of many willing hands." Leonora glanced around to include all the servants.

They beamed at her unexpected praise.

"That is most generous of you, my lady," one of the servants whispered, "for you have borne the brunt of the work."

"Nay, I could not have done it without your help." She turned to the housekeeper. "You are most fortunate, Mistress MacCallum, to be blessed with such dedicated workers."

"Aye." The elderly woman appeared flustered. She knew this English woman was a prisoner of the laird. Yet she could not help liking her. It was all so disturbing. "It is time for ye to return to the laird's chambers, m'lady. On the morrow we will begin to scour the scullery."

"As you wish." Leonora got slowly to her feet and meekly followed Rupert from the room. As she did, she noted a peg on which hung several cloaks. At the first opportunity, she would steal one, to add to her hoard beneath the pallet. She could not be expected to survive the Highlands with only the clothes on her back.

"I will need more servants to prepare the evening meal," the housekeeper announced to those who were on their hands and knees in the scullery, early the next day.

"I would be pleased to help," Leonora said.

The housekeeper was so startled, she could think of no polite way to refuse such a generous offer. Since she had joined them, the prisoner had volunteered for every difficult duty. "Aye. Ye will follow me, then."

Leonora and the others trooped out of the scullery behind Mistress MacCallum, with Rupert and Flame following. As they moved along the hallway, Leonora noted every turn. This fortress seemed to be a maze of darkened passageways and heavy doors leading to more darkened hallways and cavernous rooms. But she had begun to familiarize herself with them.

In the huge kitchen, whole pigs were being roasted over hot coals, and a deer was turning slowly over an open fire.

Leonora stepped up beside a lass kneading bread, and began to help. When that was done, she moved to a tray of partridges being prepared for the fire and sprinkled them with dried herbs.

She glanced around and, seeing no one watching her, slipped a small, sharp knife into the pocket of her gown. Then she continued working. Soon, caught up in the pleasant smells and familiar work, her sunny smile and easy chatter won the confidence of the kitchen maids as easily as her hard work and determination had won over the other servants.

"Would the laird like tarts tonight, Mistress MacCallum, or puddings?" one of the servants asked.

The housekeeper paused, considering.

"Why not both?" Leonora suggested.

The housekeeper looked at her in surprise. Then, nodding slowly, she replied, "Aye. Why not indeed?" She turned to the serving wench. "Let the lady help ye with that, lass."

Leonora gave a smile of relief. She had worked up a tremendous appetite this day. At least, if she was allowed to help with the cooking, she would be able to satisfy her hunger with palatable food.

Rupert, alone by the door, pressed a hand to his stomach. So many wonderful meats roasting. So many delightful sweets baking. Just when he thought he could bear it no longer, Leonora surprised him by crossing to his side.

"I thought you might like to try this." She handed him a steaming tart.

"Did you read my thoughts?" he asked. Biting into the pastry he closed his eyes from the sheer pleasure of it. "I have ne'er tasted anything like it, my lady."

"Then you shall have another. Gwynnith," she called.

The servant limped over, and Leonora whispered, "See that my fierce guard has another tart."

It seemed a most pleasant duty to the lass, as she carried a tart to the young guard. Their fingers brushed when she handed it to him, and he glanced at her in time to see her lashes lower in a most becoming fashion. With his gaze still fixed on her, he popped the tart into his mouth.

"Thank you, Gwynnith," he murmured.

"You are most welcome." Her cheeks bloomed with color.

They both looked up as the door was suddenly thrown open and Dillon strode furiously into the room. The sound of laughter died on the servants' lips. Heads came up sharply. Rupert chewed furiously, hoping to swallow the evidence of his indiscretion.

Dillon's voice was unusually harsh as he confronted Leonora. "Woman, I have been searching everywhere for you. Why are you not in my chambers?"

Her head lifted defiantly. "You gave your permission for me to work with the servants. And it should be obvious why I am not in your chambers. I am here, helping Mistress MacCallum with the cooking."

The servants, hearing her sharp retort, shifted uncomfortably. No one had ever dared to speak to the laird in such a manner.

Dillon allowed his withering glare to roam over her until she flinched beneath his scrutiny. Could he see the weapon she had concealed in her pocket? Had he guessed her plans?

With his gaze still fastened on Leonora, he bellowed, "Has the woman been giving you a full measure of work, Mistress MacCallum?"

The housekeeper hurried across the room and stood beside Leonora, hoping to diffuse the temper she could read in Dillon's eyes. "Aye, m'laird. The lady puts us all to shame wi' her hard work."

With no flicker of emotion, he said to Leonora. "You will come with me now to my chambers."

"I have not finished the—"

His fingers closed around her arm and he propelled her forward. "Now, woman. When the laird summons, you do not hesitate." To Rupert, he said, "I will not need you again, lad, until the morrow."

"Aye, my lord." The boy swallowed the last of his tart and watched as Dillon hauled his prisoner toward the stairway.

An uncomfortable stillness settled over the room and its occupants while they fretted over the fate of the Englishwoman. For these last few days, she had been like one of them. Now she had been snatched away, to become once again a prisoner of their laird. More than a few felt a wave of pity for the woman.

Even Flame found herself wondering why her brother always seemed in such a foul temper when he was around the prisoner. Though she despised the English, she had to admit she had been unable to find fault with this woman's behavior.

"Come now." Mistress MacCallum clapped her hands and motioned for the servants to get back to their chores. "The laird will be wanting to sup soon. Heaven only knows how many more soldiers will be at table this night."

For Flame, this brief reprieve meant she could hurry to the stables and ride across the meadows for a blissful hour of freedom. As was her custom, she slipped away unnoticed.

Chapter Fourteen

"Have you charted your escape route yet, woman?"

Leonora's heart stopped. Swallowing, she glanced at Dillon's angry profile and hoped she sounded sufficiently innocent. "I do not know what you are saying."

"Do not play with me, woman. I know what you most desire." Though he turned on her, he was careful not to touch her, for to do so always brought him a fresh jolt. "And I know now why you offered to help Mistress MacCallum."

It had come to him on his long ride across a Highland meadow, after recruiting more soldiers for his cause. With blinding clarity he had understood what the female was plotting. Would he have not done the same in her place? he thought with grudging admiration.

"I will grant you this. You are a clever female." Aye. Too clever for her own good. Now he would have to assign even more men to guard her. Men he could ill afford to spare. And all because he'd been tricked into allowing her to roam Kinloch House freely, under the guise of helping the servants. "By now you have probably noted every door, every passageway, every means of escape."

When he'd realized what she was plotting, he had ridden like the wind. His relief at finding her calmly working in the kitchens had been so great, he was still reeling from it. He had half expected to find her gone.

"I would have to be ten people to do all the things that you accuse me of." She had no choice now but to continue to deny all his accusations, no matter how dangerously accurate they may be.

After the sound of so many female voices, the silence of the hallway seemed ominous to Leonora's ears. She moved along beside Dillon, her footsteps dragging. The climb up the wide staircase was as daunting as climbing a mountain. She was certain that he had found the food and weapon she had hidden under the pallet. That must be why he was aware of her plans. By the time they reached his chambers, she found herself tensing as she waited for him to open the heavy door.

Once inside, Dillon stormed across the room to the side table, where he poured himself a goblet of ale. She glanced around, expecting to see her cache exposed. There was no sign of it. Could it be that he had not discovered it?

Seeing her pallor, Dillon filled a second goblet and handed it to her. She lifted it to her lips and drank deeply. The warmth of it flowed through her veins, restoring her flagging energy.

Feeling his dark gaze upon her, she walked to the fireplace and stared into the dancing flames. She should have known that Dillon Campbell would not long be fooled.

She jumped at the sound of his voice, low and angry, beside her. "It was clever of you to smear the dirt upon your person so that I would believe you had actually worked with the servants."

She stiffened, but said nothing in her defense. In his present state of mind, he was beyond believing her. Instead, she quickly emptied her goblet and set it aside.

Seeing the way her head lifted, he knew his barbs had found their mark. That only goaded him into hurling more.

"I was a fool to believe a noble Englishwoman would work alongside lowly serving wenches. Did you sit upon a chaise and demand tea and biscuits all day while the work went on around you?"

She gritted her teeth and thought about all the things she would like to say to this Highland oaf, but she was far too weary to be goaded into a fight. Keeping her gaze on the fire, she lifted her head a fraction more, and stiffened her spine. She would not give him the fight he so obviously desired.

Dillon drained his goblet and set it on the mantel, then faced her. She refused to look at him.

"Aye. Turn away, lying English wench," he muttered. "But it does not matter. I know what you scheme. And it will not work. You will remain my prisoner here until my brothers are free. I care not if your flesh rots and your father's heart breaks. I care only for the safety of my brothers."

At the mention of her father's heart, she turned on him, her eyes blazing with all the hatred she had stored up. "Aye. You care not that my father's heart breaks. You claim to care only about your precious brothers. I am sick to death of hearing about them. I have seen the zeal with which you make your plans, Highlander. It is not their freedom that burns in your blood. It is the thought of battle. I see you and your friends, aye, even your sister, combing the countryside for men and arms. You lust, not for justice, but for the blood of Englishmen. To declare otherwise is a lie."

For a moment, he was rendered speechless by her outburst. His eyes widened as he stared at her. Then, without warning, the corners of his lips curled upward, and he began to laugh.

It was not the response she had anticipated.

The sound of his laughter fueled her anger. "You find my words amusing?"

"Nay." He wiped a tear from his eye and struggled to compose himself. But the laughter bubbled up again. "It is not your words, woman. It is you. Look at you."

He caught her by the shoulders and turned her toward the looking glass. She saw the reflection of her soiled gown, bearing the filth of the floor and the soot of the fireplace. Her hair hung in damp tendrils, curling limply around her face. When she caught sight of the flour that dusted her cheek, and the dirt that smudged her forehead and nose, she felt the beginnings of a blush at the base of her throat. Her own father would hardly recognize her.

Dillon, too, was studying her reflection. So great was his desire to brush away the dusting of flour, he had to will his hands to remain at his sides. His smile faded as he reminded himself that this was all a sham.

"You played your part well. Now, wash yourself, woman. Then we will go below stairs and sup." His tone was abrupt, with no trace of the laughter from just minutes before.

When he turned away, she walked to the basin and filled it with water from the pitcher. Her mind was awhirl with plots and schemes. Seeing Dillon's gaze averted for a moment, she slipped the knife from her pocket and tucked it beneath the sleeping pallet.

In her mind she went over her plan of escape. From the balcony, she had seen a door in the wall of a garden. A door that no one seemed to use. She would have to find out where that door led, for that was her door to freedom.

Knowing Dillon watched her, she took a throw from the sleeping pallet and draped it around herself for modesty. She removed her kid boots, her gown and her petticoats. Wearing only her chemise, she began to wash. When she had finished, she lifted a brush to her hair and tried to arrange it, but her movements were oddly slow and awkward. The lack of food, the grueling work and the pain in her muscles conspired to weaken her. She gave up and turned her attention

to her gown. With soap and water she began to wash the
soiled areas, scrubbing at each spot until she was satisfied
that the gown was presentable. Draping it across a chair by
the fire, she decided to sit a while and allow it to dry.

She pressed a hand to her forehead. She was so warm. No
doubt it was the ale. It had dulled her senses, making it impossible to think.

She drew the fur throw around her and curled up on the
floor in front of the fire. She would not allow herself to
sleep, for she could ill afford to further incur Dillon's wrath.
She would merely rest her eyes for a moment.

Her lids closed. She could hear Dillon moving around in
the sitting chamber, but she could not rouse herself. It felt
so good to just lie there unmoving.

She must not fall asleep, she cautioned herself. She must
be ready to sup when Dillon summoned her.

That was her last coherent thought before she fell into a
deep, dreamless sleep.

Dillon stood with one hand resting atop the mantel. His
gaze was riveted on the flames.

Sutton and Shaw. He believed, strongly, that they were
still alive. If not, he would know it in his heart. But though
he had faith that they were still alive, it was not enough.
What condition were they in? He had seen proof of the cruel
treatment of Scots prisoners in English dungeons. Every day
that he hesitated was another day of torture for his brothers.

A part of him wanted to raise an army big enough to destroy anything that stood in the way of their freedom. Another part of him wanted to slip away, alone, and see to his
brothers' safety as he always had.

His army was growing. This day, another ten and five had
pledged their arms to him. But it would be a fortnight or

more before he would have the number necessary to meet the English.

God in heaven, how he hated this waiting.

His hand clenched into a fist and he turned away, intent upon venting his anger on his favorite target—the woman.

Why did she vex him so? How was it that she had the power to rouse his anger one moment, and send him into spasms of laughter the next? What mystical powers did she possess, that all who met her fell victim to her charm?

Though he had tried to ignore it, he had seen the reaction of the servants when he had spoken sharply to the woman. Already they were accepting her as one of them. And what of Rupert? The lad had every right to mistrust the English, yet he watched her with the eyes of an adoring puppy. Then there was Mistress MacCallum, as hardened an English-hater as any he had ever known. Yet she had told him that the woman had worked alongside the servants. What would induce the housekeeper to lie, if it was indeed a lie?

He knew one thing. Nothing would soften his heart. So long as his brothers were held prisoner by the English, his heart must remain hardened against this female. Her fate was tied to theirs. Her treatment would be no better.

When he entered the sleeping chamber, his gaze fell upon the figure huddled before the fire.

"Woman, what are you doing? You knew we..."

Puzzled by her lack of response, he paused and dropped to one knee. His throat went dry at the sight that greeted him.

She lay in a nest of fur. The throw had slipped from her shoulders, revealing pale flesh barely covered by an ivory chemise. Her dark hair had fallen forward to swirl over one breast. Flickering firelight played over her, casting her in light and shadow.

This was not the way she looked each night in his pallet. Always she had taken great pains to preserve her modesty, wearing not only her gown and boots, but always tucking the covers around her in such a way that no part of her was visible.

He allowed his gaze to move slowly over her, savoring the vision. A more perfect creature he had never seen. From the slope of her shoulders to the pale, creamy throat. From the rise and fall of high, rounded breasts, clearly visible beneath the flimsy bit of fabric, to a waist so small his big hands could easily span it. From the flare of her hips to the expanse of long, shapely legs. She was exquisite.

She sighed and moved in her sleep and he was startled out of his reverie by the sight of something that jarred this otherwise serene portrait. Catching first one hand, then the other, he turned her palms upward to reveal raw, bloody blisters.

He was rocked by a rush of self-revulsion. He had mocked her and accused her of falsehoods. Worse, he had assumed that her silence was an admission of guilt.

With great tenderness he pressed his lips to her palms, before lifting her in his arms.

In her sleep she sighed and wrapped her arms around his neck, burying her mouth against his throat. He stood holding her cradled against his chest, feeling a welling of tenderness unlike anything he had ever before experienced.

He carried her across the room, deposited her on his sleeping pallet and drew the covers over her. Then he went in search of Mistress MacCallum and some of her precious healing ointment.

Leonora stirred, but couldn't seem to rouse herself. She could feel the warmth of the fire, but she refused to open her eyes just yet. She felt warm and snug and thoroughly refreshed. She could not recall having ever slept so soundly.

Vague remnants of a dream seemed to be flitting through her consciousness. A sensation of being lifted in strong arms and carried like a child. A feeling of gentle fingers stroking hers. A voice, low and deep, murmuring half-remembered words of endearment.

A smile touched her lips and a feeling of joy spread through her like warm honey. She was home. Home with her father. It must be his voice, his words, for no other man had ever carried her in his arms. And the soothing strokes had to come from Moira, her old nurse. The Highlands had been nothing more than a bad dream. As was the Highland savage, Dillon Campbell.

At the thought of that name, her smile fled. Nay. Not a dream. Reality was the Highland savage. Dillon. Dear heaven. The voice in the dream was his, as was the touch. It all came rushing back. She had fallen asleep after washing herself. She had not even managed to stay awake long enough to go below stairs to sup. This was not a dream. It was actually happening.

Her eyes blinked open as Dillon settled her among the furs of his pallet and sat beside her.

"What are you doing?" She pushed herself into a sitting position, unaware of her state of undress. She shoved the heavy hair from her eyes, fighting the effect of sleep. "You must not—"

"Shh." He touched a work-roughened finger to her lips to silence her.

Shock waves collided within her at his simple touch. She tried to pull her hands away but he held her fast and began to apply a soothing ointment to her palms.

"Please. You need not—"

"It is little enough to do after what I put you through, my lady." His tone was intimate, sending tiny slivers of fire and ice along her spine. "To think that I accused you of some devious plot. Your hands say otherwise. Besides, the servants who worked alongside you sing your praises."

She felt a sting of guilt and trembled beneath its weight. If he only knew how she had plotted and schemed ... She ducked her head, afraid to meet his steady gaze. That was when she realized that she wore nothing more than her chemise. She tried to reach for a covering, but he held her fast.

Though he continued to hold her hands, his fingers had stilled their movement. He studied her bowed head and felt an overwhelming rush of emotion. "I have denied the truth long enough."

Her head came up. "The truth?"

"I want you. And have since I first beheld you in your father's home."

"Nay." She drew back, terrified of the feelings that had rippled through her at his words. Feelings that had no place between a captor and captive, between an Englishwoman and a Scot.

"Aye, my lady. God help us both, it is true."

He lowered his mouth to hers with all the power, and all the force, all the fury that, until now, he'd been holding back. Now it was up to heaven itself to stop him, for he had no more willpower left.

She had never felt such passion. Always, she had been aware that he had held something back, exerting rigid control over his emotions. Now his kisses spoke of hunger, of need, of unbridled passion.

He moved his hands along her back. The thin fabric of her chemise, barely covering her from breast to thigh, excited him. Her skin was as cool and pale as the white sand that shimmered beneath a Highland stream. Fascinated, he slipped his hands beneath the fabric and discovered her heat.

Still drowsy from sleep, Leonora's movements were slow. Though she lifted her hands to push him away, her limbs betrayed her. Her hands slipped around his waist. Her fingers dug into his back, urging him closer.

Her body hummed with needs. Needs that pulsed through her, setting tiny fires to her flesh, heating her blood until it flowed like molten lava through her veins.

How could she react so wantonly? And with her enemy. Even as she experienced a wave of shame, she couldn't seem to hold back the sigh that escaped her lips.

He brought his lips to her throat. Against her delicate flesh he murmured, "Tonight, my lady, I can no longer resist the need for you." His voice held the hint of danger, the promise of paradise. "Tonight I will have what I most desire."

He ran hot hungry kisses along the sensitive column of her throat, then lower, to the soft swell of her breast.

Instantly her nipple hardened beneath the gauzy fabric. Frustrated by even this small barrier between them, he brought his hands to the ribbons that laced her chemise. With quick, impatient movements he slipped it from her shoulders.

The realization of what she had permitted was like a dash of icy water. God in heaven, what had she been thinking of? She had permitted this savage liberties granted to no other man.

"Nay!" Frightened by her sudden arousal, she began fighting like a cornered animal, scratching, pushing, struggling against the arms that held her.

Aroused, angered, he caught both her wrists in one big hand and pinned her arms over her head. With his other hand, he caught her chin, forcing her head still as he plundered her mouth.

Blinded by rage and desire, he kissed her as no man had ever dared to kiss her before. With teeth and tongue and mouth he teased and tormented until, on a cry, her lips softened and her mouth opened to him. While he continued kissing her, he ran his hand possessively over her until he felt her gradual response.

"You see, my lady." His breathing was ragged. His voice was a low whisper of triumph. "Though you deny it, you want what I want. And tonight we shall—"

It was then that he tasted the salt of her tears.

Tears?

He lifted his head. In the firelight, her face was bathed in tears. She could not seem to stop herself. Though this display of weakness shamed her further, the tears streamed from her eyes and coursed down her cheeks in rivers.

In that instant, he knew that he had overstepped all bounds of decency. God in heaven, he was no better than those he had scorned as cruel, wild animals.

With his thumbs he wiped the tears from her cheeks. His voice was choked with pain and frustration. "Forgive me, my lady. I was possessed by madness."

Muttering a savage oath he strode from the chambers.

Chapter Fifteen

Leonora stood by the balcony window, watching as ribbons of light on the horizon signaled the arrival of dawn. She had spent the long, sleepless night huddled on the balcony, prepared to leap to her death if Dillon Campbell should return.

It was not that he repulsed her. Nay, she still blushed each time she thought about her reaction to his kisses. If truth be told, she had wanted him. Though it shamed her to admit it to herself, she had wanted him as much as he claimed to want her.

How could this be? She knew not. But this much she knew—last night, in Dillon's arms, she had almost brought dishonor to her father's name. She knew now that she could no longer trust herself with this man. Though he was a primitive savage, Dillon Campbell touched her is a way that no other man ever had. She was weak and spineless, she reasoned. A foolish romantic, who had somehow become confused in her mind about right and wrong. She was actually beginning to believe that there was a goodness, a kindness about this Scots laird that she had not found in any of the men who had tried to court her in her own land.

She had come to a decision. She must not remain under this roof another night. For to do so would be to bring shame upon herself and her father. She knew that she would not have the strength to resist Dillon Campbell's advances again. No matter what, she must make good her escape this day. Another night and she would be lost.

Hearing the servants moving about in the hallway outside her door, she hurriedly washed and dressed herself. When the door to her chambers was opened, she looked up sharply, then gave a sigh of relief when she spied Gwynnith.

"Ah, my lady. I see you are about early, as well." The servant lowered her voice. "The laird is below stairs in a fierce black temper. Mistress MacCallum has cautioned us to walk softly in his presence this day, else we shall feel the sting of his displeasure."

"And does he display these black tempers often, Gwynnith?" Leonora turned her back and busied herself with a comb and brush.

"Nay, my lady. In fact, it is not at all like the laird." The little servant giggled before coming up behind Leonora to help with her hair. "If I did not know better, I would think he had been up all night tipping a goblet. But the laird has never been known to enjoy the ale like some." After securing a jeweled comb, she took a step back to study the English lady's reflection in the mirror. "Mistress MacCallum says a temper such as his can only be because of a woman."

Leonora felt her cheeks flame and turned away quickly. That was when she realized that the object of their discourse was standing in the doorway. On his face was a scowl of displeasure.

"Do you not have chores, Gwynnith?"

"Aye, my laird." The little servant fairly flew from the room, leaving Leonora alone to face him.

He studied her for long silent moments. He still wanted her. With every fiber of his being, he wanted her. And hated himself for it. "You will remain in my chambers this day so that your tender hands can heal."

At his words, her head came up sharply. "Nay, I must not." She caught herself before she said anything more that might reveal her scheme. She must convince him that she was able to leave the confines of these chambers.

He was watching her with a wariness that unnerved her. As if, she thought, he could see clear through to her mind. He walked past her, poured water into a basin and, stripping off his tunic, began to wash.

"I . . . cannot lock myself away now." She paced to the balcony, then back. "The work is going so well. I have given my word to Mistress MacCallum that I will teach the servants how to—" her mind raced "—make my father's favorite brandied pudding."

He dried himself with a square of linen. "Mistress MacCallum will understand why it cannot be done today."

"It must."

The passion with which she protested made him curious. Tossing aside the linen, he crossed to her with the agility of a predatory animal. "Let me see your hands."

He seemed unaware of the fact that he wore only tight black breeches. But Leonora was aware. Aware of a broad expanse of hair-roughened, muscular chest. Aware of arms corded with muscles. Aware of a trim, narrow waist and flat stomach. And a face close enough for her to feel the warmth of his breath on her cheek. The rush of feeling was so swift, so overpowering, it nearly took her breath away.

Reluctantly she held up her hands for his scrutiny. The moment his fingers brushed hers she felt the jolt and had to struggle to show no emotion.

"They are healing nicely." He looked up, meeting her direct gaze. "How do they feel? Is there any pain?"

"Nay." She tried to pull away but he held her fast. "Truly," she insisted.

He gazed into her eyes and saw, in his mind's eye, the way she had looked the night before, wearing nothing more than a flimsy chemise. She would never know what it had done to him. Had it not been for her tears...

He could still recall the shock of her tears. It was the only thing that could have penetrated the lust that had driven him mad with desire. To have been the cause of this strong, proud woman's tears still grated.

The sudden urge to kiss her was stronger than ever. To cover his feelings, he said sternly, "I cannot return you to your father blemished in any way, else he will accuse me of having mistreated you."

She felt the sting of disappointment. "I should have known you did not act out of kindness, Dillon Campbell, but out of a sense of duty."

He released her and watched as she stalked to the fireplace. "It is not kindness that dictates my treatment of you, my lady. It is prudence. As you are treated, so shall my brothers be treated by your father."

This was better. Safer. Anger was preferable to tenderness. The woman must never know that he harbored tender feelings for her.

He went on in the same impersonal tone. "In a day or two, the torn flesh will heal. But until then, I cannot give you my permission to continue the work of the servants."

She was equally determined to be allowed to roam the fortress without restrictions. This must be her day of freedom. Else all was lost. "Then I shall assist Mistress MacCallum. Even if I cannot do the work, I can instruct the servants in the proper ways to cook as well as clean this hovel."

Hovel, was it? His eyes narrowed at her superior tone. Did the woman spend every waking hour thinking of ways to anger him?

The truth was, he knew his overburdened housekeeper would benefit from the Englishwoman's knowledge. But he dared not permit Leonora too much freedom, or she would devise a way to use it to her advantage. Besides, he was still smarting from his momentary lapse of the previous night.

He pulled on his shirt and tucked it into the waistband of his breeches. "I see no harm in permitting you to instruct the servants. So long as Rupert is by your side."

She turned toward the fire to hide the little smile of triumph that touched her lips. It was a victory of sorts, and one she would use.

"If you are ready," he said, opening the door, "we will go below stairs and break our fast."

She swept past him, keeping her head high, her gaze averted. In her pockets were the knife and linen-wrapped packages of food.

"You must lay the rushes like this." Leonora moved across the floor on her knees, positioning several rows of rushes in an intricate pattern.

The servants nodded and followed her example. Mistress MacCallum stood and watched, her arms crossed over her ample bosom.

When Leonora continued working alongside the servants, the housekeeper admonished her, "Nay, m'lady. The laird has said ye must give ye'r hands time to heal."

By now, all of the servants had heard of the lady's valiant efforts to hide her pain, and most had seen the evidence of her work etched on her tender palms. Their own hands had been callused and toughened by years of hard labor, but many could still recall the early years of discomfort, and admired her courage.

"Perhaps I could do something less challenging in the kitchens." Leonora tried to hide her eagerness. From the kitchens, it was a short walk to freedom.

"Aye, m'lady. A grand idea. All who tasted your tarts last night asked for more. Perhaps you could make them again?"

"I would be happy to, Mistress MacCallum."

Rupert held the door and followed the two women down a hallway that twisted and turned until it ended at the huge kitchen. Inside, the ovens were already overflowing with loaves of bread, and two deer were being roasted over a fire.

Leonora joined several other servants in rolling out the dough for the tarts, then ladled sliced apples laced with honey and flour into each delicate crust. When all was in readiness, the confections were placed in a large stone oven to bake. Soon the wonderful fragrance filled the room, making Rupert's mouth water.

With Mistress MacCallum beaming her approval, Leonora proceeded to show the servants how to make her father's favorite brandied pudding and a sweet, dark cake laden with bits of fruit.

Instead of the usual gruel to accompany the bread, Leonora made a fruit conserve that had even the housekeeper sighing with pleasure when she'd tasted it.

"Have you a garden?" Leonora asked, though she was already aware of the answer.

Mistress MacCallum nodded.

"Perhaps I might be allowed to pick some tender young vegetables to accompany the venison." The housekeeper seemed about to refuse, so she added quickly, "Your laird will proclaim your meal fit for a king."

She saw the light that came into Mistress MacCallum's eyes as the housekeeper wiggled a finger at Rupert. "As long as the lad is with ye, I see no reason not to allow it."

"Thank you. We will not be gone long. I will need a warm cloak," she said to Rupert.

"It is not that cold outside, my lady."

"Perhaps not, but I . . . I get chilled quickly," she lied.

He led her to a peg where she selected a warm hooded cloak. As she followed Rupert along the passageway that led to the outer door, she slipped the knife and packages of food into the deep pockets of the cloak. When they stepped into the garden, she lifted her head and breathed deeply. "Ah, Rupert. Do you smell it?"

"Smell what, my lady?"

Freedom, she thought. But aloud she merely said, "The scent of freshly turned earth. Herbs. Fruits and vegetables. They are scents that remind me of home."

"You miss your home, do you not, my lady?"

"Aye."

"Soon enough you shall see it. And I shall miss you, my lady."

His words pricked her conscience.

The lad picked up a shovel and began to dig into a row of carrots. As he stepped his foot on the shovel and turned the earth, Leonora bent down to retrieve the golden carrots from their nest of earth. While the lad's head was bent, she peered around, searching for the door she had spotted from Dillon's balcony. On the far side of the garden, set into the wall, she spied it. Because it led directly to the forest, no one dared use it. Thus, no guards were posted. On the other side of that door lay freedom.

She and Rupert worked the row together, with the lad digging and Leonora retrieving the carrots, until they had enough for the evening meal. As the pile of vegetables grew larger, her mind was awhirl with plans. She must find a way to elude her young guard. But how? Her mind raced.

Lifting her head, she sniffed the air. "Do I smell roses, Rupert? Are there roses nearby?"

"Aye, my lady. Would you like to see the rose garden?"

"I would indeed."

He led her beyond the vegetable garden to a small plot of land ringed by overgrown hedges and a thick tangle of vines. Roses, which had been allowed to grow wild, bloomed in profusion. Their perfume filled the air.

She made her way to an old stone bench and draped her cloak over it.

"Ah, Rupert," she said on a sigh. "There is nothing quite like a rose garden. Even one as neglected as this."

"Aye, my lady."

She began to walk along an overgrown path, all the while keeping the door in sight.

"This could be a lovely garden," she mused aloud, "if anyone loved it enough to tend it."

"With all the fighting, there is little time to tend gardens, my lady."

She looked up at the lad, who watched the flight of a bird. It pained her to misuse him in this way, but she simply had no choice if she were to assure her escape. "I believe I will pick a few roses for Mistress MacCallum. While I do that, do you think you could fetch me a basket from the kitchen, Rupert? We will need it to carry the carrots."

"Aye, my lady." The lad began to lumber away.

As soon as he disappeared from sight, she grabbed her cloak, raced to the door and eagerly pushed on the handle. It didn't budge. Leaning all her weight against it, she struggled to open it, but the door remained solidly sealed. She could see that the heavy door had not been opened in many years. Thick vines grew over it, nearly concealing the hinges.

Leonora knew that at any moment Rupert would return. Pulling the knife from the pocket of her cloak, she cut away the vines, then pushed again with all her might.

The door swung open just enough for her to squeeze through. There was no time to wrestle it closed, so she turned and began running through the tall grass. If she could reach the cover of the nearby forest, the Highlanders would never find her.

Flame stood in the doorway of the kitchens, staring hungrily at the clear, cloudless sky. The day was too perfect to be spent on loathsome household duties. She yearned to be free. Instead, she was trapped with the servants. All because of the hated Englishwoman.

Her eyes narrowed at the pair strolling in the garden. The damnable woman had bewitched every man who dared to look upon her. With those beguiling eyes and that innocent smile, she had cast them all under her spell. Father Anselm. Rupert. Even Dillon, though he would deny it. But Flame had seen the way he watched the woman when he thought no one was looking.

While she watched, Flame saw Rupert turn away and walk through the doorway that led to the inner passageway. But the Englishwoman remained in the garden.

Had he left her unattended?

While she watched, Flame saw a flutter of white gown moving swiftly across the garden toward the outer wall. As realization dawned, she raced from the kitchens, intent upon stopping the woman before she could escape. In her haste, she did not spare even a moment to sound an alarm. No matter, she reasoned as she ate up the distance between them. A fragile English kitten was no match for a wildcat born of the Highlands.

The forest was farther away than Leonora had first thought. The expanse of meadow was not so easily crossed. Briars caught at the hem of her gown, holding her back as she struggled to run. The branches of small brush snagged at her sleeves and tugged the ribbons from her hair. The heavy cloak she carried over her arm further slowed her progress, but she dared not drop it. She would need its warmth once the sun went down.

As she ran, she chanced a quick glance over her shoulder and was dismayed to see a figure behind her. The sun glinting off fiery hair left no question as to the identity of her stalker. Flame.

Gritting her teeth, Leonora pressed on. Her breathing was more labored as she crested a hill and caught sight of the tangle of dense woods that lay just beyond the edge of the meadow. With her breath burning in her lungs, she sprinted the remaining distance, determined to reach the safety of the forest. Once there, she had no doubt she could evade capture.

As the lush growth closed around her, she slipped into a world of cool dark shadows, icy streams, strange, primitive creatures. Drawing her cloak firmly about her, she stepped deeper into the forest and prayed she could become one with her surroundings.

Leonora was hopelessly lost.

For hours, she had stumbled through the forest, twisting and turning to evade the lass who stubbornly trailed her.

At first, Leonora had thought she had escaped Flame's relentless pursuit. But with each new turn, she had seen further proof that the girl was still following.

Now, in a desperate attempt to be free, she slid down a steep ravine, landing headfirst in a thicket. Nearby she could hear the roar of a waterfall, obliterating all other sounds. Gradually, as her ears became accustomed to the sounds of the forest, she heard something else. Something that had the hair at the nape of her neck prickling.

A horse whinnied nearby. As she sought shelter behind a tree, a hand clamped on her shoulder. A man's voice whispered against her ear, "The gods are indeed smiling on me this day. I have just been granted my fondest wish. I am alone with the beautiful English wench."

Leonora was spun around, and found herself looking into the cruel, laughing eyes of Graeme Lamont.

Chapter Sixteen

"How did you find me?" Leonora's eyes were wide with fear.

Graeme's lips curled into a cold smile. "Have you not guessed? These forests are my home. I walk them as comfortably as Dillon Campbell walks the halls of Kinloch House."

As his fingers tightened on her shoulder, her cloak slipped from her fingers and dropped to the ground.

"The truth is, I was not searching for you. When I caught sight of the flutter of a white gown in the forest, I thought I would amuse myself with a local wench." His smile grew, though it never reached his eyes. The effect was chilling. "My pleasure will be even greater now. I have long wanted to sample an Englishwoman's charms. And it shall be twice the pleasure, since you cannot threaten to run home to weep in your father's arms as some of the local wenches have done after I have taken my pleasure with them."

She felt an icy finger of fear along her spine. She thought of the frightening stories the servants had told, of women and even children mysteriously murdered in these forests. Now, seeing the chilling look in Graeme's eyes, it all made sense.

She looked around, desperately seeking a way to escape.

Seeing what she was contemplating he drew her closer. "Do you think you can outrun me in this forest?"

"If you unhand me, you will have your answer."

His smile fled and he brought his hand across her face with a blow that snapped her head to one side. "Aye. I shall unhand you, my fine fancy lady. But only long enough to tear away the peasant dress you wear. It offends my eyes. It does not suit you."

With a hand at each side of her neckline, he ripped the gown from her. The torn and tattered remnants fluttered to the damp moss at her feet.

"Nay," he breathed, "it does not suit you at all." He caught a handful of her hair and yanked her head back sharply, bringing a cry to her lips. He studied the swell of her breasts, visible beneath the delicate chemise, and the outline of her hips through the gauzy fabric of her petticoats. "I knew you would be easy to look at."

Shame flooded Leonora's cheeks as she was forced to endure his leering gaze. She crossed her arms in front of her bosom in a futile attempt at modesty, but he caught her hands roughly and pinned them to her sides.

"Now," he muttered, twisting her arms roughly behind her back, "I am going to pleasure myself with a taste of paradise."

Dillon dismounted in the courtyard and absently tossed the reins to old Stanton. Had he not been so deep in thought, he might have noticed that the old stable master seemed highly agitated. But he could not rid himself of this foul black mood. Even though another ten and two men had pledged themselves to him this day, it was not enough to lift his spirits. All he could think of was the woman. The damnable woman and her damnable tears.

How could he go on, day after day, night after interminable night, desiring her, and doing nothing about it? God knew he was not a saint. He was a mere man. And the thoughts that had been plaguing him were driving him to distraction.

He passed along a corridor and noted fresh candles, casting their soft glow on highly polished stone walls and wood floors. Everywhere he looked, Kinloch House sparkled with the woman's touch.

He strode to the kitchens and hurled the door wide as he entered. At once, the voices stilled. Mistress MacCallum, wiping her hands on the apron tied at her middle, waddled over, sweating profusely.

"Where is Rupert?" Dillon asked.

The housekeeper stared at a spot on the floor. "He has ridden to the forest, my laird."

"The forest?"

She looked up and nodded. Seeing his dark eyes boring into her, she lowered her gaze and began twisting the apron between her plump fingers.

"He…" Her lips quivered. For all her nagging at the lad, Rupert had always been one of her favorites. Now, fearing the wrath of the laird, she hated being the one to tell him how the lad had been duped. "…left the Englishwoman alone for a moment in the garden—"

"Alone!"

"Aye. And she—"

"She what?" he thundered.

Mistress MacCallum swallowed, afraid to go on. But when she saw the fierce look in the laird's eyes, she had no choice. "The English lady…fled to the woods."

"Fled! God in heaven. How long has she been gone?"

"A long time. Several hours, m'laird."

He swore loudly, viciously, and the old woman cringed before adding, "There is more, m'laird. And 'tis worse, I fear."

"Worse?" he bellowed. "My prisoner has escaped, and her guard has not yet brought her back. What can be worse than this?"

"Flame is missing, as well, m'laird. We did not see her go. But…" She looked as though she might break down at any moment and begin to weep. "We fear she saw the English-woman escaping and went after her."

"Two headstrong women," he muttered aloud, "and only Rupert to seek them out."

A feeling of dread pierced his heart like an arrow. Now he had two fears to deal with. Not only had Leonora escaped, but both she and Flame were treading dangerous ground. A killer of women lurked nearby.

He spun on his heel, shouting over his shoulder, "Summon what men we have within the walls of the keep. Tell them to comb the forest. I do not return to Kinloch House until both women return with me."

Flame's hatred of the Englishwoman grew with every bramble that snagged her gown or tree limb that caught her hair. She had expected the coddled noblewoman to cower at the dangers lurking in the forest. Instead, the woman had surprised Flame by displaying a rare determination.

She experienced a deep welling of despair. Why had she not sounded the alarm before rushing off? Because, she re-minded herself, she had not considered the Englishwoman a challenge. Who would have dreamed that she could evade capture for so long?

Despite the teachings of the good sisters, the young Scotswoman could swear as viciously as her brothers, and did so now as yet another bramble tore her flesh. Suddenly, she lifted her head. Was that a voice? She inched forward, straining to see through the dense foliage. Aye. A female voice raised in a cry of alarm. She gave a smug smile. Perhaps the Englishwoman had fallen and muddied herself. 'Twould serve her right.

"Take off the rest of your clothes." Graeme no longer bothered to hide behind a facade of good manners. Here in the forest, with no one to witness his deeds, he shed the last vestiges of civility. Something wild and feral glittered in his eyes.

"Nay." Leonora lifted her head defiantly, praying her lips would not tremble and reveal the terror that held her in its grip. "You will have to cut them away, as well."

"With pleasure. Perhaps I will cut your throat while I am at it."

In his hand, the blade of a knife caught a flash of late-afternoon sunshine that filtered through the tangle of leaves and vines. As he lifted it menacingly, a small figure stepped into the clearing.

Flame's voice was triumphant. "I see you have managed to catch the Englishwoman."

Graeme seemed momentarily confused. "Flame. How did you . . . ? Where did you . . . ?"

"I have been following her," the girl explained, "since she first slipped away from Rupert. But until now, she managed to elude me. Praise heaven you were here." She glanced around in puzzlement, her gaze lingering on the remains of a campfire and a bed made up of animal fur, all evidence of a lengthy encampment. Suddenly, her good fortune at having found the woman was momentarily forgotten. "Why are you here, Graeme? Why are you not out searching for an army of soldiers as you promised Dillon?"

"I have been resting."

"Resting?" Flame took a step closer and the scene before her took on a sharper focus. The Englishwoman's cloak and remnants of torn gown had been tossed aside. The knife in Graeme's hand could mean only one thing. "What is the meaning of this? Why have you misled my brother? And why are you threatening such harm to the woman when you know how important she is to Dillon's plan?"

Leonora saw the hard look that came into Graeme's eyes when he realized that his lie had been uncovered. "Alas." He shrugged. "I had not wanted you to share the fate of the Englishwoman. But now I have no choice."

"What are you talking about?"

"It is not merely my honor he intends to steal," Leonora said softly. "He intends to kill me. And you, as well."

"How do you know what Graeme is planning?" Flame asked.

Graeme fisted a hand in Leonora's hair and yanked her head back sharply. Though she did not cry out, he was rewarded by a flash of pain that glazed her eyes for a moment before she composed herself. "Aye. How do you know what I plan? Do you claim to read minds now, Englishwoman?"

"It is easy enough to see that once you have . . . despoiled me, you cannot return me to Kinloch House. In fact, you will be forced to kill me in order to silence me."

"And why do I need your silence?"

"You dare not permit me to live. For if I am allowed to reveal your wickedness to Dillon Campbell, you will have to answer to his wrath."

"You flatter yourself if you think Dillon Campbell cares what happens to an Englishwoman," Flame said with contempt.

"Think, Flame," Leonora urged. "If Graeme kills me, Dillon Campbell will have lost his only chance to barter for the safe return of his brothers. Your beloved brothers. And for that, he will never forgive Graeme, despite their years of friendship."

Graeme's eyes darkened with fury. "Do you think I fear Dillon Campbell?"

"If you do not," Flame said, tossing her head, "you are a fool."

"Dillon need never know."

"Aye." Leonora's voice grew even softer as she fought the horror and revulsion that filled her at the thought of what she and Flame must face together. "So long as there are no witnesses left. Is that not how you have managed to elude capture for so long, Graeme? It is you who murdered all those women and children, is it not?"

"Nay," Flame protested quickly. "It cannot be. For Dillon said that such a man was a monster."

Graeme smiled, a cruel, twisted smile that left no doubt as to his intentions. "A monster, am I?"

"Holy Mother, 'tis true, then," Flame whispered.

"Sad." His smile grew. "But true, lass."

"But why?"

"Why?" Graeme's face twisted into a mask of hatred. "I have a right to a little pleasure. It is little enough comfort when a lad has no father and a mother who wastes her charms on everyone save the one who most needs her."

"All in the villages have heard about your mother, Graeme, who sold her charms to anyone with coin. But none of us ever guessed that her deeds festered so in your soul."

"Festered?" His eyes narrowed. "I revel in it. I take delight in enjoying the same pleasures she enjoyed."

Flame felt a tremble of fear at the torrent of hatred in his words. "But why do you hate Dillon?" she asked.

"Dillon," he spat. "Ever since we were lads, your precious brother has always appointed himself leader. From our earliest years at the monastery, the monks always treated Dillon Campbell like one anointed by God. And now, even the greatest warrior in all of Scotland, Robert the Bruce, seems blinded by Dillon's virtues, calling him noble and honest." Graeme's voice deepened with fury. "I should have been the one sent to England. Women are taken with me. Men trust me. Why should a crude warrior with a face marred by an English sword be sent on a mission of such importance?"

Flame's voice was little more than a strangled whisper. "You called yourself Dillon's friend. You accepted shelter in his home, ate his food, shared in his joys and sorrows. And all this time, you have hated him?"

"Aye, hated him for all that he is, and all that I can never be. And because of your diligence in searching, dear little Flame, you must now share the Englishwoman's fate."

"Bastard!" Flame's hand went to the knife at her waist and she attacked with all the vengeance of a warrior. But though she fought bravely, she was no match for Graeme's strength. With quick, powerful strokes, he deftly brandished the knife in his hand until Flame found herself backed against a tree. He lunged, but she managed to move aside at the last moment, avoiding a knife thrust to the heart.

Flame was beginning to tire. As she lifted her hand to defend herself from yet another attack, Graeme gave one powerful sweep of the knife that sliced her arm from wrist to shoulder. With a cry, the knife slipped from her nerveless fingers and she dropped to her knees in the grass, cradling her bloody arm. Soon the ground around her was soaked with her blood. Graeme, with all the sleek assurance of a mountain cat, moved in for the kill.

He had momentarily forgotten about Leonora. Using the distraction to her advantage, she picked up a fallen tree limb and sent it crashing against his head with as much force as she could muster.

Graeme was momentarily stunned. The knife thrust missed Flame's heart, landing instead deep in her shoulder.

But before Leonora could hit him again, he got to his feet and yanked the club from her hands.

His voice rang with pain and rage. "Now you will pay, woman."

He advanced on her, the knife glinting in his upraised hand. He caught her roughly by the hair and yanked her head back sharply. Tears filled her eyes but she clenched her teeth, refusing to give him the satisfaction of hearing her cry out.

"First, I will have my pleasure." He cut away her chemise and petticoats, and laughed when Leonora struggled to hide her nakedness.

Though she kicked and bit and fought with all the desperation of a wild creature, she was no match for his strength. He pressed the sharp edge of the knife against her throat until she felt the warmth of blood trickling across her breasts. She stopped fighting. Her eyes were glazed with pain and loathing.

"That is better, my fine lady." He fisted a handful of her hair and lowered his mouth to hers. When she tried to evade his lips, he tightened his grasp and held her still.

"And when I have had my fill of you, you and the lass will become the latest victims of the mysterious marauding savage. And I will be the one to comfort Dillon Campbell, not only on your deaths, but on the certain deaths of his brothers, as well."

He threw back his head and laughed, a cruel, chilling sound, that suddenly seemed to die in his throat. The hand holding Leonora relaxed its grip. Leonora tilted her head up to stare at him. There was a look of surprise in his eyes. Then he stiffened slightly and began to topple forward. Leonora took a quick step aside, barely avoiding the full weight of his body as it fell. When he landed on the ground, she could see a small, deadly knife embedded in his back.

Across the clearing, Flame's bloody arm dropped to her side. In a weak, rasping whisper, she said, "You are free to run now, Englishwoman. I've no strength left with which to follow you."

Chapter Seventeen

"What are you doing? Nay! Free me!" In a panic, Flame fought against the arms that pinned her.

"You are chilled. You must let me wrap you in my cloak." Leonora struggled to restrain the wildly thrashing arms and legs that beat against her. Despite the severity of Flame's wounds, the lass fought until there was no strength left.

Some time later, bruised and battered, Leonora managed to subdue her long enough to examine her arm. The cruel gash had caused her to lose far too much blood. Graeme's knife was buried to the hilt in her shoulder. When it was removed, the wound ran red with a river of blood.

Using the strips of her petticoats, Leonora applied a tourniquet to stem the flow. She quickly poured a liberal amount of spirits from a flask she had found lying in Graeme's bed of animal furs, then wrapped the entire arm and shoulder in layers of white wool, and bound it tightly in the remnants of tattered gown.

"You had best run while you can," Flame said.

"I am not leaving you." Leonora bundled the lass into Graeme's furs, sheltered beneath an outcropping of rock. Neither wind nor rain nor cold would touch her here.

"But you must. When my brother discovers us gone, he will come searching. Mark me well, Englishwoman. Dillon

Campbell will not rest until you are once again his prisoner."

"Hush." Leonora would not allow herself to think about the consequences of her actions. She knew well enough that she was forsaking her last chance to escape. But how could she abandon the lass now? It was unthinkable.

She lifted the flask to Flame's lips and saw her shudder as the spirits trickled down her throat.

The lass's teeth began chattering uncontrollably. Shock. Leonora had seen enough wounded after a battle to recognize the signs. After the chills, a fever would soon rage through the girl, leaving her fighting for her life. Leonora shuddered as another thought struck. She had seen, too, the dead that littered the fields after a battle, due to unclean wounds. Flame would have to battle two demons: fever and infection.

Taking the blood-soaked cloak from Graeme's body, she draped it around herself to cover her nakedness, then went in search of dried sticks for a fire.

A short time later, as she coaxed fire to the kindling, she heard Flame's voice, weak but still commanding. Moving to her side, she saw the girl's eyes widen with surprise.

"Still here...Englishwoman? Why do you not...escape while you have the chance?"

"You saved my life, Flame. How can I do less for you?"

"But—"

"Hush now." Leonora placed her fingers over the wounded girl's lips, then brushed the damp hair from her forehead in a gesture of tenderness. "Sleep, Flame. Conserve your strength. The struggle is not yet over. Soon enough, you will face the battle of your life."

In the darkness of the dense forest, it was impossible to discern day from night. Through a canopy of tangled leaves and vines, Dillon saw the faint light of a distant star.

At first, the trail left by the woman had been easy to follow. Brambles and briars held bits of hair and clothing. Reeds were trampled. Thickets pushed aside. Now, in the blackness of midnight, it was impossible to find a single clue. Earlier, there had been an eerie silence, as though something evil had roamed at will, disturbing the creatures of the forest. Now, however, insects hummed and night birds cried. These normal sounds gave Dillon no comfort. Though he tried not to think about the mysterious deaths of so many of his people here in this forest, it was impossible to hold such thoughts at bay. They crept, unbidden, to torment him as he plodded onward, staring into the darkness, straining to hear anything that might alert him to the presence of Flame or the woman.

He lifted his head. Had that been a voice? Or the cry of a bird? He couldn't be certain.

Creeping through the brush, he caught the faint scent of wood smoke. Fire. Somewhere up ahead, someone else shared these woods. He moved out at a faster pace.

When she touched a hand to Flame's forehead, Leonora was alarmed by the fire that raged. She had anticipated a fever, but the lass's entire body seemed consumed by flame. Had she cleansed the wound carefully enough? Would a single careless act cost the lass her life?

After fetching water from a nearby stream, Leonora dipped a remnant of her tattered gown into the gourd and began to bathe Flame's face and neck. As she worked, she murmured words of comfort.

"You must fight, Flame. Do battle against the fever that strives to claim your life." She dipped the cloth in cold water, wrung it out and laid it against a fevered cheek. "Can you hear me, Flame? You must fight this thing. You are young and strong. You must not be overcome by this fire, else, even in death, Graeme will have won."

The thought of Graeme, and the evil he had committed against so many helpless women and children, brought a lump to her throat. Had it not been for this wounded lass, she would surely have been his latest victim. She felt tears sting her eyes and blinked them away. How could she permit such weakness, when this brave girl was fighting so hard to live?

Though she was weary beyond belief, Leonora continued her ministrations, hour after hour, fetching cold water from the stream and bathing Flame, all the while murmuring words of encouragement.

"Fight, lass. Do it for Sutton and Shaw." She saw a flicker of movement behind the closed lids and realized that at least part of what she was saying was getting through. She leaned closer, her voice growing more urgent. "Fight for Dillon. And for yourself, Flame. Fight as you have never fought before. You must not let down your guard. Because to give up the battle now is to die. And you have so much to live for."

Leonora shivered in the predawn chill and burrowed deeper into the folds of her cloak. Despite her best intentions, sleep had overtaken her, and she slumped over the unconscious form of the girl who lay swaddled in fur beside her. One hand dipped into the gourd of icy water, causing her to jerk awake. In that brief moment, she caught a flash of movement in the brush and in her confused state thought that it was Graeme, rising from his shallow grave of leaves to claim her. Snatching a tree branch as a club, she struggled to her feet.

"God in heaven, what have you done?" Dillon's gaze darted to his sister, lying at Leonora's feet.

"Dillon. Praise heaven—"

Without waiting for a reply, he charged at her with the fierceness of a wounded bear. Leonora was helpless against

such a ferocious attack. Though she lifted the club in her
defense, it was swept aside as if it were no more than a mere
willow switch.

Dillon drove her back against the trunk of a tree, both
hands closing tightly around her throat.

"I should have killed you as soon as we were free of your
father's castle," he muttered thickly. "What was I thinking
of? You are the devil incarnate!" His eyes blazed with un-
controlled fury. His thumbs pressed against her delicate
flesh, cutting off her breath. "I curse the day I met you,
woman. And now that you have killed my sister, you shall
share her fate."

"I did not—" Choking, coughing, sputtering, her words
were stilled as he tightened his grasp.

Though she clawed at his hands and struggled with all her
might, she could not budge this giant who held her in a
death grip. Her vision blurred and she felt strangely light-
headed. Her hands, which had been wrapped around his,
now dropped limply at her sides.

She closed her eyes and gave up all attempts to struggle.
Death would be infinitely better than the loathing she could
read in his eyes. She could no longer bear to be the object of
Dillon Campbell's hatred. For now, with death nearly upon
her, she could finally admit the truth to herself, which she
had struggled for so long to hide. The truth was, she cared
too deeply about Dillon to endure his contempt.

"Nay, Dillon," came a feeble voice.

Dillon's head came up sharply. For a moment, his mind
had played tricks on him. Perhaps, because he wanted so
desperately to shield his little sister from all harm, he had
imagined that she was still alive.

"Dillon."

Relaxing his grasp on Leonora's throat, he turned to
where Flame lay. Her eyes were open and burning with a

strange, fevered light. Her words were little more than a whisper.

"You are not dead? This witch did not succeed in her evil attempt?"

"The Englishwoman...did not harm me. 'Twas Graeme. She stayed...to tend my wounds—she could have...left me to die."

He looked down at the woman who leaned against the tree, taking great gulps of air into her lungs. The bruises caused by his hands stood out in sharp relief against the pale flesh of her throat. Shame washed over him. Shame at what he had almost done to her. Shame that he had been so quick to condemn. Nay. If truth be told, *eager* to condemn. And why? The answer came instantly. He had been grasping for any reason to keep from caring too deeply about this woman.

Running a hand through his hair, he whispered, "I hope you will find it in your heart to forgive me, my lady. I...promise you I will make it up to you, somehow."

She could not speak. Her throat was still too constricted. Instead, she merely moved away from him and made her way back to Flame's side. Sinking down to her knees, she picked up the cloth and pressed it to the girl's forehead. Flame's eyes flickered, and a weak smile came to her lips as she closed a hand over Leonora's.

That was how Dillon found them when he knelt beside them.

"I never suspected Graeme." Out of respect for his sleeping sister, Dillon kept his tone low.

A deer carcass roasted over a blazing fire. Dillon had insisted that Leonora replace her blood-soaked cloak with his own heavy traveling cloak, which still bore the heat of his body in its folds.

For the first time in more hours than she could count, Leonora felt snug and warm and safe. Safe. Odd, she thought, that it was her captor who made her feel safe. Yet sometime during the past hour, he had ceased being her captor and had become her confidant. Odder still, it was Flame who had helped them bridge the chasm that had always loomed between them. Once he discovered that Leonora had freely chosen to remain behind and tend his wounded sister, the last barriers between them had dropped away, to be replaced by an openness she never would have believed possible.

"Graeme had every opportunity to kill," Dillon muttered, more to himself than to Leonora. "Always volunteering to go to distant villages. When he returned, I never questioned the time it took. Since he had a reputation as a wencher, we all believed that he tarried with village wenches. When I think what he did... And what he almost did to you—"

She touched a hand to his arm to still his words. "Hush. We will speak no more of it. I cannot bear to think of those who suffered at his hands."

"Aye." But Dillon could think of only one. Leonora. He felt a fierce surge of pride that it was his little sister who had saved Leonora's life. The knowledge that Leonora had been willing to give up her freedom in payment for that heroic act only increased his admiration for her.

Dillon sliced a portion of sizzling meat and handed it to her. It was the easy sort of camaraderie between them that, until this moment, she could not have imagined.

As she ate, Leonora thought she had never tasted anything so wonderful. How long it had been since she had eaten?

Dillon handed her a flask, and she drank, feeling the warmth of the ale course through her veins.

"I never guessed that Graeme hated me," Dillon muttered.

He glanced at her and she nodded, too weary to speak.

"I accepted his friendship in the same spirit in which I gave mine. Without condition." He shook his head in wonder. "To think I would have died for him. For a man who would have betrayed me."

"There are such men in every land, it would seem." She took another sip, then passed the flask back to Dillon. As their fingers brushed, she glanced up and saw him studying her so closely, she felt a sudden rush of heat. "There are those among my father's circle of friends who would betray him, as well."

"Aye." Dillon's gaze pierced her, as though suddenly uncovering a deeply buried secret. "We are not as dissimilar as we had first thought."

She shivered at the intensity of his words. Mistaking the movement, he scrambled to his feet. "You are cold, my lady. I will add to the fire."

"Nay."

Despite her protests, he hurried away to gather more wood. When he returned a few minutes later, he found her sound asleep, her head pillowed against a rock.

Very gently he lifted her and stared down at her face, so beautiful in repose. He brushed a kiss over her lips and felt a rush of heat that left him shaken.

He carried her to the nest of furs where his sister slept fitfully, gently set her down and covered her. Leaning his back against the trunk of a tree, his gaze moved over the two women who lay side by side. So dissimilar. And yet so alike. Strong, proud, brave. Headstrong and foolish. Loyal to a fault.

Strangely enough, these two very different women had become equally important in his life.

* * *

Early-morning sunlight filtered through the leaves, bathing the damp forest in a hazy glow.

Leonora awoke and lay very still, struggling to shake off the cobwebs of sleep. Somewhere close to her, a fire raged. Why had Dillon moved her so close to the flame?

Flame. She lifted her head. Not a fire. Flame. Lying beside her, burning with fever.

The girl's head rolled from side to side, while she muttered incoherent words of distress.

As Leonora scrambled to her feet, Dillon's head came up. Though he had nodded off, he was instantly alert. "What is it?"

"Flame. The fever is worse."

"What can I do?"

She handed him a hollowed-out gourd. "I will need water to bathe her."

Dillon returned with water from the stream and watched as Leonora knelt beside his sister. After unwrapping the dressings, she poured spirits from the flask over the festering wounds and examined them closely. He saw her frown of concern when she touched a finger to the raw, puckered flesh.

"Are the wounds clean?" he asked.

She shrugged. "I pray they are. I used what little I had to cleanse them."

He helped her wrap the wounds in fresh dressings. Then he and Leonora took turns bathing Flame's heated flesh. By the time the sun was high overhead, the lass had fallen into a deep, dreamless sleep. She lay in the mound of furs, as still as death.

Flame's stillness was far more frightening than had been her thrashing around.

"The fever grows worse." Dillon's big hand rested on his sister's cheek. For a man of such size and strength, he was incredibly gentle.

"Aye." Leonora tried to keep the fear from her voice.

"What more can I do?"

"You have done all you can, Dillon. She is in God's hands now."

"You sound like Father Anselm." He turned to the woman who knelt beside him. A more devoted nurse he had not met. She was fighting for Flame as fiercely as any mother.

All day, Dillon and Leonora had eaten sparingly, and rested not at all, while tending to Flame. Though he coaxed Leonora to sleep a while, she had adamantly refused, saying she feared Flame would soon reach a crisis.

"Either the fever will break, or—" When she realized what she had almost said, she caught herself and added haltingly, "The fever shall soon break. I know it."

"Aye." Restless, he got to his feet and began to pace. He hated this helpless feeling. "Perhaps I should return her to Kinloch House, where she would have her own bed, and servants to tend her, and Mistress MacCallum's healing herbs."

"Aye, all of those would help. But I fear she would not survive the ride on horseback. The jarring motion could tear open her wounds, and she could bleed to death. I think she is better off here, Dillon."

Her words, spoken softly, had a soothing effect on him. He stopped his pacing and turned to her with a weak smile. "I am not thinking clearly." He took her hands in his and studied the way they looked, so small and soft in his big palms. "I am grateful that you are able to think for both of us, my lady."

She clasped his hands and struggled to ignore the sensations that curled along her spine. "Rest a while, Dillon. I will wake you if there is any change."

"Nay." He shook his head. "I have a need to be busy. I will tend the fire and see that we both have something to eat."

He touched a hand to her cheek. "Lest I have not told you, my lady, I am most grateful for all that you do for my sister."

Long after he had walked away in search of fallen logs for the fire, she continued to feel his touch against her cheek. And was warmed by it.

Chapter Eighteen

Storm clouds obscured what little light managed to filter through the thick foliage. With the clouds came a strange calm, as though the very air was holding its breath, awaiting the release of the storm's fury.

As an eerie darkness settled over the forest, the crisis came without warning. Flame called out in a loud voice, sending chills along the spines of the man and woman who knelt beside her.

"Mother!" she cried, grasping Leonora's hand in a death grip. Though her eyes were wide open, they seemed to stare without seeing. "You have come for me."

Leonora saw the pain in Dillon's eyes as he muttered, "Sweet heaven, she is preparing to pass into that other world." He ran a hand through his hair in a gesture of helplessness. "Is there nothing more we can do to stop her?"

For long moments, Leonora studied the lass who, though staring directly at her, was seeing someone long-dead. Squaring her shoulders, she said suddenly, "Aye, we have to. We have come so far, Dillon. I will not give up now."

"Take me with you, Mother," Flame whispered. "I cannot bear the pain."

"Nay." Leonora brushed the damp hair from the lass's temple. After her long exposure to the women at Kinloch

House, it was not difficult to shed her cultivated English accent and affect their soft Scottish burr. Had she not done it before, with only young Rupert as her witness?

After talking a deep breath, she began. "I have not come to take ye wi' me, Flame, but to tell ye that ye must live."

When the feverish girl began to protest, Leonora whispered fiercely, "There is so much of life ye have not yet tasted, lass. The love of a man. The birth of a babe."

"Such things are not for me, Mother. The sisters said I do not behave as a lady."

"Hush, lass. Some day ye will meet a man as fine as ye'r father, as fine as your beloved brothers, and he will win ye'r heart. He will see the goodness in ye, and love ye as ye are. Ye will lie with him, and the two of ye will become one in mind and heart and soul. And ye will bring forth bairns, Flame. For 'tis through ye'r bairns that ye can live forever as I do."

With a look that could have been surprise or disbelief, Dillon turned to stare at this woman who spoke so eloquently of things as yet unknown to her.

Unaware of his scrutiny, Leonora continued in that same tone of loving command. "Do ye see now why ye must live, Flame?"

The girl nodded. "If you say I must, Mother, then I shall."

"Aye, lass. Ye must fight to live. And someday, years from now, when ye have tasted all that life has to offer, I promise that ye will join me in that other world. And we will walk together forever in paradise." Her voice lowered, "Ye have my word, Flame."

As the storm clouds gathered and roiled above them, and the air became oppressive, Flame's agitation seemed to dissipate. Her breathing slowed.

Dillon pressed a hand to her forehead. "Had I not witnessed this myself, I would ne'er have believed it," he murmured. "You performed a miracle."

"It was no miracle," Leonora said softly. "Flame is strong. She would have fought to live."

"But you gave her the will to fight."

"I merely said what your mother would have said, had she been here."

"And how would you know what a mother would say to her bairn?"

Leonora lifted her head and met his look. "I was one of the fortunate ones, Dillon. I had my mother until I was ten and three. Even though there are many things I wish I could ask her now, at least I had her for those important early years."

He touched a hand to Flame's cheek. "This poor lass was but a bairn when our parents were killed."

"But she had you, Dillon."

He shook his head. "A lot of good that did her. Sutton and Shaw and I were in a monastery, while she was in the abbey."

"But she was surrounded by good women who cared for her and taught her what she needed to know." She smiled. "Though, I must admit, it is hard to imagine a high-spirited girl like Flame locked away in an abbey."

"Aye. When I brought her to Kinloch House, she was like some wild creature just set free of its cage." The smile returned to his lips. He stood and helped Leonora to her feet. "From the day I sent for her, she has filled my life with such delight. And now," he whispered, touching a rough palm to Leonora's cheek, "you may have given her yet another chance to fill my life."

"How many times must I deny it?" Instead of drawing away, she lifted a hand to cover his. "The fight is not mine, but Flame's. And now she must fight it well."

"Like another I know." He drew her closer, and lifted his other hand, so that both big hands were framing her face. Staring down into her eyes, he murmured, "You continually surprise me, my lady."

"Surprise you? How?"

Her lips were so close, he could almost taste them.

"You flee when I least expect it." His breath was warm against her cheek. "And then, when you are free to escape, you refuse to budge, but choose instead to remain and care for a lass who has made no secret of her animosity toward you."

It was impossible to stand so near and not feel the temptation. Her voice became a low whisper of seduction. "Perhaps, in her eyes, I deserved such treatment. I am, after all, one of the dreaded English."

"Aye, my beautiful, bewitching English prisoner." His thumbs brushed her lips and he saw the look of surprise in her eyes. Combing his hands through her hair, he drew her head back, his gaze burning over her mouth until she could feel the heat of passion rising between them. "But now I wonder, who is captive and who is captor?"

Before she could think of a reply, he lowered his head and touched his lips to hers in the merest whisper of a kiss.

"I think I am the one who is bound," he murmured against her mouth. "And I cannot break free, no matter how much I struggle."

"I do not hold you, my lord."

"Ah, but you do, Leonora. Do you not see? I am hostage to your lips..." He brushed his lips over hers again, this time lingering until she sighed and lifted herself on tiptoe to better reach him. "And to your throat..." He brushed feather-light kisses down her neck to the sensitive little hollow of her throat. The sight of the bruises he had inflicted there caused him to linger, as if to kiss away all pain. "And your shoulder…" He drew the cloak from her shoulder and pressed a line of kisses until she shivered.

"Dillon." His name trembled on her lips.

The first fine raindrops fell. With them, Dillon struggled to make sense of the jumble of emotions that had him tied in knots. He wanted her. God knew he wanted her. And had, since first he had seen her. But now she could no longer remain his prisoner. The debt he owed her could only be paid by setting her free. And if he were to truly set her free, there must be no bonds between them.

"You need to rest, Leonora." He saw the stab of disappointment as he drew her cloak firmly around her, hiding from view the flesh that so tempted him.

When he lowered his hand, the heavy fabric slid open, revealing one creamy shoulder. Instantly he took a step back, but not before she saw the look of hunger in his eyes. The knowledge that he desired her made her bold. "I am not tired, my lord. In fact, now that Flame has passed through the crisis, and will sleep for hours, I feel wonderfully refreshed."

Struggling with temptation, he turned away and busied himself by tossing a log on the fire. Overhead, lightning cut a jagged path through the night sky. Moments later, thunder split the heavens with such force the earth trembled.

Not even the force of the storm could dampen Leonora's happiness at the knowledge that he was not as immune to her charms as he pretended. But for some unexplained reason, he was turning away. Why?

She felt a wave of desperation. Oh, Mother, she thought, I know so little about love.

Love. She went very still. Was this what she was feeling? Love? Aye. How long she had denied it. But all the tales of noble deeds she had heard about Dillon Campbell, painting him the hero she had always yearned for in her heart of hearts, had long ago convinced her. She loved this Highlander. Loved him as she would never love another. And now she must find a way to tell him, to show him.

"Are you afraid, Dillon?"

He turned to her with a look of surprise. "Of a storm?"

"Nay, not of the storm." She took a tentative step closer. "Of me."

His eyes narrowed. He suddenly seemed aware of the haughty way she lifted her head as she moved nearer. Of the way her hips swayed. Of the slope of bare shoulder beneath the heavy cloak. The cloak. His throat went dry. He knew that she wore nothing beneath it. That thought had his heart hammering in his chest. He needed only to undo the clasp...

She placed a hand on his arm. "Since you do not reply, my lord, I have my answer."

He stared at her hand, then into her eyes. "Aye, my lady. Though I have never known a moment's fear as a warrior on the field of battle, I fear you." She felt the muscles of his forearm bunch and tighten as he clenched his fist. His voice lowered to a whisper. "In fact, I am terrified of you. As you should be of me. Of this," he growled as he crushed her in his arms and covered her mouth with his.

The kiss was hot, hungry, filled with so much longing, it threatened to consume them. It spoke of passion, of need, of deep, desperate desire.

"How long," he muttered against her lips, "I have wanted this."

"No more than I."

He held her a little away, as though unable to believe what she had just admitted. He'd wanted to spare her, to return her to her father as he'd found her. But there was no strength in him to resist. How could he refuse what she offered?

"Think, Leonora," he murmured, struggling to hold off the storm that threatened. "Think what it is you do here. On the morrow, you will not be what you are tonight. On the morrow, there will be no going back.''

In answer, she brought her arms around his waist and pressed her lips to his throat. She was rewarded by his quick intake of breath.

He brought his hands to her shoulders. His eyes were mere slits; his face as grim as though he were poised for battle. "Then God help you. God help us both," he breathed.

His hands slid along her arms. His gaze was steady on hers. Lightning flashed across the sky and he could see that there was no fear in her, only invitation.

His mouth was greedy, avid, as his lips moved over hers. He feasted on her lips, filling himself with the sweet taste of her.

Never, he realized, as he took the kiss higher, then higher still, had he been so mesmerized by a pair of lips. He continued kissing her while his hands roamed her back. Beneath the coarse texture of the cloak, he could feel the smooth contours of her tiny waist, the flare of her hips. Bringing his hands to her shoulders, he found himself fascinated by her skin, as pale as alabaster, as smooth as the underside of a rose petal. He bent his lips to her shoulder and was rewarded with a sigh that broke from her lips. He continued pressing soft moist kisses to her shoulder, her arm, the bend of her elbow, before lifting her hand and pressing a kiss to the palm. In an achingly sweet gesture, he lifted her palm to his cheek.

With infinite patience he kissed her temple, her eyelids, the tip of her nose. He followed the curve of her cheek, then suddenly took her earlobe between his teeth, tugging lightly before plunging his tongue into her ear until she writhed with pleasure.

"There is still time to change your mind," he whispered, though he knew that, for himself, the line had already been crossed.

She shivered. She understood now his hesitation at his thing they intended. It was not a rejection of her; it was his strict code of honor. The choice must be hers alone.

"Nay, Dillon. I want this. I want you."

She felt the way his hands tightened at her shoulders before he lifted his hands to the clasp at her throat. With a quick twist, the heavy garment dropped to the ground.

His gaze moved slowly over her. She was even more perfect than the image he had carried in his mind. His voice was little more than a whisper. "Oh, my lady, you are bonny. Aye, indeed bonny."

That word. That wonderful, passionate word. Never had she felt more beautiful, more cherished.

His lips burned a trail of kisses down her throat, then lower, to the swell of her breast. When she reached for his tunic, he nearly tore it in his haste to help her remove it. His clothes soon joined her cloak in a heap at their feet. Together they dropped to their knees, and their sighs, like the sighing wind, filled the night.

His fingers tangled in her hair as he drew her head back for an almost brutal kiss. For a moment she stiffened, startled by the abrupt change in him. Then her fear was forgotten and she became caught up in her own savage needs.

Hesitantly, awkwardly, she brought her arms around his waist and felt his muscles contract at her touch. With a low moan of pleasure he took the kiss deeper while his hands began a slow, lazy exploration of her body.

As their passion intensified, she suddenly understood why he had held her at arm's length for so long. This was why he had slept in the sitting chamber, isolated from her. This was why he had walked in the gardens late at night, avoiding contact with her. This dark, brooding beast had been locked inside him for so long. Now free, it would consume them both.

This dark side of Dillon would have frightened her, had her own dark desires not been aroused. But now, intoxicated by her own powers, she moved her lips across his chest and felt him tremble. Growing bolder, she began exploring him as he was exploring her. With lips and teeth and fingertips she thrilled to the tremors that rocked him.

Dillon's body was alive with need. It had been his intention to go slowly, and allow her to set the pace. But with her passion swirling as angrily as the storm that raged around them, there was no longer any need to hold back. There was so much he wanted to share with her. Not just lovemaking, though he knew this was her first taste. It was the trust that allowed her to follow wherever he led. It was more than passion without limits; it was knowing that she was his and his alone.

He thought of how little time they had. Perhaps this night was all they would have for a lifetime. This, then, would be his gift to her. A banquet of delights. A night of unbridled pleasure.

With great tenderness he laid her down and brought his lips to her breast, moving his tongue until the nipple hardened. He moved to the other, tasting, feasting, until she writhed and moaned softly, arching her body and clutching the rough cloak beneath her.

Her breathing grew more labored as, with lips and fingertips, he moved over her, exploring her body, drawing out each exquisite pleasure.

Above them the storm drew nearer. Black clouds obscured the moon, the wind grew colder. Despite the chill wind, the heat rose between them as he took her higher and higher, keeping release just out of reach.

Leonora had slipped into a world of unbelievable delight. A world of touch and taste and feel, where thought no longer existed. Here there was only Dillon. He tasted of cool Highland streams and smelled faintly of evergreen and horses. The feel of his work-roughened palms against her flesh was more pleasurable than the finest silk.

She trembled as he moved along her body, moist flesh to moist flesh, and brought his lips to hers.

Never had Dillon wanted as he wanted her. It took all his considerable willpower to keep from taking her, wildly, savagely. But he was determined to draw out the moment, until they were both mad with need.

He felt her go rigid when he brought his mouth down her body. But at the first tremors of pleasure bordering on pain, she forgot all her fears. And then she gasped as she reached the first crest. He gave her no time to catch her breath as he moved over her, allowing his lips to trail upward until they captured hers.

Her eyes focused on his. He saw the pupils, round and dark with passion. It didn't seem possible that she could want more, but she did. His name was torn from her lips as he finally entered her. She wrapped herself around him, wanting to hold him like this forever.

He was filled with her. The sweet fragrance of crushed roses filled his mind, his heart, his soul. In the years to come in his lonely Highland castle, the memory of this would remain with him, warming him.

"Leonora. My bonny, bonny Leonora." He lapsed into words she couldn't understand as his mouth closed over hers and he felt the last vestiges of sanity slip away.

She moved with him, soaring, flying free, on a path toward the stars. And as they lifted higher, then higher still, their bodies shuddered, then seemed to break into millions of tiny, fiery fragments.

Chapter Nineteen

They lay, still joined, their breathing erratic, their bodies slick. Neither of them seemed inclined to move.

The cloak, cushioned by damp moss, was as soft as any bed. The air about them was redolent of the fragrance of sweet clover.

Another jagged flash of lightning stabbed the sky, followed almost immediately by a crash of thunder. The storm was directly overhead. Already the first drops of rain had begun. Even that wasn't enough to cool their heated flesh.

And then he tasted the salt of her tears. Alarmed, he touched his thumbs to the corners of her eyes.

"Tears, lass? Have I hurt you, then? God in heaven, I am such a brute. Am I too heavy for you?"

"Nay." Ashamed, she tried to blink away the tears, but they only fell faster.

He rolled to one side and drew her into the snug circle of his arms. "What is it, love? Why do you weep?"

Love. She hugged the endearment to her heart. "It was so...wonderful. More wonderful than I had ever dreamed."

"Ah." He breathed a sigh of relief. A woman's tears were a terrible thing for a man to deal with. But tears of joy were at least understandable. His own heart was filled with a rare kind of peace.

"It is wonderful," he whispered against her temple, "when it is shared by two people who love."

"And do you love me, Dillon Campbell?" She held her breath, amazed at her own boldness.

"Aye, lass."

"How long have you known?"

He squirmed uncomfortably. "I am a warrior, lass, a man of the sword, not a man of words. Do not ask me to speak of such things."

But she couldn't control herself. It was as though an imp had entered her body and had taken over. Sitting up, she shoved the heavy hair from her eyes and leaned over him. "Tell me, Dillon. How long have you known that you love me?"

She was flirting shamelessly. And he loved her for it. With the warmth of laughter coloring his words he said, as gruffly as he could manage, "It certainly was not the first time I met you, all stiff and proper on your father's arm."

"Stiff and proper was I? And what about you? You stood there like some wild-eyed giant, looking as though you were going to devour the lot of us." She tossed her head in that haughty manner he loved and he reached up and grabbed a handful of her hair.

Watching it sift through his fingers, he said, "I could not take my eyes off you. And the thought of . . . devouring you was not far from my mind, if the truth be told."

At his admission, it seemed the most natural thing in the world to be as honest and open with him. "And I had to try very hard not to stare at you." She ran a hand along his thigh, and saw the way his eyes glazed at her touch. Growing bolder, she moved her hand slowly upward. "Especially since I had never seen such muscles before."

"Witch." He caught her hand, but not before she had discovered that he was thoroughly aroused once more.

How could it be that he wanted her again so soon? Would he never have his fill of this woman?

As though reading his mind, she pressed her lips to the flat planes of his stomach and felt his muscles contract. "Perhaps you would not mind if I explored those...muscles more carefully, my lord."

He threw back his head and roared. It was as he had always suspected. Inside this very proper Englishwoman was a wild, wanton vixen. It was another reason that he loved her.

The sky opened up. Rain pelted them, thoroughly soaking them. But neither of them seemed to take the slightest notice. They were too caught up in the wonders of their newly discovered love.

"Ah, lass, how did I manage to spend all those nights beside you on my pallet and avoid touching you?"

Rolled snugly in the cloak, they had taken shelter from the rain beneath a tangle of thick vines. The night was swiftly passing, but neither of them gave a thought to sleep. Flame had passed through a crisis. And they had passed through one of their own. The sound of the rain falling around them was a soothing symphony.

"I did not think you even noticed. You spent most of your time walking alone in the gardens."

"Aye. And now you know why."

She touched a finger to his lips, tracing the smoothness, feeling her heartbeat beginning to accelerate once again. How could the mere touch of this man arouse her so? "Do you mean you were avoiding temptation?"

"Aye, lass. Heeding the lessons of the good monks. 'Twas the worst torture I have ever been forced to endure."

She laughed, and he drew her close, running his hands slowly up her thigh, across the slope of her rounded hip, then along her side until he encountered the fullness of her breast. This was a body he was beginning to know as intimately as his own. All night he had explored, discovered, touched to his heart's content. His thumb began a lazy circle.

The laughter died in her throat and became a little moan of pleasure.

She traced a fingertip across the faded scar that ran from his temple to his jaw and felt her heart contract at the thought of what he had endured as a lad. "I wish..."

"What, love?"

"I wish I could erase every pain you have ever suffered, Dillon."

"You already have," he murmured. "I am so filled with your love, I have forgotten all else. I am so moved by your love, in fact, that I think perhaps I should take another walk," he whispered against her temple.

She clutched at him and dragged his mouth to hers for a lingering, intimate kiss. Between kisses, she murmured, "Nay, my lord. I have a much better idea."

"More satisfying than a walk in the garden?"

"Aye." She allowed her fingertips to move lightly down his back while she pressed feather-light kisses across his face. "Far more satisfying."

Without further invitation, they tumbled into a world of dark, sensual delight.

By morning, the storm had passed, leaving the Highland forest awash in color. Along with the purple of the heather, and the shiny deep green of the holly, there were colorful blueberry, ling and forget-me-nots. Snow bunting and ptarmigan darted from tree to tree, sunlight reflecting on their downy wings. High overhead a golden eagle soared, hunting a breakfast of field mouse or hare.

To these familiar sounds Dillon awoke to find the space beside him empty. The sudden swift pain he felt was a sharp reminder of what lay ahead. All night, though he had tried not to think about it, one painful fact had marred his pleasure. He knew that he could no longer hold Leonora his prisoner at Kinloch House. As soon as possible, he would have to return her to her father.

In the light of the morning, the knowledge was even more painful.

The warmth of Leonora's body still clung to the folds of the cloak, alerting him to the fact that she had only been gone a few moments. He watched as she knelt beside Flame, then hurriedly returned to his side. Shivering, she crawled in beside him, snuggling close.

"I checked on Flame. She sleeps as peacefully as a bairn."

He felt oddly pleased by her use of the Scots term for child. "I think," he said as he welcomed her with a kiss, "you have spent too much time in my land. You have begun to speak like one of us."

"Your manner of speech is most pleasant to the ear."

His pleasure grew. Perhaps, for the moment, he could forget the painful truth that lay before them, and pretend for a while longer that they would always be together.

"Are you hungry, lass?"

She shrugged. "I suppose. And you, my laird?"

"Ravenous."

"I will fetch you some venison."

She started to scramble up, but he pulled her back down for a long, lazy kiss. The moment their lips met, a familiar warmth began spreading through them, heating their blood, fueling their passion.

"It is not venison I crave, love. It is something far more satisfying."

"You are a glutton," she said with a laugh.

"Aye. I will never have enough of you."

"Nor I you."

With soft sighs and murmured words of love, they satisfied the craving of their hearts and souls.

"Something smells wonderful."

"Flame! At last you are awake." Dillon, returning to the clearing with a brace of partridges, hurried to kneel beside his sister. On his face was a wide smile of relief and pleasure.

Leonora looked up from the broth she was stirring and joined him at Flame's side. "I had hoped you would awaken soon. I thought perhaps some broth would renew your strength."

"So," Flame said, glancing from Leonora to her brother, then back again. "I did not dream it. You did stay, Englishwoman."

"Aye. I told you I would not leave you."

"So you did." The lass glanced at her brother, who was watching Leonora with a strange, unfathomable look on his face.

"How did you find us, Dillon?"

"I followed the scent of wood smoke." He paused. "Do you remember anything, Flame?"

"It is like the haze that hangs o'er the meadow on a summer morn. I recall coming upon Graeme and the Englishwoman. And realized that he was the monster..." She paused to shiver, then added, "I seem to remember your voice, Dillon, threatening to kill the Englishwoman because you thought she had caused me harm." She grew silent a moment. "There is little else I recall. Bits and pieces of memory are here, then gone."

"It will come back to you," Leonora said softly. "For now, you must eat something."

As she walked away to fill a small, hollowed-out gourd with broth, Dillon watched her, then turned to find his sister watching him carefully.

"She could have escaped," she whispered.

"Aye, I know. But she stayed to tend you."

"But even before that, she could have run, Dillon. Graeme and I were engaged in battle. Neither of us could have stopped her if she had chosen to run away. But she fought him off with a club and saved my life."

Hearing the last of that, Leonora returned and knelt at Flame's side. "You did the same for me, Flame. Had it not been for your intervention, I would have been another of Graeme's victims." She lifted the gourd of steaming broth to Flame's lips. "Here. Take this."

The girl looked up at her and said softly, "You fought well ... for an Englishwoman."

Leonora bit back the smile that tugged at her lips. "Hush now and eat. You must restore your strength."

As Flame sipped the broth, she watched her brother prepare the fowl for cooking. When he handed them to Leonora, the two exchanged whispered words, following by a long, lingering look.

With a sudden flash of knowledge, Flame thought back to the murmured love words that had drifted into her consciousness during the night. She had thought she'd dreamed them. Now she knew better.

Could it be? Aye. Even as she watched, she saw the proprietary look on Dillon's face. And the way all of the woman's features softened when she smiled at him.

God in heaven. Her strong, fierce brother, the loyal Scots warrior, and laird of the Campbells, had done the unthinkable. He had lost his heart to his English prisoner.

"Let me see your arm, Flame." Leonora knelt beside the lass and began to unwrap the dressings. "How does it feel?"

"It pains me something fierce."

"Then you are very brave, for I've heard not a word from you all day."

"The sisters taught me to offer up pain as a payment for sin."

Leonora smiled. "I would think a lass as young as you would have few sins."

The girl shrugged. "If not mine, then perhaps I can offer the pain for the sins of...others."

At her slight hesitation, Leonora's curiosity was piqued. "What others?"

Flame let out a slow hiss of pain as Leonora poured spirits over the wound. When she could find her voice, she said, "My brother Dillon seems to be in need of a sin offering."

"What makes you say that?"

The lass lifted her chin defiantly and met Leonora's steady gaze. "I think you know, Englishwoman."

Leonora busied herself with a clean dressing. All the while, she could feel Flame's eyes watching her. When the wound was dressed, she started to get to her feet.

Flame caught her hand. "By your silence, you admit your guilt."

Leonora took a deep breath. Despite the lass's obvious dislike for her, she was Dillon's sister. And she deserved the truth.

"If loving a man who risked everything to make peace between our people is a sin, then I am guilty."

The lass looked thunderstruck.

Leonora got to her feet. "Rest a while," she said softly. "I will bring your food soon."

When she walked away, Flame passed a hand over her eyes. She had feared the Englishwoman was merely using her obvious charms to obtain her freedom from her obstinate brother. But she had been wrong. So very wrong.

Love, she had said. The Englishwoman loved Dillon. It could not be more simple than that. Nor more complicated.

What strange twists and turns life's paths sometimes took.
Flame decided it might be best if she never grew up. For she
never wished to deal with such things.

Dillon piled logs on the fire until it was a blazing inferno.
Then, as the sun rose high in the sky, he added green
branches. A blanket of thick, black smoke sent its pall over
the Highland forest.

"It is a clear signal," he explained to Leonora, "to all
who are searching. Before the Angelus bells ring out this
day, my men will find us."

He saw the look that came into her eyes and drew her into
the circle of his embrace. During the long night of loving,
Dillon had told Leonora what he planned. It was time.
Flame was well enough to endure a return to Kinloch House
in a wagon. The men who had been searching the Highlands for two long days deserved to be notified that the laird
and his party were safe.

Dillon understood Leonora's dismay and shared it. Here
in the privacy of the forest, their newfound love was as precious, as satisfying as the greatest treasure. But once they
returned to Kinloch House, the fragile peace between them
might be forever shattered.

Across the clearing, Flame awoke from a deep sleep and
caught sight of the couple locked in an embrace. She had
been dreaming of her mother and father, and hearing once
again her mother's soft voice, filled with so much love and
promise.

"Ah, Mother," she whispered, "if only there was some
way I could repay Dillon for all he has done for me. Alas, I
am at a loss. I fear his heart shall surely be broken by his
love of the Englishwoman."

She looked up at the sound of a horse. When the horse-
man reached the clearing, she could see it was young Ru-

pert. His face was etched with weariness, but he gave a loud sigh of relief when he caught sight of Dillon and Leonora.

"Ah, my laird." Rupert hung his head in shame. "Though I am relieved to see the lady did not escape, I know you can never forgive me for my lapse, for I have caused untold pain."

"No apology is needed, Rupert. This was not your fault. The lady has explained how she duped you. Now." Briskly Dillon explained what had transpired, then said, "I am in need of a wagon to carry Flame back to Kinloch House."

Rupert's glance took in Flame, lying in a bed of furs. With a worried frown, he said, "At once, my laird." He wheeled his horse and took off in a flurry of hoofbeats.

No matter how weary the lad was, he would push himself until he dropped before he would disobey another order from his laird.

By the time dusk began to settle over the land, a tiny procession made its way from the forest toward Kinloch House. Rupert drove the wagon. In the back lay Flame, firmly ensconced in furs to absorb the shock of bumps and ruts. Kneeling beside her was Leonora, draped in Dillon's coarse cloak, clutching Flame's hands firmly in both of hers. Dillon followed behind on his horse.

When they arrived in the courtyard, Mistress MacCallum and the servants spilled out the doors and stood at solemn attention.

"Welcome home, m'laird," Mistress MacCallum said in a strangled voice. It was plain that the plump housekeeper was close to tears.

"Thank you, Mistress MacCallum."

Dillon assisted Leonora from the wagon. His hands lingered for a moment at her shoulders before he lifted Flame in his arms and carried her through the open doorway.

Leonora walked behind, carrying the furs folded over her arm.

"Oh, my lady," young Gwynnith cried out, breaking the silence. "We had feared that you and Flame had fallen victim to—"

The housekeeper shot her a look and the words died on her lips.

"Welcome home, my lady," Father Anselm said as he stepped through the crowd. Lifting his hand, he added, "A blessing on all those who have returned safely."

"Thank you, Father." While she followed Dillon up the stairs, Leonora couldn't help thinking how different this was from her first arrival at Kinloch House. And yet, her heart whispered, for all the friendly greetings, little had changed. She was still a prisoner. Only now it was much worse. Now she was a prisoner of love.

Chapter Twenty

Short, stout Camus Ferguson kept pace with Dillon's steps as they climbed the stairs of Kinloch House together. The anger and betrayal Camus felt was evident in his eyes and in the harsh tone of his voice.

"Word of Graeme's treachery has preceded you, Dillon. 'Tis like a raging fire, the way the word has spread throughout the Highlands. Families are breathing easier, knowing their forests are once again safe havens."

"I still find it hard to believe that such a monster hid inside the man who called himself our friend." Dillon's voice was tinged with sadness.

"Aye, Dillon. I blame myself for not recognizing him for what he was. But some good has come of all this. All the clans have sent riders to Kinloch House, offering to ride with you against the English, in return for having rid them of the one who had threatened their women and children. At last, an army awaits your command, my friend."

Dillon let his statement pass without comment. Odd. Scant days ago, he would have rejoiced at such knowledge. Now it was like an arrow to the heart. He had already come to a decision. He would not fight the English.

"Take some men, Camus. Go back to the forest and bury Graeme's body in an unmarked grave, as punishment for his unholy acts. No one shall mourn Graeme Lamont's passing. In time, none will even recall his name."

"Aye, my friend. Consider it done."

Camus summoned several men and moved out at a swift pace.

In Kinloch House, there was much rejoicing. Their greatest worry had not come to pass. The prisoner had not escaped. Their beloved Flame had been returned safely to them. And the laird had never been happier. Of course, all of this caused a flurry of gossip. It was obvious from the moment of their arrival that Flame and the Englishwoman had forged a strong bond during their ordeal.

And what of the laird and his prisoner? At first glance, it was just as plain for all to see. The two had become intimate. It was there in the way they looked at each other when they thought no one was watching. In the proprietary way they touched. In the way they spoke. In a million tiny ways that lovers communicate. Everyone was aware of the change in the laird and his prisoner.

"What is this?" Leonora returned to Dillon's chambers after seeing that Flame had been made comfortable.

On a rug of sheepskin set before the fire was a round wooden tub, filled with steaming water.

"I ordered Mistress MacCallum to have a bath ready for you." Dillon tossed another log on the fire and stood, wiping his hands on his breeches.

"A bath? Oh, Dillon, how wonderful."

He smiled. "I thought you would approve."

They looked up as Gwynnith and two other servants entered, carrying an assortment of linens and jars and vials.

Dillon touched a hand to Leonora's cheek and gave her a smile, before crossing to the door. "I will leave you to your mysterious women's rituals."

With the help of the servants, Leonora removed the heavy cloak. If the servants were surprised that she wore nothing

beneath it, they were too polite to take notice. Nor did they
mention the bruises that marred her flesh.

After helping her into the tub, they began lathering her
hair, which was matted with bits of leaves and twigs.

"Oh, how glorious," she sighed.

"Close your eyes, my lady," Gwynnith urged. "And rest
a while, for your ordeal has ended."

She needed no coaxing. After what she had been through,
the fragrance of perfumed soap, the soothing warmth of the
water and the gentle massaging of fingertips on her scalp,
were like heaven. With a sigh she closed her eyes and leaned
back, allowing the servants to minister to her.

"Were you frightened, my lady?" one of the servants
asked timidly.

Keeping her eyes closed, she murmured, "Aye. I was terrified."

"But you did not run, my lady. Flame said you were the
bravest woman she has ever known. Though you could have
fled, you stayed and helped her slay the monster."

"Hush," Gwynnith admonished. "We will speak no more
of unpleasant things."

The servants fell silent. Leonora was grateful. She had no
wish to speak, or even to move. She was content to lie very
still and allow herself to be pampered. It could have been
minutes or hours that she lay in the water, feeling all the
cares and tensions drift away.

"If you will dip below the water, my lady, we will rinse the
soap from your hair."

Leonora did as she was told, and came up laughing and
sputtering. "Oh, I feel so clean. And refreshed, as though I
had rested for days."

One of the servants brushed Leonora's wet hair from her
eyes and wrapped a linen square around her head. Another
servant entered the chambers and placed an array of feminine clothing on the sleeping pallet.

When Leonora stepped from the tub, she was wrapped in more linen, before being led to a chaise drawn up in front of the fire. While she lay, wrapped in linen, and then in fur, her waist-length hair was combed, again and again, until it was dry. Then, seated in front of a mirror, her hair was arranged in a mass of curls, held away from her face by jeweled combs.

"Your clothes, my lady."

Gwynnith helped her into a beautiful, delicately embroidered chemise and petticoats, and then into the amethyst velvet gown she had been wearing when she'd been abducted from her father's castle. It had been perfectly mended with fine, even stitches.

"Oh, my lady, how fine you look."

"Thank you, Gwynnith. And all of you," Leonora added to the others, "for all that you did to make my homecoming so comfortable."

The servants exchanged quick, knowing glances at her use of the term *homecoming*. Did the lady not realize what she had revealed?

Before they could speak, the door opened. Seeing the laird, they bowed quickly from the room.

Leonora, studying her reflection in the mirror, saw Dillon walk up behind her. For a moment, each stood, drinking in the sight of the other.

Dillon was dressed in a clean shirt of softest lawn, the collar open to reveal a mat of dark hair. Billowing sleeves could not hide the muscles of his arms. Tight black breeches were tucked into tall boots. Droplets of water still clung to his hair.

He studied the way her skin glowed from the bath. With her hair dressed in the latest fashion, and the lush curves of her body revealed in the elegant gown, she was once more the cool, regal Englishwoman he had first seen. And desired.

Drawing her back against him, he bent his head and brushed a kiss across her shoulder.

"Mistress MacCallum has prepared a special feast to welcome us home."

She shivered at the touch of his lips against her flesh. Tiny fires had already begun in the pit of her stomach.

"Must we go below stairs?"

He chuckled, low and deep in his throat. "Aye, little one. We would break the poor woman's heart. But as soon as we have supped," he added with a low growl, "we will slip away. For I cannot bear to waste a single moment, knowing what heaven awaits me in your arms."

With a last quick, hard kiss, he led her from the room.

As Leonora descended the stairs beside him, she glanced around in surprise. Everywhere she looked, the dark wood gleamed under a coat of fresh polish. The floors were cushioned with new rushes, the fragrance of herbs and evergreen perfuming the air.

When they entered the great hall, the hum of conversation died. All eyes were on the handsome couple as they made their way to table.

"Ah, my lady." Father Anselm, who had been bending solicitously over Flame's linen-swathed figure at the table, hurried forward, his coarse brown robes swirling at his feet. "I have missed your smiling face and sparkling conversation."

"As I have missed you, Father Anselm."

"This house has not been the same since you left, my lady. Flame has just been regaling us with stories of your courage and loyalty."

"It was Flame's courage that saved us, Father."

"I would say that you are both extraordinary women, my dear. I pray you will attend Mass in the chapel on the morrow. It will be offered in thanksgiving for the safe return of those we love."

"Oh, I would like that." She turned to Dillon with a joyous smile. "Will you accompany me, Dillon?"

At her easy use of his name, the priest studied the couple with new interest. So, the rumors he had heard were true. These two had not come through the danger unscathed. Their hearts had been pierced.

"Aye, my lady." Dillon closed a hand over hers, then looked up to meet Father Anselm's curious stare. "If you wish it, it shall be."

He led her toward the table and bent to kiss his sister before he helped Leonora to sit. Taking the place beside her, he called, "Come, Father Anselm. Join us."

"Thank you." The old priest sat down.

As the food was being served, he suddenly got to his feet and announced, "I would say a blessing before we eat."

Amid a loud shuffling of feet and scraping of benches, the assembled stood and bowed their heads.

"Father, we thank You for the safe return of our beloved laird and the ladies Leonora and Flame. We are grateful that You have protected us from the one who brought pain and death to so many here in our land. And finally, we ask for the safe deliverance of Sutton and Shaw from their English prison. Amen."

The serving wenches began moving among the crowded tables. As the servants approached the laird's table, they welcomed Dillon and Leonora with friendly smiles.

Mistress MacCallum waddled over to call out a greeting.

"Look, m'lady." She spread her hands to indicate the entire room. "Begging ye'r thanks, the servants have learned their lessons well."

"Aye, I see, Mistress MacCallum." Leonora gave her a gentle smile.

"What have you done to this venison?" Dillon asked when he'd tasted it.

"In honor of the lady, I ordered the cooks to try her recipe. Do ye dislike it, m'laird?" the housekeeper asked timidly.

"Nay, Mistress MacCallum. How could I dislike such perfection? It is the finest I have ever tasted."

The old woman beamed and signaled for another tray to be brought.

"And this?" Dillon asked, cutting a thick slice of whole roasted pig. "Is this also the lady's recipe?"

Mistress MacCallum nodded.

As each food was sampled, the housekeeper hovered nearby, awaiting the laird's approval or rejection. When the sweets arrived, she watched as first Dillon, then Father Anselm, and finally Flame, smiled their approval.

"It is m'lady's brandied pudding and fruited cake," she explained.

When Dillon had eaten his fill, he leaned back, replete, content. "You have outdone yourself, Mistress MacCallum," he muttered.

"Thank ye, m'laird." In an unexpected surge of emotion, she caught Leonora's hand and pressed it between both of her plump palms. "And thank ye, m'lady. Not just for all this, but for bringing home our dear Flame."

When the housekeeper waddled away, Leonora struggled to swallow the lump that threatened to choke her. What had happened to her, that she should feel such emotions at a simple meal and a few kind words?

"We have prepared an evening of entertainment to welcome you home, Dillon," Camus announced proudly.

Both Leonora and Dillon had to swallow back a little groan of dismay.

Clasping Leonora's hand, Dillon shot her a glance. Though they both yearned to escape this noise and seek refuge in each other's embrace, they could not hurt the feelings of those who had worked so hard to make their homecoming special. They would have to put off, for a while longer, the relief they sought.

As the tables were cleared, a juggler leaped onto Dillon's table and began to entertain by tossing and catching glittering knives, razor-edged swords and even a series of flaming torches. Leonora was so amazed by his skill, several times she caught Dillon's arm and pointed, much to the delight of those around them. Dillon, in turn, drew her closer and murmured words that made her blush and laugh. Both of them, it would seem, had given up all attempts to hide their feelings from the others.

When the juggler had finished entertaining them, a minstrel began playing the lute and singing. The songs, of warriors and the women they left behind, of knights and ladies, of birth and death, and mostly of unrequited love, had the women sighing and the men lifting tankards and drinking deeply.

Dillon and Leonora became more and more quiet, but the looks they sent to each other became more intense with each song. When at last the minstrel finished his last song, Dillon gave an exaggerated yawn.

"I fear the journey has caught up with me, my friends. I will bid you all good night."

With Leonora's hand on his arm, he almost ran in his haste to lead her from the room.

Behind them, Father Anselm watched them go, his forehead wrinkled with concern. "This time, Lord," he whispered, "I fear Dillon Campbell has chosen a path too steep."

The once-roaring fire had burned to hot embers that punctuated the darkened room like fiery stars. On a side table, two half-filled goblets remained. An amethyst gown, discarded in haste, lay on the floor like a wilted flower. Beside it lay boots, breeches, a hastily removed shirt.

The two figures in the sleeping pallet lay in a tangle of arms and legs, exhausted by their lovemaking, drifting on a cloud of sheer bliss.

Leonora snuggled closer, pressing her lips to the pulse at Dillon's throat. She heard his little intake of breath and thrilled to it. "Will I always be able to make your pulse quicken, Dillon? Or will you grow weary of me and look for another?"

He framed her face with his hands and kissed her with such passion, she felt her own heart skip a beat. "Do not even jest about such things." His voice was rougher than he'd intended. "I will ne'er love another woman, Leonora. No matter what happens, know that you will own my heart always."

"So serious, my love." She kissed him, then drew back, trying to see his eyes in the darkness. "Why have you suddenly become so solemn?"

He took in a long, ragged breath, then said softly, "I had hoped to wait until the morrow to tell you the news."

"News?"

"In order to show young Rupert that he is still in my good graces, I entrusted him with a most serious mission."

"Rupert?" Leonora realized that the lad had been missing at table. Wrapped in the glow of new love, she had taken no notice. "What is this serious mission you speak of?"

"I sent Rupert with a missive to your father."

"A...missive?" Her palms were sweating. Her heart was pounding.

"I assured him that you are safe. And that you are to be returned immediately to his loving arms."

"Returned." Her heart plummeted. "Why, Dillon?"

His arms tightened perceptibly around her, as if bracing her for what was to come. "Because I love you, Leonora. It is the only honorable thing I can do."

She pushed away, feeling the sting of tears. "You speak of honor? You declare your love, and then you send me away? I do not see honor, Dillon Campbell. I see a coward who stole my love when I was weak and vulnerable, and now absolves himself of any wrongdoing by sending me away." Against her will, the tears flowed freely. "You are mean and cruel and—"

He pressed a finger to her lips to silence her. "Hush, my love. We have so little time left together. Let us not spend it inflicting pain. Know always that I love you, Leonora. I could not love you more. But I must do the honorable thing, even if it means a lifetime of unhappiness for me."

"And what about me? What about my unhappiness?"

"I am vain enough to hope you will miss me. But you are a noble Englishwoman, with an enviable dowry of fine estates. Your future is secure."

"But my future does not include you? Is that what you are saying?"

"I see no other solution, love. If we are to prevent a war between our people, I must show my good faith by returning you safely to your father, without condition. I pray he will send my brothers safely home in return. Though I would not have risked such a thing before, my love for you has made me bold. I can no longer use your life to barter for theirs."

"Oh, Dillon. How can I leave you?" With a sob, she fell into his arms.

Her cry shattered all his cool control. "Aye," he muttered raggedly. "And how can I bear to let you go?"

Their lovemaking became crazed, frenzied, as they sought to hold back the inevitable dawn.

Chapter Twenty-one

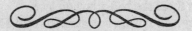

"Is it not good to feel the sun warm upon your face?"

With Flame leaning heavily upon Leonora's arm, the two young women walked along the overgrown path of the rose garden. They sat wearily upon a stone bench, and Flame struggled to catch her breath.

"I hate this feeling of helplessness. I am as weak as a bairn, and just about as useless."

"You grow stronger every day," Leonora said good-naturedly. "Besides, look at how Mistress MacCallum and the servants fuss over you."

"Aye. If I eat any more of Mistress MacCallum's pudding, I shall be as plump as she." Shading her eyes, Flame stared into the distance. "I yearn to feel a horse's hooves beneath me once more, and the wind in my hair. I want to be free to do as I please."

She happened to turn. The look of pain on Leonora's face twisted like a knife.

"Forgive me, Leonora. How can I think of myself when your heart is so heavy? I am being selfish."

"Nay." Leonora patted her hand. But the questions she could not bring herself to ask Dillon tumbled from her lips. "How can we be certain Rupert will deliver Dillon's message?"

"The lad may be slow to speak, but he is not slow-witted. If there is a way to slip into England and reach your father's castle, Rupert will find it."

"But even if he does, how can my father's soldiers enter your land without being accosted? Surely they will be delayed many nights by fighting." It was not that she wished harm to her father's men. She only yearned for more time, to spend with those she had grown to love.

"Nay. They will not be accosted by loyal Highlanders. Rupert will give them Dillon's banner to carry. That banner will assure them safe passage. As long as it remains unfurled, no Highlander would dare to attack them."

"It has been two days since Rupert left."

"Aye." Flame's eyes narrowed as she calculated. The English would, in all likelihood, be here on the morrow. She needed to keep Leonora's mind off that gloomy fact, even if it meant doing something she detested. Struggling for a cheerfulness she didn't feel, she said, "You promised to teach me how to embroider."

Seeing through her scheme, Leonora smiled gently and helped her to her feet. "So I did. And I know how anxious you are to add to the lessons of the good sisters in the abbey."

She nearly laughed aloud at the look in Flame's eyes. It would be sheer torture for the lass to spend time on such frivolous female work. "Mistress MacCallum has left cloth and thread in Dillon's chambers. Come."

For at least a few more hours, Leonora reasoned, she would keep herself busy, and for the sake of Flame and the servants, she would force a smile to her lips.

And tonight, for perhaps the last time, she would lie in Dillon's arms and pretend that their love would never come to an end.

* * *

Leonora stood on the balcony and watched as the English horsemen made their way up the steep incline toward Kinloch House. Dillon's banner of blue and green on a black background fluttered in the breeze. As Flame had promised, no Highlander accosted them. Though more than a dozen of Dillon's finest archers kept them in their sights, not a single arrow was notched into a bow. And though a line of swordsmen lined the trail, not a single weapon was raised in challenge.

While the horsemen clattered into the courtyard and dismounted, Leonora leaned over the balcony railing to see their faces. She had expected a long column of soldiers, escorting Sutton and Shaw. Instead, there were only a half a dozen soldiers. The only familiar faces belonged to Lord James Blakely, his handsome son, Alger Blakely, and George Godwin, the Duke of Essex. There was no sign of Sutton and Shaw.

She watched as Dillon stepped through the doorway, flanked by Camus Ferguson and Father Anselm.

"I am returning Waltham's daughter to him unharmed. Will he now do the same for my brothers?" he asked sharply.

"Lord Alec Waltham wishes to be assured that his daughter has not been harmed. When he has such assurance, he will release his prisoners into the hands of your young messenger," called the Duke of Essex.

Dillon's features hardened. "I would not have summoned you here to return the lady to her father if she had been harmed in any way."

"Perhaps." Essex gave a cool, calculating smile. "That is for Lord Waltham to decide when the king's own physician examines her. Are you prepared to deliver the woman into our hands?"

Camus gave his friend a wild-eyed look. "Beware, Dillon. I do not like the looks of this."

"Nor I," Father Anselm said softly.

"I have given my word to Lord Waltham." To the English, Dillon said, "You will wish to refresh yourselves before beginning your journey home."

"Nay." Essex shook his head. "Lord Waltham is anxious to have his treasure returned. We will not tarry until our mission is accomplished. Where is the lady?" His gaze lifted toward the balcony.

Leonora stepped back quickly. Placing her palms against her heated cheeks, she stared around Dillon's chambers. For so long, these rooms had been her prison. For the past few nights, they had been her refuge. And now she felt the same way she had when she'd been abducted from her father's home. Everything familiar was being torn from her.

How could this be? How had this rough Highland fortress become her refuge, her haven? How was it possible that she had found heaven in a Highland savage's arms?

When Dillon entered his chambers, he found Leonora staring around as if committing everything to memory. She turned, and the two stared hungrily at each other across the room for long, silent moments.

"Your father's emissaries have come."

"Aye."

She had her chin lifted in that familiar manner. He had once thought her haughty, aloof. Now he knew that this was her way of facing down her fears. How he longed to pull her into his arms and reassure her. But that would only make things worse. They must get through this thing with strength and dignity.

"I had hoped they would sup with us before their departure. Alas, they are eager to return you to England. I can understand your father's impatience to have you back in his safe embrace."

She nodded and took a final glance around the room, then walked determinedly toward the door. As she passed him, he put a hand on her arm. She flinched and bit her lip to keep from crying out, but did not turn toward him.

"Know always that I love you, Leonora."

Her only acknowledgment was a silent nod of the head. Placing her hand on his sleeve, she descended the stairs beside him. When they walked out into the brilliant sunshine of the courtyard, she saw the line of Highlanders waiting to bid her goodbye.

Flame, her arm still heavily bandaged, drew Leonora close and hugged her fiercely. "I was wrong about you, Englishwoman," she whispered. "I wish…" She sniffed and tried again. "I wish I had not wasted so much time hating you. In years to come, I will think of you."

Leonora smoothed back the unruly strands of fiery hair that curled around the girl's cheeks. Tears threatened, but she quickly blinked them back. She must not allow herself to cry in front of her own countrymen, who were watching her closely. "If I had a little sister, Flame, I could not wish for a better one than you."

The lass turned away to hide her tears.

Mistress MacCallum hurried over, twisting a corner of her apron between her fingers. Even before she began to speak, tears were spilling from her eyes. "Thank ye, m'lady, for all ye've done for us here at Kinloch House."

"Nay. I thank you, Mistress MacCallum, for making me feel at home here."

"Oh, m'lady." The poor woman was forced to turn away in embarrassment, clutching the apron to her face.

Father Anselm caught Leonora's hands between both of his. Peering intently into her eyes, he saw how she was struggling with her emotions.

"I would ask your blessing on my journey, Father."

"Aye, my lady." He lifted his hand in blessing while murmuring in Latin, "God go with you."

"Thank you, Father."

As she lowered her head, he whispered, for her ears alone, "Never forget that God's hand is upon all our lives. He, and He alone, can make a crooked path straight."

"But I cannot even see my path, Father," she cried. "I am too blinded by tears."

"Then take His hand. Trust Him to lead you, child."

He stepped aside, and Camus strode forward.

Taking her hand, the young soldier lifted it to his lips and muttered, "You have been a most honored guest in our Highlands, my lady. I bid you a safe journey."

"Thank you, Camus." She glanced at Dillon, who stood so stoically beside her. "He will need a friend, Camus."

"Aye, my lady. More than ever, I will be Dillon's friend."

Dillon silently led her to her waiting steed, pain and fatigue evident in his eyes. Stanton stood holding the reins. The old man bowed slightly and wheezed, "Such a wee lass, for a noble Englishwoman. But a finer lady I've ne'er met."

It was the most the old man had ever spoken in her presence. Yet his simple words touched her so deeply, she had to swallow the lump in her throat.

Dillon lifted her in his arms and settled her onto the saddle. Stepping back a pace, he looked up and said, "Godspeed, my lady."

She stared at a spot over his shoulder to avoid the anguish in his eyes. "Thank you, my laird."

A call went up from the Duke of Essex and the horses began to move smartly away. Handsome Alger Blakely caught up the reins of Leonora's horse and began to follow the procession.

"Oh, my lady," came a voice from the crowd of servants. Leonora glanced over to see Gwynnith take several steps toward her.

Lifting her head, the little servant called in a tremulous voice, "Never forget us, my lady."

Leonora lifted a hand, then turned away as the first tears threatened to fall. Keeping her head averted, she blinked rapidly. When she turned back, she saw, through a mist of tears, the crowd of familiar faces. Mistress MacCallum. Father Anselm. Camus Ferguson.

But then there was only one that mattered. He stood head and shoulders above the others, showing not a trace of emotion, as he towered, as tall as a giant, as unbending as the oak trees that spread their branches across his beloved Highland forests.

Leonora felt her composure unraveling. The tears could no longer be held back. Like a dam washed away by the force of a river, hot tears streamed down her cheeks, scalding her eyes, burning her throat. Her heart shattered into a million tiny pieces.

Clouds obscured the midnight sky. Dillon paced the overgrown rose garden, the restless hounds at his side. Everyone in Kinloch House had long ago retired for the night, but still Dillon paced. He could not bear the thought of returning to his chambers alone. And so he paced, his thoughts darker than the storm clouds above.

He would welcome the storm. It had been during a storm that he and Leonora had first come together to unleash the pent-up passion between them.

As if sensing his somber mood, the hounds growled and cried and leaped at the wall. The same wall, Dillon thought with a fresh wave of pain, through which Leonora had made good her escape. God in heaven, he could not bear to even look at it.

"Be still, fool hounds," he hissed.

But the dogs, perhaps agitated by the impending storm, cried louder, snarling and leaping at the wall.

Annoyed, Dillon started to make his way back to the keep, but the hounds refused to follow. Instead, they continued their baying until Dillon suddenly snapped to attention. What was wrong with him? Had he completely lost his senses? The hounds had heard something. Something that alarmed them.

Touching his hand to the sword at his waist, he strode across the garden and pushed open the heavy door. At once the hounds burst through the opening and began baying and whining as they raced ahead. Dillon had all he could do to keep up.

They bounded through the thicket, emerging on the far side of a steep meadow. They continued running, then suddenly came to a halt and crouched beside a darkened mound.

As he drew close and recognized what had set the hounds into such a frenzy, Dillon felt his heart stop. Kneeling in the fragrant heather, he rolled the darkened mound over. And beheld the battered, bloodied face of young Rupert.

It was Gwynnith, standing on the tower beside the cages of doves, who spotted the strange procession coming across the darkened meadow. In a flash of lightning, she could make out the vivid outline of the laird and his heavy burden. With a flurry of skirts, she raced down the tower stairs and awakened Mistress MacCallum.

"You must come quickly," she called, tugging on the old woman's nightshift until she was fully awake. "The laird is carrying someone in his arms. It appears to be a Highlander who has come to some harm."

The two women were waiting at the garden door by the time Dillon arrived. For a moment, when they realized who lay in his arms, they were too stunned to move.

Pulling herself together, Mistress MacCallum commanded, "Prepare a pallet, Gwynnith. And rouse the servants. We must work quickly, if we are to save 'im, judging by the looks of 'im."

Dillon's tone was thunderous. "I will need every potion you have ever conjured, Mistress MacCallum."

Following the women inside, Dillon laid the boy tenderly on the pallet that Gwynnith had hastily prepared beside her own. One by one the rest of the servants tiptoed into the room, then hastily scurried about preparing the roots and herbs requested by the housekeeper.

With Dillon's help, Gwynnith stripped Rupert's clothes, torn and matted with dried blood, from his battered body. It was obvious that the lad had withstood a brutal beating. His skull had been split by the blade of a sword. Both eyes were swollen shut. His arm was broken. In his shoulder was embedded a small knife. The wounds had long ago begun festering.

"How did the lad manage to survive?" Mistress MacCallum breathed while she began applying her salves and ointments.

Seeing the severity of the wounds, Dillon ordered a servant to fetch Father Anselm. The priest, groggy from sleep, hurried to kneel beside the lad, anointing him with oil, and murmuring in Latin the words of the Last Rites.

At that, Gwynnith began to weep.

"Hush now, lass," Mistress MacCallum scolded. "There's no time for tears."

"He cannot die," Gwynnith said, pressing Rupert's big hand to her cheek.

Over the young servant's head, Mistress MacCallum and Dillon shared a look of stunned revelation.

"I had not realized," Dillon said, clearing his throat, "that Rupert is so dear to you, Gwynnith."

"Aye, my laird. This silent giant of an oaf means everything in the world to me."

"Then you shall stay with him, day and night, until he recovers. Mistress MacCallum," he said sternly, "I order Gwynnith to do nothing in Kinloch House except tend to Rupert until he is strong and well. Is that understood?"

"Aye, m'laird."

As Dillon began to scramble to his feet, the lad, who until that moment had spoken not a word, suddenly reached out a hand and moaned softly. Instantly, Dillon dropped back onto his knees and said, "Rupert, lad, can you hear me?"

"Aye." The word was a mere croak.

"Tell me who did this thing to you. He will be hunted and punished at once."

"'Twas..." The lad ran a swollen tongue over his parched lips and struggled to get the words out. "The English villains..."

"English villains?" Dillon's heart seemed frozen inside his chest. "You do not mean Essex and Blakely?"

"Aye, my laird...overheard their scheming...on way back to Kinloch House...'Twas they who persuaded Lord Waltham...to remain in England and...keep your brothers at his castle until they return.... Plan to murder...the lady...lay the blame on you, my laird."

"But why? How could Waltham believe I would murder his daughter when he is holding my brothers?"

"Will claim you are...vicious madman...thus assuring that our countries will go to war."

At his words, Dillon felt as if all the air had gone out of his lungs. God in heaven. He had just delivered the woman he loved into the hands of murderers.

Chapter Twenty-two

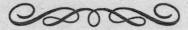

"May God forgive me, Camus." In his chambers, Dillon paced like a man possessed. "I personally delivered Leonora into their hands."

Camus filled a goblet and watched helplessly as his friend emptied it in one long swallow, then, with a furious oath, hurled it against the wall, shattering it into a million fragments.

In quick strides, Dillon crossed the room and lifted down his father's sword from above the mantel. "You must assemble my army, Camus. I cannot wait. I go after them now."

"And if they have already reached England?" Camus asked.

Dillon strapped on his scabbard and reached for a heavy traveling cloak. "I care not how far they ride. If necessary, I will go to hell and back. But this I know, I will not rest until I have rescued Leonora from those madmen."

"You must send word to the lady's father, my friend."

"There is no time."

"Listen to me." Camus caught Dillon's arm, refusing to flinch when his old friend shot him a murderous look. Had he not promised Leonora he would be Dillon's friend? At the moment, his old friend was not thinking clearly. Nor would he, Camus thought, if the one he loved was in the hands of such as Essex and Blakely. Everyone in Kinloch House had seen what they'd done to young Rupert. They were indeed heartless madmen.

"If we cross over to England, we have need of Lord Waltham's cooperation. Else we become, by murdering English soldiers on English soil, candidates for Fleet Prison, my friend."

Though Dillon was beyond caring, his friend's words penetrated the black fury that held him in its grip. He slowly nodded. "Aye, Camus. Forgive me. I am blinded." He took a deep breath. "Assemble the army. Tell them to follow my trail. Then take three or four of your most trusted men and ride to Lord Waltham's castle."

"And you, Dillon?"

"I cannot wait to assemble an army," he said, striding toward the door. "I ride now."

"Alone? In this storm?"

Dillon paused at the doorway. "Aye. And pray, Camus, that I am not already too late."

"We must take refuge from this storm." The Duke of Essex pointed to the darkened outline of a cottage up ahead. "I will prepare a shelter. James, you and your men come with me. Alger, stay here with the lady." His smile was dark and evil and full of secrets. "We will signal with a candle when it is safe to approach."

As the others rode ahead, Alger led Leonora's horse toward a stand of evergreen. The thick branches afforded some relief from the driving rain.

"Why do we not ride together to the cottage?" Leonora asked. "With Dillon Campbell's banner for protection, you need only ask and you will be warmly received by all his countrymen."

"That is not the way of the duke. Essex does not ask. He takes." Alger gave a short laugh, remembering the path of destruction they had left on their journey to the Highlands. Even the hardened soldiers among them had been shocked by the brutality of the Duke of Essex. He actually seemed to enjoy the bloodletting. By now, the word would have spread throughout the countryside that a band of English soldiers was murdering helpless peasants under the protective banner of Dillon Campbell. No door would be open to them.

Leonora could not hide the alarm she felt. "He will not harm these innocent people?"

Alger drew his steed close and dropped a protective arm around her, enjoying the swift, sudden arousal. His duties had kept him too long from having a woman. "Do not fear, my lady. He will merely...make use of their cottage until the storm passes."

She let out a sigh of relief, then deftly nudged her horse out of his reach. A few minutes later, she pointed. "There is the signal."

He felt a wave of annoyance. He had hoped for a little more time alone with the lady. With his calm assurance and good looks, he was usually able to charm his way into a lady's trust. From there it was only a step to her bed.

Taking up her reins, he led the way across a high meadow toward the small peasant cottage. At the door he helped her dismount, purposely lifting his hands high enough so that they came in contact with the soft swell of her breasts beneath the heavy cloak.

She turned away so quickly he could not see her angry reaction. But as he followed her inside, he decided that he would stay alert and hope that the others soon fell asleep. Perhaps he could still sample the lady's charms before she...reached the end of her journey.

Once inside, Leonora glanced around. The Duke of Essex was seated at table, eating what was left of some roasted fowl. James Blakely and his soldiers were drinking from what appeared to be a cask of spirits.

"Where are the peasants who live here?" she asked.

Essex looked up with a chilling smile. "They retreated to their pig shelter rather than share their quarters with the hated English."

She noticed an empty cradle. "Why did they not take the babe's bed with them?"

Essex shrugged. "Who knows how these savages think? Would you care for some fowl, my lady?"

"Nay, thank you." She shivered and drew near to the fire, gathering her cloak around her like a shield. While she stood warming herself, she could feel the silent stares from the others. Everything about Essex and his men made her uncomfortable.

"You had best sleep, my lady." Alger's voice, so close beside her, made her jump nervously.

"I am not tired."

"You are probably too excited about leaving this bloody land behind," James said bitterly, lifting ale to his lips. The ale had loosened his tongue.

"Why do you hate it so?" Leonora asked.

Tossing his cloak aside, James lifted the sleeve of his tunic to reveal a long, puckered scar. "This was given me by a filthy Highlander many years ago."

"I am certain there are many Highlanders who bear such scars delivered at the point of an English sword, as well. But that is no reason to harbor ill will for a lifetime." Leonora smiled gently. "Can you not put your anger aside and begin anew?"

James returned her smile, and for a moment Leonora thought how handsome father and son were. But at his words, her smile disappeared from her lips.

"Aye, I can begin anew. But I fear the Highlander can not do the same. Nor will his sons. You see, he thought I ought not to bed his lovely maiden daughter. I disagreed. So, after I ran him through with my sword, I not only took his maiden daughter, but his wife, as well." He looked around the room, apparently pleased that all the men were laughing heartily at his joke. Throwing back his head, he added, "And forced his young sons to watch while I did so."

That comment brought even more laughter.

Leonora reacted as though she'd been slapped. Righteous anger colored her cheeks. She thought about all the horrible stories she'd been told by the serving girls at Kinloch House. Each one had been more shocking than the last. And each time, she had experienced a sense of outrage and revulsion at the men who had inflicted such pain. She could see these men, men who called themselves friends of her father, staring at her and laughing. She felt as if she'd been violated.

"That is not all, my lady," James said between bouts of laughter. "Within a fortnight, I returned with an army of men, and we killed the entire clan while they played in a Highland meadow. I saw to it that there were none left to seek vengeance upon me and mine."

"God in heaven." She pressed a hand to her mouth when she realized what James had just revealed. He was the one who had destroyed Dillon's clan. And left his mark upon the lad's face, and upon his soul, for a lifetime.

With a look of indignation, she removed a warm blanket from the empty cradle, then strode across the room and paused beside the Duke of Essex, picking up the remains of the meal he had been enjoying.

"What are you doing?" he demanded.

"I am taking a warm covering and the rest of this food to the peasants. I would prefer to share their quarters with the pigs, rather than remain here with such animals."

She managed to pull open the door before Alger, swearing loudly, closed a hand over her wrist.

"Nay, Alger," Essex said, beginning to laugh once more. "Do not stop her. I think you should accompany the lady to the pig shelter. Let us see if she is truly ready to...join the peasants."

Alger glanced from his father to Essex. Both men were smiling broadly. The others were laughing at their shared joke.

He shrugged and took up a torch from a niche in the wall. "Come, my lady. I will take you to the peasants."

The downpour made it impossible to track the horsemen. Hoofprints were instantly washed away. Grass that had been trampled now floated in puddles. Bits of fabric that might have snagged on branches were impossible to see in the darkness. The only thing for which Dillon was grateful was the fact that the pounding of his horse's hooves could not be heard above the steady beat of rain and the rumble of thunder.

He drove his mount mercilessly. Though he knew not which trail Essex had taken, he knew one thing: the English were eager to leave the Highlands behind. But whether Leonora was alive or dead, was still a mystery to him. It was no mystery that the lady would be dead by the time the English soldiers reached her father's castle. And their lie, which had almost cost Rupert his life, would be believed without question. They were, after all, high-born Englishmen. He, on the other hand, was known to all English as a Highland savage. All of England would be ready to ride against him, once Leonora's death was discovered.

The fragile peace between their countries would be forever shattered. But though that should have been the noble reason that drove him, it was not. In his heart, there was only one compelling fact that drove him. Leonora. His beautiful, beloved Leonora was in grave peril. If she came to any harm, his own life would be meaningless.

Pulling his cloak around him to ward off the rain, Dillon urged his mount into a run.

Leonora lifted her hood and stepped outside. Despite the rain, the fragrance of heather was strong as they crossed the field toward the crude animal shelter.

"A word of warning, my lady." Alger walked by her side, holding the torch aloft to light their way. "You would be wise to tread carefully, lest you anger the Duke of Essex."

"I care not for Essex. He is not worthy of his title."

"Perhaps. But he wields great power, my lady. And you are not yet in your father's safe embrace."

She paused in midstride and faced him. "Are you trying to frighten me, Alger?"

He shrugged, and the smile that played on his lips gave her a strange, uneasy feeling. "I merely suggest, my lady, that in the company of such powerful men as the duke and my father, you are in need of a friend."

"And you would be that friend?"

He took her free hand in his and brought the torch close so that he could see her eyes. His voice was low, seductive. "If you would let me, I would be more than friend."

She jerked her hand from his grasp and turned away, lifting her skirts in the wet grass as she strode quickly toward the crude shelter.

From behind her came Alger's voice, tinged with anger and something else. Something she couldn't quite identify. There was a smug, self-satisfied ring to his words, as though privy to a secret she had not yet learned. "Remember that I offered you friendship, my lady. For in the next few moments, you shall be in need of a friend."

She pushed open the door and was assaulted by the usual barnyard smells. Dung. Earth. The fetid stench of so many creatures crowded into such a small space.

As pigs and chickens and lambs scrambled about, she peered into the darkness in search of the family that had fled the English invaders.

"Good people, I bring you food and warmth," she called out in greeting.

Her words were met with silence. Except for the bleating of a lamb, and muted animal sounds, there was no response.

She walked farther into the shelter, groping her way until she reached the far wall. In the darkness she nearly tripped over something. Pausing to reach down, she encountered the coarse texture of a peasant shirt.

"Good sir," she said softly, "forgive me for waking you, but I have brought food, and a blanket for your child."

An almost overpowering stench arose, the likes of which she had never before experienced. At almost the same moment, she lifted her hand from the shirt and shrank back. Her fingers, she realized, were covered with something thick and warm and sticky.

"Have you found your peasants?" Alger asked, stepping through the doorway.

In that instant, he lifted the torch, illuminating the interior. The walls, the earthen floor, even the roof, were spattered with blood. It stained the coats of the pigs. The wool of the sheep ran red with it. The chicken feathers were smeared with it. And on the floor, trampled beneath the feet of the animals, lay the broken, twisted bodies of a peasant family. A man, a woman and two young girls, one of them an infant.

Leonora heard the high, piercing sounds of a woman's screams, though she did not recognize the voice of hysteria as her own. Sobbing, choking, she clawed her way out of the shelter and ran halfway across the meadow before she collapsed beneath a tree, retching.

She seemed unaware of the man who knelt beside her, or of the light of the torch as he lifted it to study her. The hem of her cloak was crusted with animal waste and blood. The hood had slipped from her head, leaving her hair to fall in soaked tendrils around her face. Her eyes, red and swollen, seemed too bright in a face that had been drained of all color.

"Now," he said, taking her cold, lifeless hand in his, "do you still wish to join the peasants, my lady?"

She could barely speak. "They did that to them. Essex and your father and the others. They murdered those innocent peasants."

She expected him to share her outrage. Instead, he said simply, "Aye. As they have before. As they surely will again, until we leave this filthy, heathen land behind."

"You know what they do, and you do not condemn them?"

"Condemn them? I am a mere soldier, my lady, following the orders of my leader. What we do, we do for England."

She shrank back from him. "Nay. It is my land, as well, and you do not do it for me. You do it because it pleases you. It gives you a sense of power to hurt these helpless people."

His tone hardened. "We do it because they deserve it. They are our enemy. Now, come, my lady. It is time we returned to the cottage."

"Nay. I cannot bear the thought of being with such monsters."

"But you have no choice," he said as patiently as if he were lecturing a child. "You are in our protective care, my lady. Your fate is in our hands."

Fate. She now knew her fate. These men had no intention of returning her to her father. At least not alive. For if they did, she would speak of their evil deeds. Now that she had been a witness to their barbarism, she would have to die. She recalled the soldiers she had encountered in the forest. Though these men called themselves noblemen, they were no better.

She had never felt so alone. This time, she had neither Dillon Campbell nor her father to protect her.

"Have no fear, my lady. Remember, I will be your friend." He helped her to her feet and brushed a strand of damp hair from her cheek, allowing his hand to linger in her hair. With an arm around her shoulders, he began to lead her back to the cottage. "As long as you do not anger me, as long as you...please me, I will place myself between you and the others."

Numbly, she moved along at his side. Her tears had already dried. The tremors that had first rocked her were subsiding. But the sight that had greeted her in the barn had been seared into her memory. She would not forget. Nor would she forgive the men who had done this. Though she knew not how, she would find a way to make them pay.

A strange sort of calm descended upon her. She glanced heavenward and realized that the worst of the storm had passed, leaving a steady, drenching downpour. Far to the east, the first faint ribbons of dawn already streaked the sky. A new day was beginning, and with it, a chance to escape these monsters who insulted all Englishmen by passing themselves off as English noblemen.

So long as she had a breath left in her, she vowed, she would escape from these men. And then fight to denounce them.

Chapter Twenty-three

The rain continued, though not as heavy, throughout the next day. The party of English soldiers, who had been in the saddle since dawn, grumbled among themselves about the harsh terrain, the scarcity of food, the lack of women.

Leonora rode in their midst, her hands bound, her reins held by Alger Blakely, to prevent her from attempting to escape. Since witnessing the fate of the peasants, Essex saw no reason to continue the pretense that they would return her to her father.

Each time their party passed a crofter's cottage, each time they entered a farmer's land, Leonora held her breath, praying they would not stop and wreak more havoc on these innocent people. And yet, each time she passed another family working in the fields, she had to resist the temptation to cry out for help.

What could these simple people do for her? she reasoned. Would a scythe or pitchfork equal a razor-sharp knife or a sword? Could a farmer, no matter how muscular, be the equal of these soldiers whose strength had been honed by years of battle? And why, she asked herself, would simple Scots peasants come to the defense of an English-woman in the company of English soldiers?

She could not involve these good people in her fate. And so, as she passed each one, she met their gazes solemnly, showing no sign of her inner turmoil. But as day faded into evening, the terror grew within her. They were approaching the English border. The time for confrontation was drawing near. Alger had left no doubt that, were she to give in to his lustful demands, he could see that her life was spared. She wanted to believe that he would help her, but despite his boastful claims, it was obvious that Essex was the true leader of this band of murderers. And in the duke's mind, she had been marked for death from the beginning.

She thought of Father Anselm's last words to her. Had he sensed the danger she would face? Closing her eyes, she whispered a prayer for safety. "And if," she added, "I cannot be kept safe, at least let me face death with courage."

"I spy a cottage," Essex muttered to James Blakely, and pointed to a small building and several outbuildings across a meadow. "We will take shelter until we are rested."

Peering through the mist, Leonora's heart nearly stopped. Though the last time she had seen this place she had been nearly consumed with exhaustion, she was certain she was not mistaken. The cottage was the same one in which she and Dillon had sought shelter on their way to the Highlands.

Oh, sweet heaven, she thought with growing panic as the scene of carnage in the barn flashed through her mind. It was the cottage of Brodie of Morayshire. And his shy, sweet wife, Anthea, and little sons and infant daughter.

"You are certain, man, that they did not pass this way?"

The old man, his face the texture of aged leather, his hair as white as the delicate Alpine flowers that grew atop the Highland mountains, nodded vigorously. "There is naught that passes this way that I dinna' see, m'laird. I would know if English soldiers and an English lady crossed o'er my land."

Dillon wheeled his mount, whipping the animal into a run. He had just wasted precious time following a false trail. Though he was a man who had rarely known fear, there was a knot of it threatening to choke him.

"Where is your man?" Essex and James burst through the door of the cottage, followed by the soldiers.

The young wife looked up just as Alger Blakely, hauling Leonora roughly by the arm, entered. As Anthea's eyes widened in recognition, Leonora gave a quick shake of her head and prayed that the young woman would understand her signal.

The sight of so many drawn weapons caused Anthea to lift her squalling infant from the cradle. The two frightened little boys hid behind their mother's skirts.

"He is..." She swallowed and tried again. "My husband is in the forest hunting."

Essex pointed the tip of his sword at her. "Whoever would like the privilege of killing the woman may first use her as he pleases."

Before any of the men could volunteer, Leonora pulled free of Alger's grasp and moved to stand beside her. "Nay," she cried, clasping the palm of the frightened young woman between her bound hands. "Can you not see that she has recently given birth?"

"What is that to us?" one of the soldiers said with a sneer. "She is still a warm body."

Leonora's mind raced. "Which would you rather satisfy first? Your hunger for the flesh, or your hunger for food?"

"The lady has a point," Essex said as he warmed himself by the fire. The cottage was redolent of the fragrance of biscuits baking and a kettle of stew simmering over the fire. Leonora's generous gift of jewelry had obviously supplied them with the finest of flour from the mill and more than enough food to feed their hungry family. "We can always take our pleasures later, on a full stomach. You will feed us, woman. But first, I would savor a sip of spirits."

The young woman produced a wooden cask of finest Scottish whiskey. The men gathered around and began to drink. As they did, Leonora lifted her bound hands.

"If you would free me, I could help this woman prepare your food."

"Aye. And be quick about it." Essex pulled a knife from his waist and cut away her bindings.

When he returned his attention to the spirits, Leonora beckoned Anthea to the other side of the small cottage, where they began to prepare a meal. While they worked, they spoke in whispers.

"You must pretend we have never met."

Anthea nodded and glanced down at the boys tugging on her skirts. "I have heard the rumors about these English. They will kill us all."

"Aye. And I will fare no better. How soon will your husband return?"

"Perhaps not until the morrow, depending upon his good fortune."

Leonora felt her heart tumble. By then, they would all surely be dead. "We must devise a plan."

The young woman's fear was evident on her troubled face. "I would gladly die if they would but spare the wee ones."

"These men are monsters who will leave no living thing in their wake. We must find a way to strike the first blow." Leonora's eyes narrowed in thought, then suddenly widened. "You are a healer, Anthea. You know herbs and plants. There may be a way, but if it should fail, our punishment will be horrible indeed."

"Tell me, my lady." Anthea clutched her sleeve. "So long as there is a thread of hope, I will do anything."

Leonora shivered at the enormity of her plan, then whispered her instructions. The young woman nodded in silence, drew the infant close to her breast and knelt down to hug her young sons. If she failed, they would pay with their lives.

Leonora moved among the soldiers, filling their tankards each time they were emptied. After such a tedious journey, they were only too happy to sprawl around a cozy fire and enjoy the warmth of ale snaking through their veins. Even the Duke of Essex and Lord James Blakely seemed ready to relax their guard now that they had made it to the border.

"On the morrow, we shall be on English soil," James said, lifting his tankard.

"Aye, home," Essex muttered. "And none too soon. Even these scrawny Scots women are beginning to look tempting." He cast a glance at Anthea, who quickly ducked her head and continued preparing their meal.

"More ale, your grace?" Leonora had cast aside her coarse traveling cloak to reveal the regal velvet gown. Her long hair, spilling over one shoulder, gleamed blue-black in the firelight.

"Aye." He held out the empty tankard.

As she bent to refill it, he gazed longingly at her high, firm breasts, exposed beneath the low rounded neckline.

"But no one," he announced to the others, "can compare to the beauty of our lovely English ladies."

"Aye." James, seeing the lustful gleam in the duke's eyes, said sadly, "I had hoped for a match between the lady and my son Alger. With her wealth and beauty and his ambition, they could have left a legacy for my progeny."

"Alas," Essex said with a laugh, "poor Alger will have to look elsewhere for a bride."

"The king's cousin has an impressive dowry," Leonora said, pausing to fill James's tankard.

"She is but ten and three," he said with a trace of scorn.

"The perfect age for your son." Calling on all her skills, she slanted a look at Essex, the man who wielded all the power in this small company of soldiers. "Clumsy lads do not interest me, your grace. I prefer men who have spent enough years learning how to pleasure a woman."

Essex blinked. "You, my lady? I had heard that you have managed to resist all the men at court."

"Aye." Leonora sauntered closer to pour more ale into the duke's tankard. She saw his eyes follow each movement of her hips. "I was waiting for one special man to pay heed."

Across the room, Alger sat brooding as he watched Leonora flirt with Essex. He drained his tankard in one long swallow and she quickly moved to refill it. After only a few drops, she gave him a look of exaggerated disappointment. "Forgive me. The cask is empty."

"No matter," James said, "There is another with the horses. We did not travel all this way without fortification."

"I will fetch it." But as she started across the room, the duke's hand clamped around her wrist.

"Nay, beautiful lady. Let the peasant retrieve it." He motioned with his empty tankard to one of the soldiers. "Gather together the peasant's children and keep them here until she returns. That way, we can be assured that she will not attempt to run."

When one of the soldiers caught up the children, the infant began wailing and the little boys joined in, howling for their mother, who was shoved out into the night.

James roared with laughter. "You are sly, Essex."

"Aye." He joined in the laughter and ran his hand possessively along Leonora's arm. "The woman was not born who could outwit me."

Leonora swallowed back the terror that clawed at her throat. Forcing a smile to her lips, she perched on the arm of the duke's chair, exposing a length of ankle. She knew she played a dangerous game that might easily turn violent.

While Essex stared at her ankle with lecherous fascination, she mentally ticked off the passing moments until, at last, Anthea returned, carrying the cask. At once, the soldier released the children into the arms of their mother.

"I will pour," Leonora said, springing to her feet.

When she filled the duke's tankard, he watched her with a frown of concentration. "This ale is going to my head," he muttered. "It is time for some food."

"Aye, your grace." Leonora glanced at Anthea, who had wrapped a strip of linen around her hand and was lifting the heavy kettle from the fire, while at the same time emptying something from her apron into the kettle. Then the young woman bent over, stirring furiously.

When Leonora had filled each tankard, she crossed the room and began to assist Anthea in ladling stew into wooden bowls, which were passed out to the hungry soldiers. Along with the stew she offered hot steaming biscuits.

The men, made careless by the ale they had consumed, and ravenous from their long journey, ate quickly, barely tasting their food. As soon as their bowls were empty, Leonora and Anthea filled them a second time and watched with satisfaction as the men emptied them yet again.

"There is more stew, your grace," Leonora said, reaching for his bowl.

"Nay." Shaking his head, the Duke of Essex set aside his bowl and reached for Leonora's hand. "It is not food I crave now."

"But it is too soon," Anthea cried.

"Too soon?" he asked suspiciously.

Leonora licked her dry lips and glanced quickly at Anthea, whose wide eyes registered absolute terror. "She means, your grace, there is still so much food to savor."

He relented. "One more serving, then."

As she moved about the room offering more stew, Alger caught her by the wrist and said, "Do not think I have not noticed the invitation in your eyes for Essex."

"What makes you think it is only for Essex?" she asked, knowing this game became more dangerous with each passing moment.

He got to his feet. "Come, my lady." A look of hatred darkened the duke's features as Alger said loudly, "It is time you tasted the kisses of a real man."

The others, emboldened by drink, laughed and looked from Essex to Alger. Perhaps, if they were lucky, they would get to witness a fight between these two.

Essex stood so quickly, his bowl of steaming stew up-ended and sprayed across several nearby soldiers. "I am leader here," he roared, reaching for the sword at his waist. "Let no man usurp my authority."

"You promised her to me," Alger shouted. "All during this tedious journey, you assured me I would sample her charms before she met with her...untimely death." He turned to his father for support, and seeing none, reached into the fireplace, grasped the end of a flaming tree branch, and held it aloft threateningly.

Essex blinked and backed away. "I see the woman has made your blood hot."

"Aye. Be warned, your grace. Let no man try to stop me. I will have her."

He shoved Leonora ahead of him toward the sleeping chamber, brandishing the flaming stick like a sword. When they reached the doorway, Alger pushed Leonora inside, then tossed the stick aside. He closed the door firmly and leaned against it. Taking a small, deadly knife from his waist, he lifted it aloft until the blade glinted in the reflection of the fire on the hearth.

"Essex will kill you," Leonora said.

"Essex needs me and my father," he boasted. "Remove your garments, my lady. I would see this precious jewel who was held in such esteem by her proud father."

"Do not speak my father's name at such a time," she whispered.

"And why not?" His high, shrill laugh scraped across her already tautly stretched nerves. "My father and I have long hated your father. And the king he so loyally serves."

"What you speak is treason, punishable by death."

"Nay, my lady. What I speak is the truth. Our king is a coward and a weakling, who would prefer to talk peace instead of defeating his enemies on a field of battle. But, as Essex said, your death will change the course of history. When your father sees the proof of the Highlander's deception, there will be no more talk of peace. Now we have wasted enough time. Remove your garments."

She tossed her head. "You promised to be my friend. You said I would be safe with you."

His lips peeled back in a feral smile. "I indulged in a falsehood. Remove your clothes."

"You will have to tear them from me."

"It will be my pleasure." He advanced on her, wielding the knife. He pinned her hands behind her, grasping them painfully in one of his hands. With the other, he lifted the knife to her throat and in one smooth movement slit her garments from top to bottom. The torn remnants fell away, revealing pale, smooth flesh.

"Ah, my lady. You have been worth waiting for." With a look as evil as the devil himself, Alger tossed her down on the sleeping pallet and levered himself above her.

Tears stung her eyes. All her prayers, all her schemes, had not been enough to save her. But at least, she thought, scraping her fingernails across his face, she would die fighting.

"Wench! You are no better than a tavern slut." His brutal slap snapped her head to one side. "Now you shall pay." He gave another shrill laugh, and reached for her. But just as his fingers closed around her shoulders, his grip slackened.

With a look of surprise and confusion, he released his hold on her and turned away. He rose, staggered a few paces away, then fell back to his knees.

Scrambling from the pallet, Leonora took up his knife, and without giving herself time to dwell on what she was about to do, she plunged it into his shoulder.

He looked up at her, his eyes wide with shock and pain. With a roar of fury, he pulled the knife free and lumbered to his feet. When he reached for her, she managed to step aside and began racing for the door. He lunged at her and brought her to her knees. But as he lifted the knife, prepared to plunge it into her heart, his eyes glazed over and he wavered, nearly toppling. In that moment, Leonora brought her knee against his hand, and plunged the knife into his chest. As he lay in a pool of his own blood, she pulled on her tattered remnants and tore open the door.

And stepped into a blazing inferno.

Dillon's fury built with every meadow he crossed, every cottage he visited. He had witnessed the brutality of these men. The bodies of the murdered peasants had been a ghastly reminder of what Leonora faced at the hands of her captors. Though his heart wished otherwise, he was convinced that she had not managed to escape. At each farm, each crofter's cottage, the stories were the same. Of a beautiful Englishwoman, hands bound, being led by a band of English soldiers.

As he headed toward the English border, he lifted his head. From across a high meadow came a pall of thick, black smoke. And lighting up the twilight sky, a bright orange ball of fire.

He spurred his horse into a run, praying that he was not too late to save the woman he loved.

"Anthea, where are you?"

With her eyes burning, Leonora dropped to her knees and began crawling across the floor of the cottage. Everywhere she looked, men were either crawling groggily or sprawled unconscious.

Flames licked across the wall, then ignited the thatched roof, which blazed into a blinding fireball.

"I am over here." The young woman lay in a corner of the cottage, her terrified children clinging to her.

"Hurry! You must run."

"I cannot. I am trapped."

Crawling closer, Leonora realized the young woman's legs were pinned beneath a wooden beam that had collapsed inward. Though she struggled with all her might, she was unable to budge the heavy timber.

"Never mind about me," Anthea shouted above the roar of the fire. "Save my children."

"I will be back," Leonora promised as she caught up the infant and ordered the terrified little boys to hold tightly to her skirt.

With their eyes and lungs burning, Leonora and her little party stumbled through the thick black smoke, tripping over bodies, dodging falling sparks, until at last they made it to safety.

She set the squalling infant in the grass and commanded the little boys to remain at the babe's side. Then she took a deep breath and dashed back into the inferno.

The smoke was thicker now, and the entire roof was ablaze. Sparks had fallen into the infant's cradle, igniting the blanket. As she inched her way across the floor, Leonora could see that the roof over Anthea's head would soon collapse right onto the young woman.

Frantically she struggled to lift the heavy timber. At last, using a piece of burning wood as a lever, she ignored the pain to her searing hands and managed to pry the timber high enough to allow the young woman to slide free.

"Oh, my lady, it is too late," Anthea cried just as the roof began to cave in.

"Nay! Run, Anthea." Leonora dragged her toward a wall of flame. When the young woman refused to go through, Leonora pushed her to safety. But when she started to follow, a hand closed over her wrist and she was held fast.

With a cry she turned. And found herself facing the Duke of Essex. In his hand was a small, deadly knife.

Chapter Twenty-four

"We must flee," she cried.

"Nay, my lady. I must die. And so must you."

"You are mad."

"Nay, merely dedicated to saving England from a king who would destroy her. For so long, I have plotted and schemed. When the Highlander stole you away, I had the perfect plan. It could not fail to bring down our king. And now," he cried, eyes narrowed in fury, "I will not have it snatched from my grasp. If I must die, my lady, so must you, so that my plan will not be thwarted. You will never see your father again."

More of the roof collapsed around them, sending up a spray of sparks into the darkening sky. Essex seemed not to notice.

Leonora's mind raced. "They are all dead. There are none left to follow you into battle."

"But there will be others who will rise up and demand retribution for what happened here. We are on Scottish soil. Your savage will still be blamed for this bloody massacre." He faltered for a moment, but shook his head to clear it. He seemed to remain standing through sheer force of will. "I know now what you and the peasant woman did. It was very clever. You poisoned our food."

"Aye. But she is a healer, as well, your grace. Come with me, and Anthea will save you."

"Enough of your tricks. You speak falsehoods."

"Please, Essex. The fire—"

"Aye." He laughed. "The woman, following Alger's lead, tossed a flaming stick at me when I tried to pleasure myself with her. And then..." He shook his head again. "Then the fog came over me. It is so hard to..." He staggered again and his expression grew darker. "It is...too late." His eyes were glazed, and she saw his hand tighten on the hilt of the knife. "For both of us, my lady."

As he lifted the knife, Leonora saw the flash of brightly colored jewels reflected in the firelight and wondered idly why her mind was playing such tricks on her. Then she saw the hand holding the jeweled sword, and Dillon's tall figure loomed before her, passing right through a wall of flame.

"Release the woman," thundered Dillon's voice.

"Nay. You have lost, Highlander." The duke tightened his grip on Leonora and prepared to plunge the knife.

The jeweled sword found its mark. With a gasp, Essex stiffened, then dropped to his knees. With one quick motion, Dillon pulled the sword free, but from behind him came a ghost from his past.

"Dillon!" Leonora shouted.

He turned and found himself facing James Blakely's sword.

"It was he who murdered your clan," Leonora cried above the sound of the fire.

Dillon's eyes blazed in fury. "Though I resisted the knowledge, my heart knew."

"I thought I had killed every last one of you," James said, lunging toward Dillon.

Sidestepping, Dillon avoided his thrust and began to circle, all the while feeling the heat of the flames. One part of his mind noted that Leonora's only means of escape was being blocked by this English soldier. But another part of his mind could focus only on the fact that this was the man he had waited a lifetime to meet.

"At last," Dillon said in that deadly quiet way all men had learned to fear, "I will avenge the death of my parents. Know this, James Blakely. You and your son will die this day, and there will be none left to carry on your name. But though you murdered nearly an entire clan of Campbells, our name will be carried on proudly for generations to come."

With one smooth motion, he thrust his sword through Blakely's heart. For a moment, the soldier seemed surprised. Then, clutching his chest, he fell into the flames.

Dillon lifted Leonora in his arms and carried her through a wall of fire to safety.

"Oh, Dillon," she murmured against his cheek as he cradled her against his chest. "You are truly free. Free of the past. Free of the ghosts of your father's murderers."

"Aye."

"I prayed you would come for me, Dillon."

"Ah, love, how could I not?" He was still trembling at the thought of how close he had come to losing her. "I told Camus I would ride to hell and back for you."

"This truly felt like the fires of hell." She gave a weak sigh and watched as the last of the cottage went up in flames, collapsing in on itself with a blaze that leaped taller than the line of trees in the nearby forest.

They looked up as a long line of soldiers crossed the border and raced across the meadow. When they drew near, Leonora recognized the rider in the lead.

"Father!" she cried.

He slid from the saddle and crossed the distance separating them in quick, impatient strides.

"Leonora. Oh, my beloved daughter. I had feared, when I saw the flames..."

Dillon released her and she fell into her father's arms, laughing and crying. It was several minutes before either of them was able to speak.

While they kissed and embraced, Dillon let out a cry of joy when he spotted two figures riding on either side of Camus.

"Sutton! Shaw!"

The two brothers leaped from the saddles and launched themselves into Dillon's arms. With a roar of delight, he embraced them, then held them a little away, as if to be certain that they were really here with him.

"How have you fared?" he demanded.

"We are fine, Dillon," Sutton said.

"Truly?"

"Aye," Shaw assured him. "Lord Waltham is an honorable man. Though we were held within a chamber in his keep, we were neither shackled nor imprisoned. We were fed and clothed."

"And the food was served by very... accommodating wenches," Sutton added.

Dillon shook his head, unable to hold back the smile that touched his lips. "I see that some things never change, my brother."

"Rupert arrived just as Lord Waltham was about to leave for the Highlands with the king's own army," Shaw added. "The English had been preparing for a bloodbath."

Lord Waltham approached them, with his arm still firmly around his daughter. In his eyes were tears, which he did not even bother to hide.

Extending his hand, he said, "Dillon Campbell, I give you my heartfelt thanks. My daughter assures me that she was well treated while in your Highlands. I know now that it was you who saved her life."

"And I am equally grateful, Lord Waltham, for my brothers assure me that you treated them in like manner."

Lord Waltham's voice deepened with emotion. "Though I was loath to believe him at first, Camus persuaded me of the villainy of Essex and James and Alger Blakely. I should have questioned why they were so eager to go to the Highlands without the king's army, but my mind was clouded by concern over my daughter. Now that I see clearly, I realize so much more. It was Essex and Blakely who struck the first blow against the Campbells, thus assuring that the Highlanders would be forced to fight back. With men like that slaughtering innocents, peace could never be achieved. When the king learns of their misdeeds, he will see that their heirs are stripped of all lands and titles. And because you risked your life to save my daughter, I will ask my king to reward you handsomely."

Dillon's gaze was riveted on Leonora's face. His voice trembled with feeling. "No reward is necessary, my lord. It is enough to know that the lady is safe."

At the roughness of his tone, both his brothers turned to study him. This open display of emotion was something they had never before seen in their brother. But Dillon was unaware of anything except the pale young woman who stood quietly beside her father, returning his look with a hunger that matched his own.

"Well." Lord Waltham cleared his throat, uncomfortably aware of the highly charged emotions between Leonora and Dillon. "We will take our leave of this scene of death and destruction. I have long waited to welcome my daughter back to her rightful place in my home. I am certain you are just as eager to return with your brothers to your Highlands, Dillon."

Dillon stood very still, watching as Leonora was led to a waiting horse and wrapped in an elegant, sable-lined cape before being helped into the saddle.

Anthea and her children made their way to Leonora's mount.

"Thank you, my lady," she said. "It would seem that we are once again in your debt."

"Nay," Leonora said softly, "it was your courage and your clever use of herbs and plants that saved us all."

"You are too modest," Anthea said. "I merely did what you suggested. But it was you, my lady, who showed such courage. Without you, none of us would have survived."

"There are no more debts between us," Leonora said. "Only a deep and abiding bond of friendship."

As she made ready to leave, Dillon crossed the distance between them and caught her hand in his. At once, a flicker of hope leaped within her. At last, he had found his voice. He would not, could not let her go.

"Farewell, my lady," he murmured.

"Farewell, Dillon?"

"Aye. We both know it must be so. But know also that I will think of you always, Leonora Waltham."

She swallowed. "And I you, Dillon Campbell."

Oh, Dillon, Dillon. Tell my father how you feel, she thought. *Ask me to stay,* her heart begged.

She felt tears spring to her eyes and cloud her vision, and still he stood, watching her in that silent, watchful way he had. He infuriated her. She hated him. She loved him. Oh, sweet heaven, how she loved him. And there was no way to speak of the things she held in the deepest, darkest recesses of her heart.

"Godspeed, my lady."

"And you, my laird."

A call went up from the head of the column of soldiers, and they began moving out at a smart pace. Lord Waltham wheeled his mount and returned to his daughter's side.

"Are you ready, my dear?"

"Aye, Father."

With a last, lingering look at Dillon Campbell, she was forced to follow the line of soldiers. At the top of the meadow, she turned for a final look. He was still standing where she had left him. He lifted his hand in a salute, and, her heart breaking, she waved and turned away toward home and England.

"Ye're not hungry, m'laird?"

Mistress MacCallum stared at the perfectly roasted venison, the tender vegetables from the garden, the brandied pudding. All untouched on the laird's plate.

He had been this way ever since he'd returned home with his brothers. Instead of the rejoicing they had all anticipated, a dark pall seemed to hang over Kinloch House.

"Nay, Mistress MacCallum. I have no appetite."

"But—"

"Let it be, Mistress MacCallum," Father Anselm said softly.

With deep sadness, they watched as Dillon pushed away from the table and summoned the hounds, who trailed eagerly as he led the way to his chambers. Once there, he closed the door, shutting out the sounds of laughter between Sutton and Shaw, closing out the sounds of life. He wanted no part of life or laughter. They merely reminded him of what he had lost.

He had not lost her, he reminded himself sternly as he crossed to the balcony. He had sent her away. His damnable sense of honor had cost him the only woman he had ever loved.

Leaning a hip against the ledge, he glanced toward the tower and could make out the silhouettes of Rupert and Gwynnith, feeding the doves. The little servant spent an inordinate amount of time these days up in the tower with Rupert. The lad's wounds had miraculously healed, and to hear Mistress MacCallum tell it, it was all due to the love and devotion of the young servant.

Love and devotion. Perhaps they were some sort of miracle. They were indeed rare. Without them, life was little more than bleak existence.

The two silhouettes turned toward each other, the taller head bent, the shorter head lifted. Then the two merged and Dillon turned his gaze away, feeling like an intruder.

The land below was a sight that had always stirred his blood. These fierce Highlands had never failed to thrill him. The weather had gentled, leaving the countryside bathed in brilliant colors of summer. Vivid purple heather covered the meadows. The leaves of the oak and alder, pine and birch were deepest emerald green; the lochs a clear, clean blue. And yet...he turned away, unable to bear the beauty of the scene below him.

From his chaise, he idly lifted the tapestry Leonora had discarded...how long ago? Could it really be a fortnight? He and his men had remained in the Lowlands, helping Brodie of Morayshire rebuild his cottage. It had postponed, for a few more days, his return to the emptiness of his life in the Highlands. But every day, Anthea had talked endlessly about the English lady's courage in the face of danger. She had described Leonora as the most magnificent woman she had ever met.

Magnificent. Aye. The thought of her brought a fresh stab of pain.

Dillon studied the heavy tapestry of rich crimson and gold. The stitches were fine and even, the images amazingly lifelike, depicting a man and woman on horseback. The woman wore a gown of deep purple, and above her head was the seal of England. The man wore the rough garb of a Highlander and carried a jeweled sword. Dillon glanced toward the sword hanging above the mantel. She had captured it perfectly.

The tapestry told the story of her abduction from her father's home to a Highland fortress. There were the En-

haunted me. Everywhere I look, I see you. Even in sleep, I find no release from the pain. I feel lost and lifeless."

"Aye," she whispered. "I have felt the same way. Oh, my love, what are we to do?"

"What can we do?" He clenched his hands at his sides, afraid to touch her. For if he did, there would be hope for them. "'Twould break your father's heart if you were to renounce your land and live here with me."

"It will break my heart if I do not, Dillon."

Her words, spoken so simply, stunned him. "You would leave your father's home? The home of your birth?"

"Is that not what women have done from the beginning of time, my love? Is it not right that I embrace all that you love, and make it my own?"

He lifted an open palm to her cheek, touching it lightly before drawing his hand away abruptly. "I would not wait for approval from your king, nor the blessing of your father, Leonora. I could not bear to send you back to England until proper arrangements are made. I would demand that we wed at once."

Because of his stern demeanor, she tried not to laugh. "I would expect no less, my laird."

"You have thought this over carefully?"

"Very carefully."

He sighed deeply, feeling a welling of passion that threatened to swamp him. "Ah, my beloved Leonora. I had given up all hope of having my dream fulfilled. And now..." He framed her lovely face with his hands and pressed a kiss to her lips.

At once, the heat danced between them, and he drew her into his arms, kissing her with a hunger that startled them both.

As he took the kiss deeper, she whispered, "We will notify Father Anselm that we are to be wed at once."

"Nay." As she started to pull back, he dragged her against him and savaged her mouth with kisses. "The morrow will be soon enough to go in search of the good priest." He dropped to his knees, pulling her down with him. "As for tonight, I have far better plans, my love."

With a sigh, she gave herself up to the pleasure of his love. Love. It filled her heart, her soul. She would not question how it happened, nor when. She knew only that she would love this savage Highlander for a lifetime. And beyond.

Epilogue

"A rider just arrived bearing a missive from your father." Dillon hurried into his chambers, then stopped in midstride to savor the view of his wife, seated in a chair by the fire, holding the tiny infant to her breast.

He crossed the room and knelt beside them, lifting his hand almost reverently to stroke the small round head covered with a thatch of dark auburn curls.

Leonora smiled and Dillon was reminded of a portrait of a Madonna and Child in Father Anselm's chapel.

"Shall I read the missive?"

"Aye."

He unrolled the parchment and began to chuckle. "It says that your loving father will be arriving within a fortnight to welcome Modric Alec Waltham Campbell, his new grandson. He carries greetings, as well as many gifts, from a grateful king, and looks forward to a long visit."

"I am glad that summer has come to our Highlands," Leonora said. "I want my father to see this land at its loveliest, so that he will love it as I do."

Dillon smiled at her use of the term "our Highlands," and wondered again at this wondrous gift he had been given. The lad who had been stripped of home and family, and taken in by monks, had never dreamed of finding such happiness. All he had wanted was justice. Instead, he had been given so much more. A place of his own in this proud, free land. A clan who trusted his leadership, and in return gave him unquestioned loyalty. Family and friends who returned his affection. And most of all, this woman who had given him his most precious gift of all—a son named after the one whose death had begun this long, arduous quest. This woman, who had turned her back on her own proud heritage to embrace his, owned his heart and soul, and filled his life with a love that would endure beyond the grave, beyond time, into eternity.

*   *   *   *   *

Author Note

Scotland's nationhood was forged during the Wars of Independence (1296-1314). In my research I discovered that one clan emerged from obscurity at this time to play a key role in the history of Scotland: the Campbells.

When I began my Highland series four books ago, with *Highland Barbarian,* I was not aware of this significance. I had merely chosen Brice Campbell as a fictitious name that appealed to me. Or did I? Perhaps my Scots and Irish ancestors planted the seed of knowledge that grew into these fantasies. At any rate, so many readers asked for, not only the story of subsequent generations, but the story of Brice's predecessors as well.

The Highlander takes us back to the beginning.

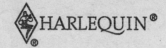

® HARLEQUIN®
®

Weddings, Inc.

Harlequin Books requests the pleasure of your company this June in Eternity, Massachusetts, for WEDDINGS, INC.

For generations, couples have been coming to Eternity, Massachusetts, to exchange wedding vows. Legend has it that those married in Eternity's chapel are destined for a lifetime of happiness. And the residents are more than willing to give the legend a hand.

Beginning in June, you can experience the legend of Eternity. Watch for one title per month, across all of the Harlequin series.

**HARLEQUIN BOOKS...
NOT THE SAME OLD STORY!**

This July,
Harlequin and Silhouette
are proud to bring you

by Request ™

CONVENIENTLY
Yours

WANTED: Husband
POSITION: Temporary
TERMS: Negotiable—but must be willing to live in.

And falling in love is definitely not part of the
contract!

Relive the romance....

Three complete novels by your favorite authors—in
one special collection!

TO BUY A GROOM by Rita Clay Estrada
MEETING PLACE by Bobby Hutchinson
THE ARRANGEMENT by Sally Bradford

Available wherever.
Harlequin and Silhouette books are sold.

HARLEQUIN®   *Silhouette*®

HREQ6

DESTINY'S WOMEN

Sexy, adventurous historical romance at its best!

May 1994
ALENA #220. A veteran Roman commander battles to subdue the proud, defiant queen he takes to wife.

July 1994
SWEET SONG OF LOVE #230. Medieval is the tale of an arranged marriage that flourishes despite all odds.

September 1994
SIREN'S CALL #236. The story of a dashing Greek sea captain and the stubborn Spartan woman he carries off.

Three exciting stories from Merline Lovelace, a fresh new voice in Historical Romance.

Fifty red-blooded, white-hot, true-blue hunks
from every State in the Union!

Look for MEN MADE IN AMERICA! Written by some of
our most popular authors, these stories feature fifty of the
strongest, sexiest men, each from a different state in the
union!

Two titles available every month at your favorite retail
outlet.

In July, look for:

ROCKY ROAD by Anne Stuart (Maine)
THE LOVE THING by Dixie Browning (Maryland)

In August, look for:

PROS AND CONS by Bethany Campbell (Massachusetts)
TO TAME A WOLF by Anne McAllister (Michigan)

You won't be able to resist MEN MADE IN AMERICA!

Where do you find hot Texas nights, smooth Texas charm and dangerously sexy cowboys?

Crystal Creek reverberates with the exciting rhythm of Texas. Each story features the rugged individuals who live and love in the Lone Star state.

"...Crystal Creek wonderfully evokes the hot days and steamy nights of a small Texas community...impossible to put down until the last page is turned."
—*Romantic Times*

"...a series that should hook any romance reader. Outstanding."
—*Rendezvous*

"Altogether, it couldn't be better." —*Rendezvous*

Don't miss the next book in this exciting series:
LET'S TURN BACK THE YEARS by BARBARA KAYE

Available in August wherever Harlequin books are sold.

**Harlequin®
Historical**

LOOK TO THE PAST FOR
FUTURE FUN AND EXCITEMENT!

The past the Harlequin Historical way, that is. 1994 is going to be a
banner year for us, so here's a preview of what to expect:

* The continuation of our bigger book program, with titles such as
Across Time by Nina Beaumont, *Defy the Eagle* by Lynn Bartlett and
Unicorn Bride by Claire Delacroix.

* A 1994 March Madness promotion featuring four titles by
promising new authors Gayle Wilson, Cheryl St. John, Madris Dupree
and Emily French.

* Brand-new in-line series: DESTINY'S WOMEN by Merline Lovelace
and HIGHLANDER by Ruth Langan; and new chapters in old favorites,
such as the SPARHAWK saga by Miranda Jarrett and the WARRIOR
series by Margaret Moore.

* *Promised Brides*, an exciting brand-new anthology with stories by
Mary Jo Putney, Kristin James and Julie Tetel.

* Our perennial favorite, the Christmas anthology, this year featuring
Patricia Gardner Evans, Kathleen Eagle, Elaine Barbieri and
Margaret Moore.

Watch for these programs and titles wherever
Harlequin Historicals are sold.

HARLEQUIN HISTORICALS...
A TOUCH OF MAGIC!